Praise for

LAWS OF THE BLOOD
DECEPTIONS

"An exciting vampire tale. Every book in the series is better than the last as the author continues to develop the culture of the vampire society."   —*Midwest Book Review*

"The author knows how to write 'realistic' vampires. Her characters are three-dimensional and intriguing. Recommended."   —*All About Romance*

"Excellent! Very well executed! Book four is even better than the last, and that is definitely saying something. I hope to see these main and secondary characters again in future books. With all that I am seeing, this is shaping up to be a series that fans will want to keep reading for years."   —*Huntress Book Reviews*

"Ms. Sizemore's breed of vampires is intriguing and her delivery compelling. Overly helpful civilian psychics serve as comic relief in an otherwise tense and fast-paced plot."   —*Romantic Times*

LAWS of the BLOOD

DECEPTIONS

SUSAN SIZEMORE

ACE BOOKS, NEW YORK

THE BERKLEY PUBLISHING GROUP
Published by the Penguin Group
Penguin Group (USA) Inc.
375 Hudson Street, New York, New York 10014, USA
Penguin Group (Canada), 90 Eglinton Avenue East, Suite 700, Toronto, Ontario M4P 2Y3, Canada
(a division of Pearson Penguin Canada Inc.)
Penguin Books Ltd., 80 Strand, London WC2R 0RL, England
Penguin Books Ireland, 25 St. Stephen's Green, Dublin 2, Ireland (a division of Penguin Books Ltd.)
Penguin Group (Australia), 250 Camberwell Road, Camberwell, Victoria 3124, Australia
(a division of Pearson Australia Group Pty. Ltd.)
Penguin Books India Pvt. Ltd., 11 Community Centre, Panchsheel Park, New Delhi—110 017, India
Penguin Group (NZ), 67 Apollo Drive, Rosedale, North Shore 0745, Auckland, New Zealand
(a division of Pearson New Zealand Ltd.)
Penguin Books (South Africa) (Pty.) Ltd., 24 Sturdee Avenue, Rosebank, Johannesburg 2196,
South Africa

Penguin Books Ltd., Registered Offices: 80 Strand, London WC2R 0RL, England

LAWS OF THE BLOOD: DECEPTIONS

An Ace Book / published by arrangement with the author

PRINTING HISTORY
Ace mass-market edition / October 2002

Copyright © 2002 by Susan Sizemore.
Cover art by Cliff Nielsen.
Cover design by Annette Fiore.

ISBN: 978-0-441-00984-8

ACE
Ace Books are published by The Berkley Publishing Group,
a division of Penguin Group (USA) Inc.,
375 Hudson Street, New York, New York 10014.
ACE and the "A" design are trademarks belonging to Penguin Group (USA) Inc.

PRINTED IN THE UNITED STATES OF AMERICA

10 9 8 7 6 5 4 3 2

For Team LOTB—Jane, Marguerite, Terri, and Chris—who get to see all my typos, missed words, grammar disasters, forgotten plot points, and research screwups before anyone else. Thank you, ladies, for making me look good . . . even if I do pout when you point all this stuff out.

Law: For each city, there is but one Enforcer, whose word is to be obeyed in all things.

Prologue

"LISTEN—"

"Not here."

"You don't even know—"

Sara put a finger over Gerry's lips. "You've got that fanatical look in your eye again."

"I—" he said around her finger.

Why did he have to be this way? Why here? Gerry Hansell wasn't any good at giving up. About every six months he brought the subject up to Sara. "Come on," she said. "Outside."

Sara stood, lunch bag clutched in her hand, and marched Gerry through the crowd in the cool interior of the building. It was always crowded, full of tour groups, but since it was such a huge place, the hordes of tourists went almost unnoticed. She came here because she lived in the neighborhood, and it had become a convenient meeting place for her and her colleagues.

They went out into the muggy summer air and down a long flight of steps to the herb garden. It was a quiet place, redolent of sun-warmed lavender, almost deserted, but for the black squirrels that spotted them the moment they sat on a bench near a wall fountain. Sara was too soft not to toss cold greasy fries to the little beggars out of her fast food bag as Gerry started up again.

"We ought to talk to her. We can make it work."

"She doesn't want to hear it, and no, we can't."

"You could talk to her. She listens to you."

"Nice wheedling, kid, but it doesn't match the facts. She's the boss. I live to serve."

"So do we all, but you're—"

"Her liaison, carrying out her bidding without power or influence."

Gerry laughed.

Sara frowned at him. They had other things to discuss; things they could actually do something about. But instead of putting a firm damper on his enthusiasm for this particular subject, she asked, "What do you want to try this time? Put together some polling numbers? I can just imagine the phone calls to focus groups. 'On a scale of one to ten, sir, do you believe that vampires exist?' "

"Yes," he answered with ringing enthusiasm.

" 'If vampires exist'," Sara continued the imaginary poll, " 'would you, A) Stake them through the heart, B) Expose them to sunlight, C) Use them in medical experimentation, or, D) Allow them to run for Congress.' "

"We wouldn't want vampires in Congress," Gerry answered. "They're all Republicans."

"Fiscally conservative does not necessarily translate as Republican." Sara defended their mistress and all their mistress's kind. "The point is, we can't poll public opinion of—" She looked around the quiet garden. "—vampires."

"The point is," Gerry said, "that the time is not *coming* when there is nowhere left for them to hide, the time is here." He slapped a hand down hard on the bench for emphasis. "They need to face it."

"They won't."

"The world has grown too small, technology is too pervasive. Discovery is inevitable. They should do it on their own terms. They have to come out before somebody without their best interests at heart does it for them. We need to introduce the idea to the public slowly, build a positive image."

"Positive image?"

"It can be done."

Sara knew Gerry was not joking, and the thought terrified her. "Death by cigarette can be made palatable, Gerry, sexy. You can make people ignore their mortality with a big enough ad campaign. But let the public know that immortality is possible for a tiny, tiny, minuscule fraction of the population, but nobody else can play, and that minority of immortals won't stand a chance."

"We can make it work."

"Right. Let's see, how do we sell the public on accepting a small group of psychically endowed immortals whose very existence depends on their periodically hunting, killing, and eating mortal victims?"

"Televise it."

He was joking this time. She was sure of it, but she didn't answer. Sara crumpled up the greasy paper bag and began shredding it into tiny little pieces. "Let's talk about that census data, shall we? You do have the information I asked for, right?"

"With the grudging cooperation of every nest I contacted, I do indeed have most of the information on the local population."

Sara noticed that she was holding the crumpled shreds of the paper bag tightly in her fists and wondered what to do with this mess. "Most?"

Gerry shrugged. "I am a humble, vulnerable—delicious—mortal servant. No way am I approaching any of the strigs in this town."

"There are no outlaw vampires in the area." Sara laid down the party line.

"Which is why you want me to find out how many there are."

"Our mistress asked for a census, starting here. We live to obey."

"To a point. No one's calling me an Uncle Igor, darling."

She sighed rather than snarl the answer that came first to mind. She wanted to remind her fellow slave that he belonged to the vampire who let him taste immortal blood, but she was aware that her hunger to serve and protect the strigoi community was a deeper commitment than that of many who served the rulers of the underneath world. She'd been accused often enough by fellow staff members of being ambitious, of wanting to be a vampire when she didn't have the psychic gift for it. She knew there were those who said she served so devotedly because she hoped loyalty could somehow win her a pair of fangs. That wasn't true, she told herself. The snide remarks and whispered accusations were the result of envy of her position. Still, she was not going to give in to frustration and snap Gerry's head off because she didn't think he was showing proper subservience. She was not going to leave herself open to accusations of being an Uncle Igor.

Sara let the balled up paper fall to the ground and rubbed her sweating palms on the edge of the bench. Her muscles were very tense, and she made herself relax before speaking again. "You're right," she told Gerry. "Finding out if there are any strigs in the area is not either of our business." She sat back on the bench, made herself enjoy the shade and the lavender-scented air. She wouldn't let herself think about the hunger inside of her. "Let's concentrate on what we mere mortals can do."

"Fine," he answered. "But I'd rather talk about vampires revealing themselves to the world."

"I know—and I don't care. Give me the numbers, Gerry."

Chapter 1

*"Outside of the killings, Washington has one of the
lowest crime rates in the country."*
— *Mayor Marion Barry, Washington, D.C.*

AN OWL HOOTED over his shoulder. There was no other
sound anywhere in the Walking world. Nothing but the
dark of vision spread out before him, pregnant with pos-
sibilities, the details as yet hidden. He could go or stay.
Staying was safe, sane, normal. Falconer took a deep
breath, though he neither heard nor felt himself do so,
and stepped onto a path lit by moonlight. He automatically memorized details as he walked farther and farther
beyond his body. The woods on either side of the narrow
asphalt path were thick, but he could hear traffic all
around the wooded area. Night sky held a sprinkling of
stars and lots of low-flying airplanes. The nearby sound
of rushing water masked some of the city noise in the
distance. He found it hard to move, even though he knew
he was Walking and nothing should have gotten in his
way. It wasn't like he was really there. This just felt more
real than usual, that's how he knew it wasn't a dream.

Falconer came upon the man suddenly. One instant
Falconer was on the path, the next he was standing by
the creek, looking at a man outlined by moonlight. The
man was standing up to his waist in the center of the

fast-moving creek. Falconer automatically memorized details despite the darkness. The man in the water was young, with long dark hair, wearing a denim jacket over a dark shirt. Good looking in an unremarkable way. Then he turned his head and looked straight at Falconer. There was no mistaking that he saw the Walker in the woods.

Falconer changed his mind immediately about the young man's looks being unremarkable. People with fangs and glowing red eyes were anything but unremarkable.

He didn't normally wake up with a start, but he blinked and told himself the reaction wasn't unwarranted. After all, he wasn't supposed to go Walking outside of business hours, but his subconscious never had taken orders very well. He wasn't happy about it, as he didn't want to bring his work home with him. Falconer was unpleasantly surprised to find himself in bed, to realize that he had been sleeping. He let himself hope for a moment that he'd been dreaming, but he knew the difference.

It was a windy night, and the bedroom curtains weren't completely closed. A tree outside the house was caught in the light of a streetlamp. The combination threw stiff tentacle shadows across the wall and ceiling and the top of the chest of drawers covered with framed family photos. The long-dead people in the pictures seemed to move in a dance with the wind. On another night Colonel Michael Falconer might not even have noticed; tonight the moving shadows seemed like an invasion. They seemed to claw toward him as he stared in sleep-drugged fascination. His thoughts spun, his senses followed. The dizziness eventually became so bad he had to rush to the bathroom to throw up. Walking always made him nauseated, but rarely to this extent.

When he came out of the bathroom a glance at the clock told him it was eleven in the evening. He'd only been in bed for about half an hour before his dreaming self strayed into the psychic territory where the subconscious moved in the real world. Falconer guessed he'd suffered stronger side effects than usual, because what his mind had done had been unintentional and uncontrolled. He hoped it never happened again. He certainly wasn't ready to go back to bed and risk falling into the same nightmare.

And maybe that was all it had been, a dream of Walking, no matter how real it had felt. After all if he'd been Walking he wouldn't have seen—

No. Not going to think about any of the dream images. He wasn't going back to bed, either. He was weary and still a little dizzy, but habit almost drove him to sit down and start making notes—but he was at home. The Georgetown row house he'd inherited from his mother was nowhere for him to carry on classified activity. And it didn't feel big enough to hold him at the moment, either. It felt—creepy. He needed fresh air, the open sky. He needed to run. The least he could do was get dressed and go for a walk.

"I had a situation in Chicago."

No greeting, no preliminaries, no suggestion of anything between them in his voice. Olympias smiled as much as she ever did. There was glee in that gruff voice on the telephone, and animosity, and that said all that was necessary about their relationship. "Hello, Istvan," she answered, brittle, bright, and polite. "What about Denver?"

"It was the same situation. Moved to the Midwest."

"I don't do situations. Certainly not Midwestern ones. What happened?"

"The bad guys are dead. Your secret is safe."

Which was what she expected to hear. "It's your secret too, Istvan."

"So I'm told. Now I'm taking a long vacation."

Which she hadn't expected to hear. Olympias coordinated the activities of vampires in North America, and Istvan was her chief Enforcer. Istvan didn't take time off.

"What's the matter? Are you feeling all right?"

"I think it's time to get in touch with my inner vampire."

"You told me you don't have an inner life."

"I lied."

"Where are you going?"

"A honeymoon."

He had to be joking. "Did you bite a nice person?"

"A nice one? No."

"Are you teasing your old mother?"

She wished she hadn't asked, hoped he wouldn't answer. He'd been hiding something from her for quite a while now. She hadn't probed. She didn't now. It would hurt her to discover the cord finally cut from the last great love of her long, long life. It was even more annoying to think she might be losing his very skilled services, even for a little while.

"Yes," he answered her after a significant pause. Then he hung up.

Typical.

Bitch put her huge black head in Olmypias's lap, and Olympias scratched the hellhound's ears for a few moments, until she remembered what she was wearing and pushed the animal away. Fur on a Badgley Mischka gown. Great. Her own fault for kicking off her shoes and settling on the floor in the narrow front hallway of her house. The house rule was that what was on the floor belonged to the dog. Fortunately, Olympias had just returned from the fund-raising party at the Kennedy Center, so Bitch's shedding on her clothes was aggravating more than disastrous. Sara wouldn't see it that way, Olympias supposed, since she would be the one who took the dress to the dry cleaners.

Sara was overworked, and didn't hesitate to complain about it. Olympias suspected she too would be overworked soon, if her best Enforcer was thinking of leaving the force. She'd suspected that was what he was calling about even before she answered the telephone. The phone had been ringing as she came in the door. She almost hadn't picked up the cordless receiver sitting on the entrance hall side table, since she'd had a feeling she'd be hearing from her most difficult offspring this evening. The foreknowledge had put her in a mood to bite something all night.

"You're home. Have a good time?"

Olympias looked up as Sara came into the hallway from her office. "Until a moment ago," she answered her slave. "Now I'm feeling a bit peckish."

Sara smiled hopefully. "I'm always available."

The girl didn't know how tempting she was, but Olympias had learned the hard way to resist temptation. Olympias scratched the dog's ears and relaxed against the wall. She had her black velvet skirt hiked up around her long legs, and the black and white floor tiles were cool beneath her bare thighs. "I'll keep you in mind," she answered Sara, but didn't really mean it. Sara deserved other rewards for her service. Service. Olympias sighed. "You have something you want to talk about, don't you?"

"Afraid so," her right hand answered. "There are situations that need your attention."

"Situations. What an awful word."

"Better situations than crises. You could have a few of those if you like."

"No thanks. Forget Istvan, I'm the one who needs a vacation," Olympias complained. She pushed the big dog off her lap and rose to her feet. "There's very little you can't handle on your own," she told Sara as she tossed the phone back onto the table.

"I appreciate your confidence, but flattery won't work. You have to decide—"

"In the morning. Talk to me about—whatever—in the morning."

"You won't be awake in the morning."

Olympias smiled. "How about that?" She glanced at the black dog that was eyeing her dropped shoes. Olympias scooped them up. "Your auntie Sara is being such a pain—all right, I'll say it—in the neck. I don't want to play dictator tonight." Bitch, of course, merely looked at her devotedly, then raced up the stairs ahead of her as Olympias went to change clothes. She could feel Sara watching her as she went, but ignored the mortal's frustrated displeasure. The night wasn't all that old. Olympias decided she had plenty of time to take a long run.

Whoever was behind Falconer wanted him to know they were there, he was sure of that. The cool breeze blew her thoughts to him, like a sharply scented perfume. Whoever she was, she wanted him to feel vaguely uneasy, perhaps a little threatened by the presence of a nearly silent stranger in the darkness. There was a hole in the moonlight where she was. He knew that if he turned around he wouldn't be able to see anyone, even though the narrow cobblestone street was quite well lit. He had the feeling that she—and he was sure with no proof that it was a she—had been waiting for him to leave the house. She'd been watching him for a long time. From the outside, not in his dreams.

Falconer shook his head. This was all post-Walking paranoia, of course, some odd flight his imagination chose to run off on when the only objective fact was that there was someone walking behind him at one in the morning.

Falconer was a careful man, carefully trained as well, though his commando years were behind him. He was still confident of his own abilities, certainly not afraid to walk the streets of his own neighborhood at night. Georgetown was as safe as you could get in the Washington area, anyway. Sometimes it was said that there were more police than citizens in this affluent neighborhood of embassies and historic houses.

He'd been rattled and restless when he started out, distracted certainly, by more things than he wanted to think about, but he wasn't so bad off that he didn't soon realize that someone was following him. For a few minutes he let himself think that the person moving so quietly behind him was simply going in the same direction, then the paranoia set in. It wasn't a long walk from his house to the Canal. The long street that fronted the Canal was a popular place; the almost silent footsteps came from that direction. Maybe it was some lost tourist. Maybe he should pause and ask if she needed help.

Maybe or not, he began to walk faster. The darkness got darker, though the light from the frequently placed streetlamps still shone as brightly. When he heard the laughter in his head, there was an unmistakable undertone of sex to it. The silent sound told him this was neither dream nor Walking, but waking nightmare. She wanted him and would have him and then he would know what it was like—

Falconer did not panic, but he did begin to run. He went past Christ Church and up P Street, but from that point on he had no idea where he was. The world around him simply grew darker and darker and filled with the scent of a spicy perfume. Her arousal bit into his self-control, and her anger seared him. Anger at him because he refused to let terror overwhelm him, anger because her arousal sparked no answering heat in him. She could catch up to him anytime, she wanted him to know that. He believed it, but he didn't let it matter. He concentrated, fought to punch through the surrounding darkness. He could hear his own ragged breathing, and the pounding of his heart, and her bubbling, vicious laughter. For a long time they were the only sounds in the world.

But they weren't alone in the world; they were still in the heart of a great, noisy city. Even in the quiet evening streets of Georgetown, there was plenty of traffic. Hunter and prey were not the only people in the world. He wouldn't let himself forget that. The thought brought him back to sanity. It lifted the suffocating darkness a little. He listened for the sound of cars and the pounding of his footsteps on the hard pavement, and not to the drumming of his heart. Falconer hunted for the outer reality and found a wisp of it in the sight of a black gaping hole. For a moment he thought he was running toward the mouth of hell, then realized it was only the entrance to a park, a simple iron gate flanked by tall old trees. He pelted through the gate and into the silence of the park, knowing it was a mistake even as he did so, but he couldn't make his feet go any other way.

She was close on his heels, and her hungry laughter grew even louder as the world narrowed down to the two of them again.

"What the hell?"

Bitch shot away from her side even as Olympias halted and swung sharply around at the scent of the hunt. She sniffed the air in the dark emptiness of the quiet side street, tasted the tang of fear and arousal with a swift flick of her tongue. It took less than a heartbeat for her senses to spread out and flow through every living thing in the crowded neighborhood. Olympias sorted easily through the mortals and discarded them as pale imitations of real thought and emotion. It was the electric wave of ecstasy and hunger from one of her own kind that tingled through her blood, bones, and mind, washing through her, jarring Olympias to the core. Her stomach churned and roiled so hard that she gagged and had to lean against a building for a moment to get herself under control. Her claws scraped against the wall, going through thick layers of grime and paint to gouge narrow channels in the old bricks.

She hadn't experienced this for a long, long time, and would be happy never to feel it again. She brushed the reaction aside, forcing the old ache down. It was only residual lust, nothing to do with her. All she'd thought she'd wanted was to take her dog for a quiet run around the neighborhood; it seemed her restlessness had had another purpose all along. It was nice to know that her gifts were still intact, even if she didn't have to use them all that often.

She took a deep breath and let her claws extend farther as she turned to follow the hellhound. She grew hunting fangs, as well, though she didn't go so far as to make the full transition to her Nighthawk form. Nobody messed around in her town. Olympias kept pace with Bitch, coursing with her, a partner in the hunt. She didn't need the dog's help to follow the scent, but knew the animal might need her for protection if it tried to interfere with a hunting vampire on its own.

She passed the hellhound at the entrance to a nearby park. Bitch followed her past an overturned bench and into a stand of trees. Traces of mortal fear grew stronger with each step she took, but they didn't lend any exciting edge to her emotions, and the vampire's hunger disgusted her. The only thing she felt was fury when she reached the downed man on the ground and the creature kneeling over him.

The vampire shot up with a snarl, swung around, and leapt at Olympias. Olympias slammed the smaller woman against a tree with all the force at her command. The tree shuddered, wood splintered and cracked, and small branches and leaves rained down from the impact. The female vampire slid to the ground. Olympias stood over her and planted a Nike-shod foot on her chest. By this time Bitch was standing on the mortal's chest, bared teeth resting at his throat.

Olympias ignored the man to concentrate on her own kind. "What do you think you were doing? You do know where you are? You do know who I am?"

The woman glared up at her, full of lust and hate and hunger, but with their gazes locked, Olympias had the advantage. She remained calm, but for the righteous anger that she let burn into the woman's brain. Moments passed into minutes, minutes in which the intruder was allowed to know that Olympias was letting her live. She let the young vampire know that she allowed her to regain control. Finally, the girl's glowing eyes changed back to something closer to a look that might pass for human. Her hysterical need tamped down to a controllable level. The girl's fury remained, but she managed to put it on a leash.

Finally, she answered Olympias. "I know who you are."

"And you know where." Olympias spoke very, very quietly. She stepped back and let the younger woman get to her feet. Bitch lifted her muzzle from the prone mortal's neck, just enough to watch. The man took this small opportunity to try to move, but the hellhound let out a warning growl, and he subsided. Olympias left the dog to do its job. "I believe I have a dagger on me somewhere," she said, and she backed the girl up against the tree once more. "You have five seconds to explain before I use it, strig."

The girl bridled at the insult. "I'm no strig!"

"Three." She put a hand under the girl's jaw and pricked claws into her exposed jugular. "Two."

"I wasn't going to kill him! It wasn't a hunt! You know damn well—!"

Olympias squeezed the young vampire's throat. "Quietly," she whispered. She was within her rights to kill this trespasser in her territory, but she felt the woman's need through the heat of her soft skin and the pulsing blood so close beneath aching flesh. Her longing perfumed the night, stinking against more than one of Olympias's senses. "Puberty," she said in disgust, and took a step back. While the girl shuddered in reaction, Olympias finally took a look at the mortal man the girl'd set her sights on. "Who's the bunny?"

"Mine."

Olympias laughed at the girl's intensely jealous reaction, and the man's gaze slowly, carefully, lifted over the dog's head and met her own. He shouldn't have been able to move. He was big, broad-shouldered, and rough-looking. He had a wide, narrow mouth and narrow pale eyes. Someone had broken his nose once upon a time. She figured that standing upright he'd be at least six feet four. The young woman who'd been chasing him was maybe five two, not that controlling him would have taken any effort for her. At least not physically.

She nudged him with her foot, and the girl snarled and moved up behind her. Olympias laughed again. Ah, to be so young! Thank the goddess she was not. She looked over her shoulder. "What's your name?"

The girl's eyes looked like two dull coals in the night, her breath came in sharp, hard gasps, cutting through the gentle evening breeze. "Lora."

"From where?"

"He's mine," was Lora's insistent answer. "My right. You can't stop me."

Olympias put her hands on her hips and reminded Lora of the rules. "You have a right to claim a companion if you're ready, but not in this town. Not without my permission."

Lora made a sharp, furious gesture. "My nest leader said I could—"

"Your nest leader didn't talk to me."

"I want him!" Lora pointed at the bunny. "That doesn't interfere with your rule, your highness."

Olympias had been a queen more than once in her life and took the title as right rather than as the sarcasm it was intended to be. She nudged the man in the ribs.

To her surprise he had will enough to grab her around the ankle. "Don't." The word was barely even a whisper, but he shouldn't have been able to speak at all. Bitch stirred, looked at her questioningly, but she didn't order the hellhound to rip his throat out.

Instead, she stepped back and smiled down on Lora's intended trophy. "Well, well, well." She didn't want to probe too deeply, but didn't have to to realize what a psychically gifted prize Lora was defending so tenaciously. Tough with it. Trained to use it? "Quite a find you have here."

"He's mine."

"You're getting boring." She made herself concentrate

on the girl. Olympias backed Lora up against the tree, slowly, revealing to the young vampire the knowledge of just how powerful she was, step by torturing slow step. The girl hadn't shown much respect up until now. Lora was crying like a suckling by the time the back of her head hit the shattered trunk of the tree. "Maybe he's yours," Olympias conceded once she'd put Lora in her place. "Maybe he's a dead man."

"No!"

The girl's concern was touching and disgusting. Olympias didn't know whether to sneer, snicker, or give Lora a reassuring hug. What she didn't give was an inch. "You have no right to hunt even for a companion in this town. I could kill you for stepping over the border into my territory."

"Not your—territory." Lora fought against terror, and Olympias's control. "Not here—"

Olympias grabbed Lora by the jaw again, made her meet her eyes. "I could kill you, couldn't I?" She didn't wait for a nod, but forced Lora's head to nod up and down. "I'm glad you agree." She backed off and gave in a little to the girl's obvious need. She could remember what it was like to be so young, more's the pity. "Maybe I'll let you have your love bunny, but I have to check him out first. See if there are any complications. Your nest leader should have given me a call, then this would have been settled already."

She waited for Lora to give her the name, but the girl said nothing and was able to block Olympias's quick probe. All Olympias was able to discern was that the block had been enhanced by a stronger talent than Lora's. So whoever her leader was didn't want any part of this trouble? Slacker. Olympias took as little interest as possible in nest politics. She preferred to concentrate on the mortal kind, so she didn't bother to express her disgust.

She jerked a thumb toward the park entrance. "Get out of here," she told the girl. "I'll be in touch."

"But—how? He—"

"Bitch."

The hellhound sprang at the young vampire, all fangs and red-eyed ferocity, and two hundred pounds of sleek, immortal muscle and fierce loyalty to its mistress. Lora shrieked and ran, the hellhound close, but not too close, on her heels. Olympias had every intention of calling the hellhound back as soon as Lora was out of the park.

In the meantime she glanced down at the mortal lying on the ground. She was going to have to be very firm with this one to get him to forget. His eyes were wide and too alert for the situation as she bent over him. "Who needs a companion?" she asked rhetorically, brushing fingers over his short-cropped hair. "When you can have a dog?"

Chapter 2

"SOMETHING HAS GOT to be done about that woman!"

Roger Bentencourt couldn't have agreed more. He'd thought so about Olympias many times before. This time, however, he was determined to do something about it. He nodded understandingly and patted Lora's hand sympathetically. The sympathy was real, even if his thoughts were not as intensely focused on the young vampire's problems as she would have liked. Vampires were vain creatures. He thought it was a good thing that the legend about their not being able to see their reflections in a mirror was indeed a legend. Of course, even if it were true, he supposed they'd find satisfaction in seeing their reflection in their adoring companions' and slaves' eyes.

Lora failed to notice any distraction on his part as he patted her hand again. Rather, he patted her claws as Lora nervously snatched her hand away. Her flesh burned to the touch. The girl was suffering, but he found the contact electric and quite pleasant. She left the patio and paced the long length of the walled garden, while he remained seated on the patio. It was pleasant here in Alexandria this evening, with a breeze coming up from the

Potomac to stir the leaves and cool the patio. He gazed up at the sky, more mindful of the time than the young vampire. Living at night was something he'd been getting used to for the last several years; his time sense was certainly heightened. He found it very advantageous to be a vampire's companion. Though, of course, there were a few minor drawbacks.

"I'm not looking forward to carrying you inside if you're out here when the sun comes up," he called to Lora. "Maybe I'll let you get sunburned and mosquito bit."

She stalked back to the patio. "Don't tease." She sat back down, and he poured her a glass of iced tea from the pitcher on the glass-topped table. She raked her fingers—fingers now, not dagger-tipped claws—through her short brown hair. She was a pretty girl at the moment, with gamin features that rather reminded him of a young Audrey Hepburn. Dressed in a denim skirt and sleeveless pink oxford shirt she certainly didn't look like the sort of person you'd suspect of being a vampire. Not that anyone was likely to suspect anyone else of being a vampire in this day and age. One of the many things the strigoi got wrong was their paranoid belief that, in a world grown increasingly jaded as horror after human horror mounted through the twentieth century, anyone would actually consider a minor nuisance like themselves a serious threat at the beginning of the twenty-first. The world, of course, would be quite wrong about the threat, or could be, if the strigoi would abandon their fears and outmoded Laws and get on with claiming their natural destiny. Well, it wasn't up to him to preach the error of their ways to them. He was but a lowly companion, after all. A servant. A concubine. Or, perhaps "boy toy" was a more apropos term in this age. He chuckled at the notion.

Lora brought him out of his reverie with a sharp snarl. "What are you laughing about? The Greek bitch is going to wreck everything, I know it!"

"Would you like Rose to talk to the Enforcer?"

His mild question was met with the derisive laugh he expected. She shook her head. "I love Rose, I really do, but . . ." They were seated in the garden of Rose Shilling's house. Rose was the leader of this Virginia nest and Bentencourt was her companion. Lora was one of the two fosterlings in the household. Alec was away on a business trip. Rose was inside reading; he was aware of the contented hum of her thoughts. The temptation was, of course, to be by her side, but she was a woman who found a great deal of contentment in being alone. It had taken him a great deal of work to court and seduce the reserved English vampire into taking him as her boy toy. Now that she had him as her devoted possession, half of the time she seemed embarrassed by the situation, the other half, she didn't seem to know quite what to do with him. Bentencourt found Rose's diffidence quite delightful, but Lora was right, Rose was no match in any way for the Enforcer of the City.

"Rose thinks everyone is as reasonable and civilized as she is."

"Turned out she was wrong about Olympias. They're of the same blood, you know," Lora went on, and laughed again. "Our mild Rose and that bitch queen who won't let the rest of us enter her precious city."

He couldn't hide his own sneer at the sound of the woman's name. "Rose is of the Nighthawks?" he asked. Despite all he knew about his mistress, this information came as a surprise. He drummed his fingers on the table, the sound sharp on the thick circle of smoky glass. "Really? Two of them so close by? It's a wonder they haven't fought it out. Don't they avoid each other?"

"I don't know. Nighthawks don't all turn out Hunters, I guess. I think there's some kind of change they have to go through. Like getting made into a queen bee or something," Lora added.

Bentencourt nodded, tucking this new bit of information away. It was so hard to draw even little bits of information from any vampire, harder still to sift legend from rumor from lie when he did. He'd have to do more research of course about the change that turned an ordinary vampire with the Hunter mutation into one of them. He wasn't surprised Olympias had turned into a monster's monster. After all, she'd been a power-hungry man killer in her mortal life; the transition to strigoi wouldn't have changed her much.

He glanced off to the east. "Sky's getting light. You better get to bed."

She was strigoi, he was mortal. He should not be the one giving the orders, no matter how mild and solicitous his tone. Alec would have noticed; that was why he was currently away on one of the frequent business trips Bentencourt arranged. Lora didn't notice that he'd given her a command as she rose from her seat. Obeying Bentencourt was something that was becoming habitual in Rose's household. Besides, Lora's mind was on the man he'd decided she should take as a companion. Colonel Michael Falconer would be an invaluable source of information of certain classified operations within the Pentagon, if Lora could manage the mating. If not, well, Falconer could still be sacrificed to the cause.

"Sweet dreams," he told Lora as she went off to her room. He looked toward the sunrise, his mind already busy with plans for the day. Lora would attempt to spend her sleeping hours inside the mind of her future lover. When the attempt proved less than successful her frustration would be even harder to deal with when she woke. It was likely that Lora would be driven to do something foolish that would probably get her killed. What happened to the young vampire and her mortal victim wasn't important; distracting Olympias was. Destroying her would be even better. Someone should have destroyed her before the vampire found her in the wild forests.

No, no, he warned himself as he watched the sky lighten, don't let the hate control you. Tuck the schemes to rule the night away, put it deep, deep down where

Rose will never try to look for it. You don't own Rose yet, she owns you still. Let yourself love her, that's easy, and all Rose cares about. Live your daylight life where there's so much to do. He had an appointment to keep today, on Rose's business, but first he'd settle down for a few hours' sleep beside his vampire lover.

He took a long sip of tea from which the ice had long ago melted. "And for the gods' sake," he murmured, resisting the urge to lift the glass and salute the chariot of Apollo, "whatever you do, don't let yourself live in the past."

He prided himself on his honesty and clarity of purpose, so he let himself recall that in the past, Olympias had always won.

"Can you believe it?" Grace spoke to the rest of the Walking team as though Falconer wasn't there, as the three stragglers shuffled in and took places around the meeting room table. "Mike was mugged last night."

He lifted his aching head and said, "*Colonel Falconer*." It would not do any good, of course, to remind the assembled crew of loons that he was their commanding officer. Even though he wore a suit—not his uniform during business hours—he did occasionally try to tone down the loons' enthusiasm with reminders of his rank. Maybe all he really could claim to be was the senior loon, but he tried.

He wished he hadn't told Grace someone had attacked him, but she'd made such a fuss about his bruises when he walked into the meeting room and found her already there. Maybe he'd blurted out the answers to her volley of questions because he'd been in such shock at seeing one of his people in early. Now that Sela, Jeremy, and Donald had dragged themselves one by one into the meeting room on the second floor of the highly classified Walker Project's Rosslyn office space, Grace Avella began to regale them with the story.

Grace was a California girl who'd come to Washington

to go to college. Donald was from the Midwest and studied at Gallaudet. Jeremy had been involved with various government psychic development programs for a long time before being accepted as a Walker. Sela was a single mother with kids in college. She'd been an admin assistant with the Bureau before taking on the same sort of job with the Walker Project as well as being one of the Walker team. Sela, Grace, and Donald had become involved with the project through volunteering for a university paranormal perceptions study that had initially screened more than two thousand people. Though these three were the only ones who'd made the cut into this highly classified program, none of the three seemed to realize how very special they were.

"Well, maybe not mugged, since he wasn't robbed," Grace rushed on. "Attacked. He doesn't remember the details," she explained to the others, her big eyes and pretty Hispanic features conveying righteous outrage. She gestured expressively at Donald as she spoke. "He remembers that it happened not that far from his house. In Georgetown, can you believe it? Okay, maybe it's not that hard to believe; people get mugged even in nice neighborhoods. At least he wasn't hurt too badly—but look at those bruises on his throat and jaw. This could be useful, though."

Grace took a deep breath, which gave the others around the table a chance to jump in and get a few words out before Grace got going again. Falconer sat back and watched them. If he didn't ache all over, both body and brain, he might have smiled with a certain paternal fondness at the four Walkers. Okay, they were loons, but they were his loons.

Donald was deaf, but he could sign as fast as Grace could talk, and he did so now. Everyone else on the team more or less understood and used American Sign Language. "Useful how? You're looking gleeful about our leader's getting hurt. Why?"

Grace's enthusiasm flowed out and filled the room.

Falconer thought even the psychically blind could have felt it. What Grace had in spades was what could be called charisma, he supposed. Everyone in the room had it, in one degree or another. He guessed even he qualified.

He looked suspiciously down the table at Grace. "What brings on this wave of emotion you're leaking? Joy at my pain?"

"No! But I think your pain offers us an opportunity." Her glance took them all in. "Why don't we try to find out who mugged Mike?"

"I don't think that's—" Jeremy began.

"We've been talking about trying some nonlinear Walking, haven't we?"

The others nodded.

Jeremy cast a sheepish glance at Falconer. "In unofficial discussions, sir."

"What do you mean nonlinear?" Falconer asked. He hated when they tried to change procedure on him, which they frequently did. "The parameters of our project clearly delineate—"

"Don't you just love it when he talks like that?" It was Sela who interrupted this time.

They had no respect, no discipline, none at all. And they were all too blasted clever. How was he supposed to impose order on psychic chaos when—?

"I've met this guy who works at the GAO a couple of times," Grace said. "Very psi-positive, very intelligent. Cute, too. We ought to recruit him." She held her hands up before her. "Not that I've ever mentioned the project to him."

"And what has this guy got to do—?"

"He's done a lot of experimenting on his own with projecting consciousness. Been Walking, astral projecting, but without controls or goals or documentation. There is literature out on the Internet about the sort of thing we do."

Jeremy snorted. "Not that Distance Viewing crap. Those experiments were terminated—"

"Doesn't mean the theory wasn't sound," Sela said.

"From the documents I've read—"

"Yes, yes, your clearance is higher than our clearance," Grace teased Jeremy. He had a tendency to be pompous, and the others loved pricking his self-importance. Grace was a natural born experimenter and risk taker. Falconer generally encouraged her to be innovative. But this time he wasn't too happy when she proposed, "Let's concentrate on pinpointing an incident in the past. I think it could be done using a variation of this man's technique. He's run some nonlinear experiments that I've participated in."

"What?" Falconer demanded in growing alarm. "You are not supposed to participate in anything outside this building."

"I have a social life." She grinned at him. "Never fear, beloved leader. These were past-life regression workshops."

Sela laughed. "You met this guy at a New Age fair, didn't you?"

"I met him at a bar . . . which has New Age classes in the back room," Grace admitted. "But the point is," she hurried on, "his methods worked for me."

"You discovered you were Nefertiti in a past life?" Sela asked.

"No. Normal people with normal lives."

Which is more than can be said about your life now, Donald signed.

"True." She looked thoughtful. "Come to think of it, it wouldn't be a good idea to recruit this guy. He's brilliant and incredibly psychic, but he's way too into believing he used to be some ancient Greek king." She looked around the table at her Walking comrades. "Don't think he has the mental stability that showed up on all our test scores."

"And I'm still wondering how each of you cheated on those," Falconer contributed. "Except for you, of course, Jeremy," he added when a dark look was turned his way from the one member of the team who would never think of breaking a rule. You'd think someone like Jeremy would be a stabilizing influence on this group, but even Falconer, who was supposed to approve of people who followed orders, thought of Jeremy as something of a pest. Jeremy was very good at Walking, however, and they all respected his psychic talents.

"What we're supposed to be doing today is more important than trying to Walk into the past." He doubted it could be done. Besides, he didn't want to go there. Whatever it was that had happened—he couldn't think about it. There was blackness when he tried to think about what had really—

Sweat broke out on his forehead, fear gripped him, the room went dark and disappeared—

"You feel that?"

"Brrr . . . temperature must have dropped twenty degrees."

"Something wrong with the air conditioning?"

"No. Thermostat's fine."

"That cold's not from this world, children. Look."

The first voice Falconer recognized was Sela's. The touch of her warm hand on his shoulder was the first thing he saw when he opened his eyes. No, when the blackness went away. His eyes had not been shut. His gaze focused on a round, dark-skinned face. The concern in Sela's coppery eyes was palpable. He smiled, not to reassure her, or the other three Walkers crowded around him. He smiled, because he knew, knew though thinking about it was painful, that someone had been messing with his mind.

Sela returned his smile and stood back as Falconer got to his feet. His emotions were shaky, but he didn't let it show in how he moved, or in his voice. "Maybe we will give Grace's nonlinear Walking a try. But," he added, duty coming first, "not until after we get today's assignment over with. Study the satellite photos in the files your controllers have prepared for you, do your Walk and report. Then meet me back here afterwards, if you're feeling up to it."

Mess with me, and I'll turn every paranormal resource of the U.S. military on your ass, he thought at the unknown source of his fear and disorientation. As far as he knew that resource included five psychics and a small staff that were facing budget cuts, but any weapon against the dark was better than none.

"We'll be here," Grace promised for all of them. Sela gave him a long, worried look, then shepherded the others out of the meeting room.

"What do you think?" Maggie asked anxiously, her voice hardly above a whisper.

Sara exchanged a look with Gerry. He sighed. Sara handed the file back to Maggie and said quietly, "What do I think? I think he's perfect."

Maggie Donner smiled. She tucked the file back into her briefcase, then she noticed Sara and Gerry's tense expressions. "You asked me to find her some new recruits. If this guy's perfect, what's wrong with him?"

"He's not a permanent resident," Sara said,

"I could introduce him to Olympias," Maggie suggested. "Let her decide."

"She'd agree with me," Sara answered. "He has great potential, but recruiting him would be a waste of our resources."

"I see your point, Sara, but good help is hard to find. With only a few of us, we're getting more spread out all the time," Gerry said to Sara. "I'm bogged down with the census at the moment."

"Trying to find out the exact number and location of every strigoi in the country is a pretty big job," Sara agreed with him. "Especially with the trouble the data you came up with is going to cause the locals. I've been thinking that it might be wise for you to be out of town when the natives get the news. Don't want any nest leader taking a dislike to a lowly slave who was only

obeying orders. Maybe you could go to Denver to personally check out what happened to the missing nest
there. Olympias isn't happy with the Denver Enforcer not
knowing where they went."

Gerry nodded. "But I can't be gone too long. Too
much to do here." He crossed his arms and said all too
casually, "About Maggie's potential recruit—"

"He's a congressman," Sara cut him off.

"Which would make him useful," Maggie said.

Sara looked around the cool, shadowy interior of the
cathedral. The three of them were standing like a group
of tourists beneath one of the lovely stained glass windows. No one was nearby, but she waved them to a row
of pews where they'd have a bit more privacy. Once they
were seated on the needlepoint cushions in the middle of
the long pew, Sara explained. "Congressmen come and
go. If Olympias chose to make him a slave, we'd have
to work for him as much as he'd work for her. The point
is to lighten our workload by recruiting new blood—not
to end up adding keeping this guy in office to what we
already do. We serve Olympias, not a congressional re-
election committee. Right, Gerry?"

He gave a reluctant nod. "I'd love to have a congressman on staff, but I suppose we can't spare the resources
to maintain him in office. I think we should keep him in
mind. Let's stick with career bureaucrats for now. We do
need to build up a larger organization before we can pro-
mote our agenda within the elected federal government."

"We don't have an agenda," Sara reminded the gung
ho slave. "We live to serve Olympias's agenda." She
thought they'd been through this yesterday and he'd
leave it alone for a while.

"She doesn't have an agenda. All she cares about anymore are the Enforcers. Grant you, that's plenty of work
for one vampire, but her responsibilities entail so much
more. She's ultimately responsible for every strigoi in the
country."

"She's responsible for keeping the underneath world

secret," Maggie cut in. "Having a congressman on staff could help that. But I do see the problems it would entail as well," she conceded. She brightened. "Can we bag him if he gets elected to the Senate? Six years are better than two."

"I could see going with that," Sara replied.

Gerry nodded at Maggie. "Good idea. We'll introduce him to Olympias and see what she thinks."

"I don't suppose he's companion material?" Sara asked. She had to fight down a pang of jealousy at the thought of Olympias with a companion—but she did live to serve, and her mistress had been without a psychic lover for a long time.

Maggie shook her head. "Sorry. I haven't met anyone talented enough to ring our lady's chimes."

"Keep looking."

"I think she needs more people like us than she does a bunny," Gerry went on. "There is so much more she could accomplish with a larger staff and a more active role in the daylight world."

Sara gestured for him to calm down. She whispered when she said, "That isn't the strigoi way."

"But we could help her see that it should be. She has blinders on and is far too content with the status quo set down hundreds of years ago."

"Then so are we." How Sara hated that she and Gerry got into this argument. "Let it go. I mean it. Do what she tells you."

"But—"

"Can we get back to current business?" Maggie asked. She checked her watch. "I'm due back on the Hill in an hour." Maggie never missed the chance to act the high-powered Washington career woman. She was an attorney with a large lobbying firm, as well as a vampire's mortal possession. She was also a slave in charge of other watchdog slaves in various agencies, PACS, and committee staffs.

"Gerry and I have a lunch meeting," Sara said. "Then

I have a great many things to report to Olympias tonight. Anything else?" she asked Maggie.

"There's a party in a couple of nights that Olympias will want to get to. A lot of needy program heads will be wining and dining and whining to a lot of appropriations people. There's a few black ops types who'll be begging there. Might be a good place for her to read some dirty military minds."

"I'll mention it to her," Sara said.

"I know a congresswoman on an appropriations committee. I'll make sure she gets an invitation to Olympias," Maggie said.

They all got up and checked their watches. "Time to go," Maggie said.

Sara and Gerry let Maggie leave the cathedral before them. When she was gone, Sara said, "Let's go have a talk with this companion from Alexandria." She wasn't looking forward to it, but a slave had to do what a slave had to do. Besides, all she and Gerry had to do was deliver the bad news. It was up to Olympias, Enforcer of the City, to enforce it.

Chapter 3

"YOU ARE DEAD."

"I make it a habit not to stay that way."

She looked away from the thick-bodied man, with his scarred face and its one mocking eye. She noticed that she wore a dress of dark red wool; heavy gold jewelry hung from her neck and her ears, while gold snake bracelets wrapped her arms. Though the wool of her clothing was finely woven, its texture was rough and barbaric against her skin. The colored tiles of a mosaic floor pressed against her bare feet. The chill of mountain air pricked her skin. She shivered and recognized that she was in her bedchamber, though the walls were made of mist.

"You are a barbarian," the man, her enemy, said. "Don't you remember?"

"I've never denied it." She held her head up proudly, graying curls tumbling around the chiseled planes of her face. She never showed him fear, not even when he beat her. Especially when he beat her.

He was drunk, she could smell the sour wine, and saw it in the evil glint in his one good eye. He was always at his worst in his cups. That ran in his blood, the love of drink and the viciousness that came with it. He'd passed that on to their son. That, and a genius for killing. She blessed the gift of war and cursed him for giving any weakness to her strong, beautiful boy.

He touched her, his callused thumbs tracing her cheeks. He was still a hard man, muscle and gristle beneath a layer of middle-aged fat. His hair was thin, his teeth going rotten. "I heard you were taking a new wife," she said. "I pity her."

His thumbs continued to caress. "You're still beautiful," he said. His hands settled at the base of her throat. "If I stop your heart right now, you'll always be beautiful."

"You'd rather see me a shriveled hag."

"I want you to live with the knowledge that I bed beautiful girls and that they give me sons. The more sons I have—"

"You have only one son that counts."

"I'll kill him before your eyes. Then I'll kill you." He laughed, and his hands tightened on her throat. "But why should I wait?"

He had threatened her before. "You won't do it yourself," she said. "Not yet. You haven't worked up the courage to do it yourself."

"Someday I will." He laughed. He dropped his hands to his side. "Why should I do it myself?"

They had played out this scene so many times before that even the hatred and fear were stale. She knew that it was a dream even as they went through the motions. Knowing it didn't make it less real, less painful. She hated hating him so much, it showed that he still held some control over her.

"You are dust and bones," she said, bringing something new into the dream. "You have no power over me."

He smiled, a deadly, dangerous smile that sent a shaft of fear straight through her heart. "Oh, I have my little ways," he said mildly. Stepping back, he gestured, and she was suddenly encircled by a wall of swords.

In the dream all the blades were made of iron, and they surrounded her in an unbreakable circle. She had always feared being trapped, hated being helpless, but in dream, and in daylight, what could she do? Olympias's body did not belong to her in daylight. Dreamwalking she could control, but never true dreaming. Priestess she had been, but never a true seer, not in mortal life. Sorceress she had been called, seductress, and far worse. She had always been hungry, for power, for love, for all the world and everything in it. Her appetite had been her Gift, and she had wielded it with no great wisdom.

Dreams had significance, any fool knew that, but repetitive nightmares were a nuisance. You'd think that after a few thousand years the traumas of mortal life would recede into vague memory and leave a person alone when she had more important things to think about. But the subconscious was a primitive bitch with blood-soaked hands and too much passion, and it would have its way with her when it willed.

But it was damned inconvenient.

She had work to do, and while even vampires needed a certain amount of sleep, Olympias's plans for lolling around in bed today had not included falling into a dream that belonged to the woman she'd been more than two thousand years before. Why dream of past failures now? She'd seen the man who'd tormented her mortal life catch fire on his funeral pyre and placed his charred bones and ashes in the gold funeral chest herself. She had even grieved, if not for the death, at least for the passing of the youth and passion they'd shared. Her life had taken many a complicated twist and turn since the day his tomb was sealed.

She should have died herself long ago, but the assassin Cassander sent had been a creature with an appetite for more than killing. He had meant to kill her, to Hunt her. He had heard a great many evil stories about her and thought it a good thing for her to die under his fangs and claws. She remembered to this day how it felt to wake up to the prick of the vampire's claws on her breast. She was an old woman, a long, skinny bag of bones, her black curls long gone gray, her passion burned down mostly to embers, but for the hot coal of grief where her heart had once been. Her son was dead in a distant land, she knew his son would be put to death by a usurper soon enough. She could do nothing more to protect her family. Battles for power were being fought throughout the lands her son had won by sword and force of will. Her death was inevitable, but no more than an afterthought, a tidying up by whoever it; was who won the kingdom. It had always been that way; when a king died it was likely his family and followers died with him. She understood this, and waited, not even bothering to place guards outside her quarters in the palace where she'd taken refuge as an exile at Pydna.

She did not think she would be surprised when the killer came, but she was. She expected a knife, or poison at the very least, even though they were not a subtle people. What she got were claws, and hungry eyes shining out of the dark. Something raced in her blood when she saw him, but it wasn't fear. Truth was, it had been so long since she had known desire that she didn't recognize it when it beat in her veins. She had felt as one already dead, until her killer made her feel alive again.

He took her from her bed and out into the moonlight on the mountainside. He left her in a clearing and folded the shadows around himself. Out of the night he listed her supposed crimes and told her to run for her life. He called himself her Nemesis, said he was one of the gods' own furies.

The legends of the Furies came from ancient vampire custom to take the most wicked and sacrilegious of mortals as lawful prey for sins against gods and humankind. Even now it was Lawful for a strigoi to accept that sort of contract, though the Strigoi Council discouraged anyone knowing about this ancient custom. The Council strove for neutrality in all mortal affairs and would force Enforcers to submit triplicate forms requesting a Hunt to go through a screening committee if they could manage to wrest any more power from the Nighthawks. It was hardly any fun being a vampire anymore; at least she hadn't had any fun for a long time.

She'd had fun that night, the night she'd died as Olympias the queen and become Olympias the companion. She'd seduced the dear, idealistic boy. She hadn't known she still had it in her to make men want her, but the one who Hunted her was no man; his needs were different, more complex than mere hunger for soft, youthful flesh. He'd come to eat her, but she'd run at the head of a pack of maenad priestesses in her youth in Epirus; she understood the Hunt. Old woman she might have been, but her spirit was strong, and she knew how to call up the magic within her, though the flame of it had been beaten down long ago by the husband she'd buried. Hers had been the final triumph, for her place beside him in his tomb was never filled. Instead she'd gone into the bed of a vampire. First he gave her back her youth, slowly, sip by sip, then he gave her immortality. Lover or executioner, at least he'd accomplished his mission to take her from the mortal world, which was how he justified his conscience and taking Cassander's gold to himself.

Except she'd never quite completely slipped away from the stage of mortal affairs. She was too well versed in the power games and politics mortals played. She understood kings and generals and the intrigues of courts and harems. Her bloodsire could go about his merry way—he didn't call himself Orpheus anymore, and the last she'd heard he'd moved to Alaska and was running with a wolf pack . . . she really ought to send him a note—but Olympias carried on the work she'd taken up helping to protect the strigoi from mortals when she was barely more than a newborn Hunter.

And, frankly, she could use a vacation as much as Istvan could.

And here she was, thinking about her lurid past, when she'd planned to spend her resting hours dreamwalking in search of the horny Lora's potential love bunny. Last night she'd had too much work getting him to forget about what happened to get information out of him as well. The man's mind was strong, the strongest she'd encountered in centuries. Lora was right in believing that he'd make a magnificent vampire, but Olympias was not in the recruitment business. The world had more than enough strigoi already, in her opinion. He was a magnificent specimen. Though she hated playing matchmaker, Olympias couldn't blame anyone for wanting him. If she still had interest in that sort of thing . . .

She had made a promise to check the man out, and though she'd wasted most of the day with dreams and recollections, she managed to slowly turn from her side onto her back—because a vampire her age wasn't as dead in the daylight as she seemed—and attempted to focus her psychic energy on traveling outward, into the minds awake to the world. It didn't help that Bitch decided to jump up on the bed when she moved and tried to get her to wake up by licking her face for at least an hour.

"This is not going to be pretty," Gerry whispered to Sara as the first of the people they were meeting entered the restaurant's private dining room.

"It never is," she whispered back.

"True. I'm here to insult you to your face while you buy me an expensive lunch," Gavivi said, going to a seat at the head of the long table.

She either had amazing hearing, or no compunction about showing off her psychic talent before them. Either way, this did not put Sara in her place. It pricked her pride, of course, but she also thought it was stupid for anyone higher on the food chain to be impolite to Olympias's chief slave. They tended to forget that the Enforcer of the City was one of the Strigoi Council. Olympias was among the most ancient and dangerous of their kind, and

Sara was the person they had to see first if they wanted to ask anything of her mistress.

Gavivi was an elegant, tall, chocolate-skinned woman with short curls dyed golden blonde. She wore a turquoise silk suit, and her long nails and eye shadow perfectly matched the vibrant color of the silk. There was nothing inconspicuous about this particular companion.

"You have excellent hearing, and terrible manners," Gerry said, though he rose to stand politely while Gavivi took her seat. It was clear from the look she gave him that Gavivi wasn't sure if the action was gentlemanly, or that of a mere servant of a vampire acknowledging a vampire's lover's higher status.

The status thing bothered Sara in the oddest ways. She knew that if she were a companion she wouldn't be one of the ones that rubbed it in to the less psychically gifted. She'd be very serious about the whole thing, aware of the honor and responsibility of someday having companions and slaves of her own. She'd prepare for the future rather than just reveling or groveling in the throes of companionship.

"You look sad," a voice she'd never heard before said.

She looked up, not realizing that she'd been staring at the tablecloth or that anyone else had entered the dining room. She saw that the man who'd spoken was distinguished looking in a bland way. He had the look of a high-level bureaucrat, a tall man with nondescript features, commanding and utterly forgettable all at once. He had a high forehead and fading blond hair, and wore wire-rimmed glasses over pale blue eyes. He was dressed in a gray suit, his shirt and tie a matching ice blue, the tailoring subdued but expensive. If Sara had not known exactly who he must be she might not have recognized him for what he was. He did not display the glow of charisma that shone around Gavivi and every other companion Sara had met. There was power there, she realized, but it was as restrained and subtle as the cut of his clothes. The look he gave her was full of sympathy, the sort of look she would normally have found offensive, but—

There was such deep understanding in his eyes. He was the sort of person, that, when he looked at you, he looked at you.

Oh, yes, he had a great deal of psychic talent all right. Sara managed to shake off the spell and remember that she and this companion weren't the only people in the room. She even managed a small, knowing smile—that the companion returned with a full-wattage grin and a deep, rich laugh.

"I'm with Rose Shilling," he identified himself. "Sorry if my comment was presumptuous, but you were looking sad, Ms. Czerny. I see it as my duty to try to make a lady smile." He then shook Gerry's hand before he turned to Gavivi and finished introducing himself. "Roger Bentencourt."

From the admiring look in Gerry's eyes and the way Gavivi preened, Sara could tell that the others were affected by the man's concentrated attention, while she wondered how he'd learned her last name. Mind reading was the explanation she preferred, as she hated the notion that such a companion would take any interest in anything outside the immediate wants and needs of his vampire lover. Sara was certain that Rose, a contented, complacent, retiring, and decidedly old-school strigoi, wouldn't be bothered with anything so déclassé as learning the names of another vampire's slaves. Sara didn't like the idea of a companion taking initiative of any sort. Rather, Olympias wouldn't like the idea; she didn't like the idea of anything that might make her job more complicated than it already was.

Making my life more complicated, that is. Sara tried not to think that thought, not in this room full of psychics far stronger than herself, but the bitter words flitted through her mind before she could stop them. Chances were good that neither of the companions noticed. She was only a slave.

Bentencourt took the seat opposite Sara and turned his intense scrutiny on her once more. "Do we have this sort of get-together often?"

She was saved from making any immediate answer when the last companion that had been invited came into the private room and slammed the door behind her. "This had better be good, maggots," Cassandra from the Bethesda nest announced. She took a seat, snatched a warm roll out of a linen-shrouded basket, and finished it off in a shower of crumbs before adding, "My lover won't forget the insult from your mistress." She wiped the back of her hand across her mouth, then turned and slapped Gerry, who'd dared resume the seat beside her. "You can stand, maggot boy."

Sara sighed and gestured Gerry to take the chair next to Gavivi.

"How did a sow like you get to be a companion?" Gavivi asked.

One moment Cassandra was pouring herself a glass of water, the next, the crystal pitcher shattered on the wall behind Gavivi's head. Shards of glass and ice flew around the room, a sideboard and the green floral wallpaper were splattered with water.

Note to self, Sara thought. *Cassandra is close to popping fangs.* Olympias would want to know that a new baby vampire was about to enter the underneath world. Some made the transition smoothly, others got a little more—tense. It looked like Cassandra was going to be one of the difficult ones. Too bad the Hunt necessary for the rebirth would have to be put off a few weeks. By the time the woman couldn't take the pressure anymore, making the arrangements would not be Olympias's problem—meaning it would not be Sara's problem—other than making sure the Bethesda nest settled in an area where an Enforcer was available to oversee the transition process.

Which brought her to the crux of this meeting. There was a dense silence following Cassandra's outburst, and everyone was carefully not looking at each other. Sara said, "The Enforcer of the City wishes me to convey a decision about each of your nests to each of your nest leaders."

Cassandra banged a fist down on the table, rattling dishes and silverware. "We don't run errands for slaves."

"We aren't being asked to," Roger Bentencourt spoke up reasonably.

"Try to listen to what the woman says," Gavivi added.

"You're being told to convey the message," Gerry spoke up. "We realize that the method is circuitous and rather old-fashioned, but we are—as the saying goes—only following orders."

Sara wondered what demon of insecurity had let her talk herself into bringing Gerry along to this meeting. Strength in numbers didn't mean anything when she and Gerry were equally lower forms of life to the vampires' companions. Facing these people was tough, but so what? She was Olympias's representative. These people didn't have to like her, and she shouldn't want the support of a friend and equal when facing the companions. Especially not when Gerry wasn't in a mood to back Olympias up. The subversion in his words wasn't that overt, but tone, body language, and the psychic energy he projected spoke volumes to this very gifted trio about his frustration with the world as it was. As Olympias's representatives they needed to be careful not to do or say anything that could possibly undermine her authority. A word, a hint, a look—Gerry needed to remember that the strigoi were predators.

Sara felt the intense scrutiny from the three companions like bruising pressure on her skin. The newcomer, Bentencourt, was the one whose interest seemed to reach deepest through her inadequate shielding. Sara turned her full attention on him. The sympathy she saw in his eyes was nothing like pity for the poor state of her feeble psychic talent. His look conveyed understanding that she was doing her best to perform a difficult job. She couldn't help but give him a small, ironic smile and shrug, which got an encouraging nod in reply.

Before she could continue with the explanation the companions waited for, a trio of servers entered the room. Meals were placed before everyone at the table, wine and coffee was poured, the mess from the broken water pitcher was efficiently cleaned up, and then the wait staff exited. Sara was aware of Cassandra's foot tapping impatiently during this interlude, and she was also aware that the tension in the room eased somewhat, while they waited for privacy once more. Gerry and Gavivi even engaged in a bit of flirtatious small talk. Roger Bentencourt discreetly studied everyone, and Sara discreetly studied him.

Once they were alone again, Sara dropped the bombshell. "You all have to move," she told them. "Olympias has decided that the three remaining nests in the Washington area pose a threat to the whole strigoi community. You are to inform your nest leaders of her decision. The nests have a month to relocate."

That was when all hell broke loose. And these three dangerous, furious creatures Sara and Gerry had to deal with were still mortal humans. Lord knew what it would have been like if there were vampires in the room being told they were being evicted. No wonder Olympias sent the help to deal with this. Sara knew she wouldn't have wanted this job if she'd had any choice in the matter— but she didn't. That was what being a slave was all about.

"Okay, maybe it wasn't such a good idea," Grace conceded to the room full of stunned, staring, pale Walkers.

She'd been the control who'd talked them through the session, so she wasn't in as bad a shape as the others. There was buoyancy in her attitude that told Falconer she was ready to try again—as soon as the aftereffects wore off. He sighed. He wasn't as bad off as the rest of them, but there was a lingering sense of disorientation and a dark anger he didn't understand. Though the very real bruises from the attack were a constant dull ache, his own head was not aching from trying to relive the experience. He knew all the others were suffering various layers of pain and nausea. He could sense the pain without actually going through it, a kind of odd empathy he'd never felt before.

Michael Falconer had been through many types of testing over the years that confirmed he possessed many forms of psychic talent, but mostly he didn't give a shit. Having a new talent crop up was the last thing he wanted. All he'd ever really wanted was a career as a soldier, and as a soldier his duty was to serve where his superiors chose to send him—as a leader of loons. He shook his head. Maybe this surge of bitterness was another after-effect he experienced from Grace's little experiment gone awry.

"I threw up," Jeremy muttered, his gaze fixed firmly in the tabletop. "I don't throw up—a Walker shouldn't be physically ill in the performance of his duty."

"That wasn't real walking," Sela said. "That was—nightmare country."

"It wasn't that bad," Grace protested.

"You were awake, I wasn't. I know a nightmare when I have one."

"Off limits," Jeremy rambled on. "Unprofessional. We had no authorization . . ."

Falconer listened to Jeremy's muttering and sympathized with the time-serving bureaucrat's outrage at a known procedure being shot to hell. The sour aroma that filled the meeting room where they'd convened to conduct the regression experiment confirmed Jeremy's re-action to the experience. Donald leaned back limply in his chair, with his eyes closed. Falconer looked away when Donald lifted his hand and began to sign the letters of a word Falconer didn't want to think about.

Sela rubbed her temples as she glared at Grace. She pointed to the floor. "I ain't cleaning that up."

Grace ignored this implication. "We need to analyze

results." She reached for the tape recorder they'd used to document their experiences.

"No," Falconer said before she could rewind and play the questions and answers she'd posed to each of them on their attempted psychic journey back to his being attacked the night before.

He leaned forward and snagged the tape recorder from in front of her. He popped out the cassette and put it into his shirt pocket. Grace turned a pleading look on him. Grace Avella had big, brown, expressive eyes, and the emotions she aimed at him were full of intense trust, hope, and curiosity. It was not easy to ignore her.

"No," he said again. "We are not analyzing this. We are not going to even listen to it. It was an unauthorized experiment. It didn't work. We aren't going to try it again."

"But—"

"We're wrecked." Sela cut Grace off. "Mike's right." She stood up. "I'm going home. I'm not going back to a park full of—"

"Nothing but our imaginations." Falconer cut her off.

"My imagination is not that sick!" Jeremy protested. He glared at Grace. "You don't have the training to be a control. You influenced us somehow, made some sort of improper suggestion that led us to impossible conclusions."

Grace popped up angrily out of her chair. "I did no such thing! Maybe we picked up on Mike's subconscious reactions to whoever attacked him. It came out as freaky imagery, but you all went to the same place, witnessed the same event and—"

"Can it," Falconer intervened. "Everybody go home. Forget about this. We'll get back to our real work tomorrow."

"It's weird, but not as weird as this," Sela said. She helped Jeremy to his feet. Then tapped Donald on the shoulder to get his attention. When he opened his eyes, she pointed to the door. Donald didn't waste any time before getting out. Sela and Jeremy followed quickly after. Grace lingered for a moment. Falconer frowned sternly and pointed. She flounced out like a disgruntled teenager, but at least she did go without any further argument.

Chapter 4

"I HATE TO speak ill of the dead, especially when she's standing over my shoulder and hasn't yet had a cup of coffee," Sara said, without turning from the desk where she was going through a stack of mail. "But there are some things, boss, that it would be better for you to handle."

Behind her she heard Olympias yawn, not for the first time since she had come into the office. Sara'd been expecting Olympias's arrival since she'd heard the shower go on upstairs a little after sunset. Now, here Olympias was, and Sara was prepared for their usual evening briefing, even if Olympias wasn't quite awake yet. There was also a grunt and heavy breathing behind her, but that came from the huge dog that had crowded into the small room at the back of the house with Olympias. Sara continued sorting envelopes for a few more minutes. When she turned around her long-limbed mistress was seated cross-legged on the office's hardwood floor. Bitch's head was in Olympias's lap, and she was lovingly scratching the ears of the creature that ran her life.

"You could make me a cup of coffee," were Olympias's first words of the night.

"Have you been in the kitchen?" Sara answered. "The coffeepot has a timer. It started brewing around sunset."

"Oh. I always forget." She pushed Bitch away and stood with a speed that was dizzying to watch. "I hate technology." She was gone and back with two blue mugs of steaming coffee within the space of a few heartbeats. "Good coffee, though," she added after handing Sara one of the mugs and taking a sip from her own. "Remember the first time I tasted this stuff. There was this Turkish prince who got himself bit—he introduced me to all sorts of Ottoman decadence while we were hanging out together. I'd been avoiding getting addicted to coffee, even though it was the drug of choice in the underneath since the Arabs brought qahwa from Ethiopia, but Selim looked at me with those big brown eyes of his and smiled an 'I dare you' smile—and here I am, hooked to this day."

"Fascinating," Sara said.

Olympias either didn't notice the sarcasm, or chose to ignore it as she went on. "I took against coffee early on, when a companion of mine used it as an excuse to divorce her husband. Did you know there was an Islamic law that allowed women to divorce their husbands if they didn't provide them with a daily allowance of coffee?" Olympias drained her cup and settled back on the floor again.

"There are chairs," Sara pointed out. "They're all covered in paperwork," she admitted. "But I could move it." There was a shredder in one corner of the office, and Sara always burned what she'd shredded, and vampires didn't put a lot of things in writing, but there always seemed to be a lot of paper around.

Olympias sipped coffee and looked thoughtful for a while. When she spoke, it was with a deep sadness that tore at Sara's heart. "It was a flimsy excuse, but she hated her marriage long before I came into her life. She wanted

out, and more than just to be with me. I could have made
arrangements. What's the use of having a companion if
you don't protect them? But she went to her husband
while I was away—on damn Council business. He killed
her, killed the mother of his children, rather than let her
go." She shrugged. "Needless to say, he paid for it. I
raised the children, but never tasted them." Another
shrug. "Mortality can be a gift, you know." She sighed.
"Damned Council. And why do I keep remembering old
companions lately?"

"Maybe because you're lonely and could use a new
lover?" Sara answered.

Olympias looked up. "Maybe that was a rhetorical
question."

Sara attempted to look innocent. "Really? I've never
been very good at recognizing those."

Olympias looked at her sharply. "Uh-huh." Having finished her coffee, she put the mug down on the floor
where Bitch proceeded to dip her huge tongue into it to
finish up the dregs. "A hellhound with a caffeine buzz,
won't the neighbors love that."

Sara didn't recall any neighbor having actually complained about the huge dog in the five years she'd been
living in the house in this very quiet neighborhood. Bitch
wasn't much of a barker and generally only went out at
night. She'd terrified a few delivery people with her sheer
size and the spooky intelligent look in her eyes when she
appeared at the door when Sara opened it, but she'd never
done any harm. Okay, she chewed up shoes, shed like
mad, and had a name Sara found unpleasant, but human
prey didn't interest the hellhound at all. The neighbors
didn't complain, but there were others . . .

"Maybe this is a good time to mention the werewolves," Sara said.

Olympias sneered.

"There's an animal rights convention coming to town
next month," Sara explained. "It seems that there are
quite a few lycanthropes that are animal rights activists."

Olympias snickered. "I can see that saving the wolves would hold a certain appeal for them, especially during the full moon. There's going to be werewolves at this conference I take it?"

"Closeted, of course."

"Of course." Olympias rubbed her hands together. "And housebroken. Please tell me this convention's during a full moon."

Sara could imagine a group of shape-shifters suddenly turning from peaceful demonstrators into truly radical animal rights activists and taking off after members of Congress on all fours. The image certainly held appeal. "Of course not," she answered. "They're as careful as vampires not to call attention to themselves."

"I know, I know. We never get to have any fun around here." Olympias made an effort to look serious. "Nor should we. What about the furballs?"

"I think it might be best if we sent Bitch out of town during that convention. If not, they'd be sure to catch scent of her and there could be trouble."

Olympias crossed her arms and showed just a hint of fang. "They could try hunting my dog."

"No need to provoke them. As I understand it there's always been a certain tension in the lycanthrope community over vampires keeping hellhounds—"

"You mean the furballs kill the dogs every chance they get and have for two thousand years. A compassionate vampire saved their little evolutionary mistake from extinction, and they've given us nothing but trouble over it." Olympias pulled her huge pet to her and threw protective arms around her. "You're a good girl."

"Of course she is," Sara soothed. "But it would be wiser for her to be elsewhere when the animal rights—"

"Hypocrites come to town," Olympias finished for her. "Fine. It's my job to keep the peace treaties unbroken. I won't be the one to provoke the fleabags. Bitch and I will go for a long camping trip that week." She noticed

Sara's frown, and added, "Or you can arrange for someone else to take her if I'm busy."

Sara nodded.

"Right. What else do you have for me tonight?"

"You know very well what—"

Olympias held up a hand. "Easy stuff first." She tilted up a brow ironically. "That's always how you feed it to me."

Sara noted that Olympias looked tired, and instead of being perked up, the vampire had become melancholy with her first cup of coffee. Sara was grateful she'd gotten a reaction from the mention of werewolves. Now that she had her mistress's attention, she continued the evening's briefing. "Gerry's en route to Denver. He'll have a look around then talk to the Enforcer of the City."

"Tell him not to bother," Olympias replied. "I'm pretty sure Istvan ate whoever caused the trouble in Denver." She glanced up toward the wall safe tucked away behind a framed picture. "On second thought, tell Gerry to find me a missing coin."

Sara was quite puzzled. "No coin's been reported missing."

The safe held an ancient carved wooden box. The box contained a supply of gold coins. Each coin was unique, but each coin portrayed an owl. Each strigoi that became the head of a vampire household, a nest leader, received one of the gold coins from an Enforcer as a symbol of authority within the nest, acceptance within the strigoi hierarchy, and pledge to obey the laws of the Strigoi Council. The Enforcers received the coins from Olympias, and it was her responsibility to know who held each coin. While Olympias swore that she carried all the information about nest leaders in her head, as was traditionally prescribed by the Council, Sara had been working to put the information on all North American vampires into a coded database. Listing nest leaders was easy enough; the tricky part was in trying to find out how many vampires, nestlings, companions, and slaves lived in each nest. Nests were private territories where even Enforcers feared to tread. For a mere slave to attempt to find out such closely held information for the sake of making her mistress's duties easier to carry out was not safe or wise, perhaps, but Sara was quietly determined. Gerry wasn't the only one who thought the strigoi needed to be dragged out of the thirteenth century and at least into the middle of the twentieth century. She simply wasn't so vocal about it.

Olympias tapped a finger on her forehead. "I'm psychic, you know. Something tells me that a coin is missing and that it's going to come back to bite my ass eventually. Have Gerry see what he can find out, but it's not top priority for the moment."

"Yes, boss."

"Next."

"Maggie's getting you an invite to a black tie black ops party. Seems like there's an exclusive little gathering coming up where the spooks and military types will be quietly lobbying for funding for their more esoteric projects. Maggie thought you might be interested in showing up, showing off your legs, and reading a few convoluted minds. You in?"

Olympias nodded. "Might be fun. Tell her I'm in." She held up her mug. "More please."

"I'll get you a fresh one." Sara stepped over the dog lying in front of the door and went into the kitchen. When she came back she found Olympias standing by her desk reading the very formal handwritten letter that had arrived that day. Sara paused in the doorway and studied Olympias's expression while the head of the Enforcers read. Sara hadn't been sure what to expect, but when Olympias put the paper back on the desk she looked weary and sad.

"I wasn't sure how to approach you with that," Sara told her. "I'm not quite sure what all of it means and—"

"Is it the lyrics of the song he put in at the end that you don't understand?"

"No. I do. I remember that the song's used in the opening credits of an old movie."

"*M*A*S*H*" isn't that old a movie."

"It was out before I was born."

"Really? How time flies."

"But the implication of his adding those lyrics—"

"Is obvious."

"Someone asking you to—"

"I need a drink."

Sara handed her the coffee mug. Bitch came over and butted Olympias in the thigh, getting Olympias to start rubbing her head. Sara supposed insisting on being petted was the dog's way of offering comfort. Olympias perched on the edge of the desk and sipped coffee, and silence stretched out until Sara couldn't take it anymore.

"He is, isn't he? I didn't think this sort of thing—you have to apply to—I mean . . . I don't know what I mean," she admitted when Olympias's dark eyes came up to meet hers.

"This is a magical ritual the man's asking for." Olympias shook her head. "I'd say it was good to see someone going through the proper channels, but, as you say, the implication . . ." She shook her head again. "This has happened so rarely in the entire history of our kind. When someone does ask for the ritual we're supposed to have a very strict process of determining if the person really wants what he is asking for. Rather like the Catholic Church determining if a person should be declared a saint."

Sara wasn't quite sure the analogy comparing vampires to saints really worked, but didn't bring it up. Sara sensed that Olympias was very disturbed and unhappy about this development. You'd think an Enforcer would jump at this sort of chance. Sara was glad that the chief of North American Enforcers took such a serious approach to the matter. "Are you going to—do what he seems to want?"

"Maybe. Since it's a formal request I have to at least go through the motions of finding out whether or not he's sincere." She picked up the letter and handed it to Sara. "Which is where you come in."

Sara dropped the piece of paper onto the floor as though it had burned her. She was more than appalled, and just a touch rebellious. "Me?"

"You're the best person for this."

Sara tried to remember that she was facing an ancient, dangerous creature of magic and myth that owned her body and soul. She tried, but couldn't keep the petulant annoyance out of her attitude. She pointed a finger at Olympias. "You're the vampire! You can't expect me— mere mortal—to decide a strigoi's fate!"

"Of course not," Olympias answered before Sara could get revved up for the tirade that had been building for a while.

The anger went out of Sara in a whoosh of breath. Her shoulders slumped. "But—"

"I remember this kid from when he used to live in the area. He was a beatnik musician who was companion to one of the local nest leaders . . . Rosie, I think. He seemed sweet, always had a social conscience, very— liberal." She touched a finger and thumb delicately to ever-so-slightly extended canines. "I never liked him much. And that means I'm not likely to be as objective as I should be if I rush into talking to him. This is a serious matter. If he'd walked up to me on the street and asked for it, the temptation would be to say, sure, let's go somewhere for a snack. But he didn't do that. He's thought through his options, made a formal request. Chances are he's having a crisis of conscience. It's fairly common, and he's just the type to get all whiny and guilt ridden."

Sara looked long and hard up at her lovely, tall mistress. "And what has this got to do with me?"

"Have a talk with him. Have several. Let me know if you think he needs me to whack him upside the head or

rip his heart out. Actually, I'd rather find someone else
to do the counseling. I'm excellent with ripping and rend-
ing, but I've never been any good at that mothering crap.
You could ask my son about that, if he hadn't been dead
for a couple thousand years."

"But—I—"

"Besides, my evenings are filled with cocktail parties
and another local boy I've got to vet. While I'm checking
out the love bunny, you can talk to the vampire. I can't
do it all."

If Olympias hadn't laughed then, Sara didn't know
what frustration might have driven her to. It still took her
a couple of seconds to fully digest what her mistress had
said. Then, on a dual flash of enthusiasm and jealousy,
Sara said, "What local boy? You finally interested in
somebody? You're taking a new companion?" *Am I going to have to move out of the house?* She wondered,
while simultaneously, thinking, *It's about time she found
somebody she can love.*

Olympias caught the girl's thoughts, and threw up a
hand in utter consternation. "Hold your horses, sweetheart! You don't have to empty out your closets. I'm not
bringing anybody home." How could anyone think that
she'd be even vaguely—

"But, boss, it's been years—"

"Decades. Many wonderful, peaceful, contented decades. I'm an old broad, you know." The mating urge
had lain dormant, and, for the most part, Olympias
wanted it that way.

Every now and then she'd hear a familiar voice on the
other end of a telephone conversation and be reminded
of nights of blood and passion and the burning joy of
sharing in the chase, sharing the fear and the death that
brought the lust they satiated during and after the kill. So
many Enforcers out there had come to her as young vampires burning for something more. They'd needed her
magic to bring them through the final ritual that brought
them birth into the Nighthawk line. Other Nighthawks

had been her mortal companions once. She'd shared her blood and bed with them for as long as she could, then she'd been their bloodmother and seen them born into the underneath world. The Nighthawk blood and magic was strong. Most who came from a Nighthawk parent eventually felt the pull, the overwhelming need to hunt vampires, to climb up one last rung on the foodchain, and become the predators who hunted the predators who hunted the mortals who thought they were masters of all living things.

Actually, mortals were at the top of the food chain. Numbers talked, and they said that strigoi were too few and mortals too many. But it certainly made vampires feel better to cultivate a false sense of superiority.

These days Olympias rarely felt the urge to Hunt, or the urge to love. She took pride and pleasure in knowing many of the Enforcers who held power over the nests on this continent were her children, grandchildren, and great-grandchildren. "Only they never send cards on Mother's Day," she murmured.

"What?"

"Nothing." Sara, who was far too discerning, probably detected a certain amount of wistfulness and yearning, but Olympias had no intention of explaining that her loneliness did not have anything to do with longing for a fresh bed bunny to sink her claws and fangs into. "If this bunny works out, he's promised to a local girl who came Hunting where she shouldn't be. He's a big, strong, smart psychic boy with more mental shields than I've encountered in a long while. Too good for the girl who wants him, I think."

"Good enough for you?" Sara asked eagerly.

It was an eagerness born out of duty, Olympias knew. Sara wanted what was best for her mistress, but what she really wanted was to be a companion herself, not that she would ask. Sara tried to be content with what she was, as it was all she could be to Olympias.

"Is he handsome?" Sara persisted.

"No." Better than handsome, he was—tough. Olympias fought down a weary yawn. "I spent much of the day trying to get into his head. I don't know how that vampgirl found him, 'cause he managed to elude me."

Sara was smiling broadly now. "Oh, good, a challenge. You could use a challenge."

"No, I couldn't. What I'm going to do is find out if this mortal qualifies as rightful prey. If he doesn't turn out to be involved with the government or military in any significant way, I'll let the girl have him. Then she can move with her nest to somewhere far away from my town, and they can live happily ever after. Which brings us to the most important topic of the evening."

"Nice segue," Sara acknowledged.

"And?"

"I've laid the groundwork for getting the nests to move via an initial meeting with the companions of all three nest leaders. They were not happy."

"Doesn't matter if they were happy. Their duty is to deliver the news to their nests."

Sara radiated stubborn, impatient annoyance at her.

"You think I should have taken a more direct route, don't you? Gone to each of the nests and had a little chat to explain why their abandoning home and territory is so important to the survival of our kind." Olympias shook her head. "You have no idea how territorial we really are, Sara. We can be mindless savages when it comes to defending what is ours. If I went to each nest leader with the news that they had to move, I'd have a fight on my hands with every one of them. They couldn't help but see red and attack me. Even knowing who and what I am, they'd respond to the instinct to defend what's theirs. I'd respond the same way if some vampire walked in here and told me to take my household elsewhere. Sending word through their companions makes it less of a threat. Those nest leaders aren't going to kill their own companions." She shrugged. "They might beat the crap out of them, but they aren't likely to kill them."

Indignation blossomed around Sara like a red flower. "Beat the—"

"Better them than me having to beat the crap out of the nest leaders. I don't want them believing in the black depths of their hearts that I'm displacing them from rightful territory. I just want them to leave. I'm long over the era when I thought it was fun to make and defeat enemies. I will have to deal with each nest leader directly eventually, but in theory, delivering the order this way will make them amenable to it sooner than if I were to show them my fangs and tell them to get out."

"In theory."

"I thought it was worth a shot."

"You could have told me."

"You were going to be humiliated and patronized by the companions anyway. Always remember who you belong to."

Sara was not impressed. She was, in fact, quite bitter. Her unspoken emotion left a bad taste in Olympias's mind. Sara's tone was mild despite the feelings she couldn't shield. "Please don't give me a lecture on how being a slave to an Enforcer is better than blah-blah-blah."

Olympias admired the mortal girl's ability to appear calm. She'd liked Sara since the moment she'd followed the scent of psychic talent out of the DuPont Circle Metro station. Olympias had given the girl one wild night, and Sara had been paying for it ever since. Suspecting that an attack of conscience might be in the works if she spent too much more time in her slave's presence, Olympias decided it was time to wrap up the nightly meeting and get out of the house as quickly as possible.

"How did the companions take the news?" she asked.

"Does it matter?" Sara wondered.

"Companions always reflect their lovers' current interests and moods." *And vice versa,* she thought. "How did the little mirrors react?"

"There were tantrums. Dishes were broken. There were

threats. Gerry got punched out by Gavivi."

"That sounds promising."

"Well, there was one sane person in the bunch. Roger Bentencourt, he's Rose's boy. He was the only one who seemed to understand the necessity of what you want from them. He promised to present the facts rationally to his mistress."

"Rose is as sensible as any of us can hope to be," Olympias answered. "Let's hope the nest in Alexandria won't give me any trouble." She scratched the hellhound's ears. "Time for us to go for a walk, Bitch."

Chapter 5

"I DON'T SEE why you should have to put up with this," Bentencourt said to Rose. "The so-called Enforcer of the City has no right to dictate to you. You don't live in her city. She's high-handed, rude—I cannot believe the contempt and arrogance she showed you of all people in having a slave summon me when she should—"

"It would hardly have been polite for a slave to summon me," Rose said reasonably, interrupting his well-rehearsed tirade.

Fortunately he knew that Rose would read his very real frustration as being for her rather than at her. They were alone in Rose's large upstairs bedroom. The lovingly polished dark wood Federalist furniture was original, built for Rose when the city of Washington was new. The Audubon bird prints on the teal green walls had been purchased new, as had all the leather-bound books in the tall bookcase. The rugs were hand-braided on the Virginia plantation Rose had owned since before the Civil War. About the only furnishings less than a century old in the nest leader's private sanctuary were the heavily insulated drapes that covered the tall, narrow windows that looked out on the back garden. The mattress on the finely carved bed was new as well. Bentencourt had insisted on a certain amount of creature comforts—though his pretext, as always, had been that Rose deserved to treat herself better.

He'd almost been surprised to discover the place had plumbing, electricity, and a telephone when he'd moved in. Fortunately Bentencourt's two predecessors, as Rose's lovers in the last century, had persuaded her to make a few concessions to the times. Bentencourt wondered what excuses they'd used, since Rose was conservative to the point of stagnation. She actually believed in the ancient laws that forbade strigoi from sharing in the technological advances of the mortal world.

These days even the Enforcers ignored laws that had been forced on the Council sometime in the Renaissance by a group of religious fanatics who'd still believed they'd been turned into vampires by the wrath of an ancient goddess. This bunch believed vampires existed to punish evil mortals, but didn't deserve to share in any good thing that came from the still pure and holy daylight world. Bentencourt didn't know what had become of that particular faction of strigoi, but at least their influence had significantly waned in recent centuries. This didn't stop some vampires, like Rose, still having a penitential streak in their natures.

Rose was also shy and demure, unworldly even by underneath world standards—especially strigoi standards. She Hunted no more than once a decade, did not take companions very often, and her only slave was a lawyer who managed her finances. His family had belonged to Rose for generations. She took in only enough nestlings and young vampires to retain her standing as a nest leader. Bentencourt found her useful. Because he'd seduced her into sharing her blood with him, he really couldn't rouse up the contempt she truly deserved. He loved his Rose even as he used her.

He took a seat beside where she lounged on the bed,

propped up by a pile of tapestry, satin, and floral chintz
pillows. He took her long-fingered hands in his and
kissed them one at a time. Heavy, jeweled rings gleamed
on every finger of her hands, gifts from former lovers.
He'd given her the three-carat diamond set in platinum
she currently wore on the third finger of her left hand.
She was such a romantic.

"Perhaps I haven't conveyed the gravity of the situation to you," he confessed, gentle and contrite. "You, my
love, are being ordered to leave your home. You, me,
and everyone in your nest have been given an eviction
notice. We must go, and it is not right."

"Go?" Rose caught his gaze, and he felt her looking
deep into his mind—or, as deep as he would let her. A
part of his mind was open, the thoughts he placed there
easy for her to read. For all her great psychic talent, Rose
was a simple person. He saw worry finally begin to
crease her lovely, smooth brow after she had examined
his thoughts for a while. She drew her hands from his
and sat up from her languid pose, pushing herself away
from the luxury of the pillows. "This cannot be true," she
declared.

He nodded slowly. "It is, my love. The hag's slave
gave the order as if it meant nothing. As if you meant
nothing."

Rose blinked huge blue eyes at him, eyes that finally
held a hint of comprehension. "This is my home. This
has always been my home."

"I know how you love this place."

She rose up off the bed, not with her usual grace, but
with the speed of a vampire. She moved across the room
to stand before the fireplace and gaze at the portrait over
the mantel. From the style and the dress of the man in
the portrait, Bentencourt guessed that the painting dated
from some time in the late seventeenth century. The man
in the painting was fine boned and had a square, cleft
chin, but was not particularly handsome. The style of his
clothing showed that he was a well-off merchant or land-

owner, a solid, middle-class gentleman, perhaps. And probably a vampire, for he was pale, a candelabra blazed on a table beside him, and a full moon showed through an open window behind his head. Bentencourt assumed this was a portrait of the vampire that had sired Rose, but he had never noticed her pay any attention to it until now.

"This is my home," she insisted. Her fingers stroked the finely carved wood of the mantel, then she picked up and put down several pieces of the bric-a-brac that rested on the shelf beneath the painting, including a small, tapestry-covered box. "Our home." He got the impression she spoke not to him, or even to herself, but to the man in the painting. "I'm an American vampire." She chuckled. "Sometimes I've even thought about applying for membership in the DAR. That's how long I've been here. Longer. A good American. In England I was just an ignorant girl who told fortunes in a highwayman's tavern. When the king's soldiers cleaned out that thieves den, I was loaded onto a ship without so much as a trial. Sent as a bondservant to the new world. I made it my world. I was worked hard, and I nearly starved that first year. I nursed the sick when the swamp fever came. I hated the man who owned me and loved the land like I'd never loved the place where I was born. Then one night I heard a call in my head and ran away from the farm, ran into the woods, into the night, into the arms of a good man who took my blood and taught me how to kill to survive. I learned how to love, how to think, how to fend for myself. Ours was the first nest in the colonies. Only one for a long time. When I made the change, we stayed together because there was no one else who could foster me. We obeyed the laws, never touched each other again, and we both took companions when I was old enough to feel the need. We cleared the land and worked it, and our slaves were bought with blood, not caring about the color of their skins but the spark of magic that makes the weak need to serve the strong. The tobacco merchants built their port town around our land. We fought in the war for independence and the war with the British in 1812 and used our magic to call up the storm that kept the city from being completely burned when the English set fire to it. You felt the need to wander out west, my first true love, but I stayed with the children, with the nest we founded. This is my place."

Rose turned back to face him. "The Greek woman came with the turn of the twentieth century, after the Great War. This is not her land. She works for the Council. She's an ambassador, not an American. She can't make me leave. She can't mean me."

"She can. She does." His words were emphatic, final. He put all the regret he could into his voice. "I'm sorry, but she's ordering you to leave your home."

Rose crossed her arms beneath her ample bosom. "Is she?" she asked. Her voice was ominously soft, and for the first time her eyes took on the glitter of a very dangerous animal. "Is she indeed?"

Bentencourt almost laughed with glee at Rose's reaction. Satisfied that he had his vampire lover's attention directed where he needed it to be, he immediately turned his attention to other factors in his plans. He didn't need to worry about Lora right now. She was in her room, frantically pacing, trying to control the heat coursing through her blood. Lora didn't have to do anything but seethe with pent-up hormones. All he had to do was wait for Olympias to refuse to let the young vampire take a mate. That should take a few days yet. In that time he would continue to work on Rose.

He'd also spend the time cultivating the lovely Ms. Sara Czerny. He'd read her vulnerabilities earlier in the day. The slave was going to be invaluable to him. It was going to be so delightful to seduce Sara away from Olympias and use her as the knife pressed to the bitch queen's throat.

• • •

Alone in his house on a very quiet Georgetown street, with the door to his office locked behind him, Falconer took the tape out of his pocket and tried to decide exactly what to do with it. As he tossed the cassette from hand to hand, every sense he had told him that Grace wasn't going to give up digging into what they'd recorded on this cassette, despite what they agreed on, despite the orders he'd given. They'd gone someplace they shouldn't when they'd tried her little regression experiment. Someplace logic told him could not be real. Grace was going to want to go back, he knew that, maybe to prove that it was all a group hallucination. He hoped it was.

Falconer put the cassette down on the desk in his home office. He glanced at the wall safe and thought about locking away the strange, eerily similar statements made by each of the Walker Project staff. Those similar statements would have been eerie on a normal Walk, though Walking was a psychic phenomenon they were trying to refine into a science. *Astral projection* had been the term for what they did once upon a time. Then some bureaucrat trying to get funding for a study of the phenomenon had coined more obscure and prosaic terms, which certainly sounded a lot less weird when going begging for funding. The people who became involved in these programs were certainly obscure, and anything but prosaic. With the Walker Project they had gone out of their way to find participants that were psychic but sane. Until today Falconer had thought that he and his loons were basically stable personalities, despite the extra added something that made them special.

Until today he hadn't thought he believed in vampires. Consciously he certainly didn't, but his traumatized subconscious had come up with a pair of fanged women who'd fought over him like a pair of bloodsucking bimbos in a B movie. These could not be real memories, of course, but he'd managed somehow to convey his mind's ravings. Every member of the Walker team had tapped into their own view of the same scenario—him on the ground with a huge dog at his throat, while two female vampires, one a small blonde, the other tall, dark, sharp-featured, and utterly fascinating, argued. None of the Walkers had picked up the vampires' words, audio was generally not a part of the Walking experience.

The aching bruises on his body were the only thing he knew for sure to be true. But this fantasy, this group hallucination—there was no way Grace wasn't going to want to go back there, despite any direct orders to the contrary. She could get the project in trouble, discredited, canceled, and those were the least dangerous conse-quences Falconer could think of. Because—what if it was true?

Impossible. Ridiculous. But so was Walking, if you thought about it.

Maybe the others wouldn't let her try to go Walking into the past. Maybe they wouldn't go with her. Maybe she was scared enough by the hallucinations they'd run into to back off and continue doing things by the rules. Maybe she wouldn't run off and talk her friend who did the past life regressions into exploring this new area of research with her. Walking techniques were classified. Falconer didn't think Grace would share them with any-one outside the project deliberately, but she was such an enthusiastic, unconventional kid. More unconventional than all the others combined, come to think of it, which was saying quite a lot.

He really was too fond of her, he admitted with a smile. Maybe she took the place of a daughter he'd never had. He was long divorced, and they'd never had kids. He'd been married to the military rather than to the woman he loved, and she eventually figured that out. The lesson had taken him a lot longer to learn.

Falconer considered listening to the tape, but what good would hashing over the nonsense on it do him in trying to remember what had really happened? He con-sidered destroying it, but it was evidence of—something. A gut reaction told him it might come in handy, or be the most dangerous thing he could possibly possess. His head told him it wasn't evidence of vampires, but something else far riskier for the future of the Walker Project. This tape was evidence that the Walkers could be easily led into a group hallucination by an inadvertent suggestion. That was dangerous news for the project. He feared the bureaucrats in charge of funding far more than he did vampires. He wasn't ready to give up on the project yet, not when there was plenty of other objective, verified evidence that this time the mix of psychic talent and scientific method promised to yield valuable espionage and reconnaissance data. This was a glitch, an anomaly. He could destroy it, listen to it, or lock it away.

He decided to lock it in his office safe, but that still left him with the nagging certainty that Grace wasn't going to abandon trying to repeat the exercise. *Don't worry about it now,* he instructed himself after he turned from locking the safe.

He left the office and considered having dinner, but settled on a glass of iced tea and flipping channels for a while. He ended up watching a cooking show, which didn't seem like a manly, soldierly sort of thing to do, but the WNBA game on ESPN couldn't hold his attention, and he couldn't understand why anyone needed three golf channels when one was more than enough to cure insomnia. Eventually he changed channels and found himself staring at a dog show on Animal Planet.

It was the sight of a group of rottweilers in the show ring that sent the adrenaline rush of terror through him. Falconer was out of the chair, out of the room, and halfway down the hallway to the front door before he came to himself. When he halted he was breathing hard, and sweating, and he had a hand clutched protectively around the bruises on his throat.

"O-kay," he murmured, looking around the narrow hall while his heart pounded in his ears.

He didn't pretend that he imagined the shadows moving on the walls, or that he felt the hot breath of a hound from hell fading behind him. He didn't imagine it, but that didn't mean it wasn't real all the same. As real as the crazy scene he'd relived and the others had witnessed in the exercise in the meeting room this afternoon. He lowered his hand and stood there, making the terror drain away.

All right, that did it. Mike Falconer turned on his heel and marched back into his living room. He switched off the dog show and flipped off the lights. Seated in the dark in his comfortable leather chair, he propped his feet up on the coffee table, closed his eyes, ran through the exercises that brought on a state that was something like light sleep, and let himself do the thing he'd been consciously avoiding since he had had the dream that was akin to Walking the night before.

All right, he thought stubbornly. If there are any vampires in town, I'm going to find them.

Sara cleared her throat. "Uh . . . hello?"

Her voice was so dry with nerves that she barely got the words out. Sara took another step farther away from the path. Branches from a bush caught at her hair, and a mosquito buzzed around her ear. She could hear the creek nearby, and traffic on the high bridge that spanned the stream. There were lights and people, in the distance, leaving her feeling alone and more than a little bit terrified. This was so embarrassing. Sara had no idea how to go about a clandestine meeting at midnight in the dark and spooky woods. In truth it was a well-used national park, and not all that far from where she lived, but homeless people, junkies, and crazy people slept in the more secluded areas. Even without vampires, Washington wasn't the safest city in the world. The point was, there weren't supposed to be any vampires in Washington. The one she was trying to find was breaking the Law simply being in town. Which made him technically a strig, beyond the protection of strigoi law and technically lawful prey for the Enforcer of the City to take at her leisure.

He knew all that, and Sara had to admit that this was actually rather reasonable behavior for someone who wanted to die anyway. Maybe not reasonable, because an immortal being who wanted to die seemed completely unreasonable to her, but she supposed his acting like a strig was logical.

"Hello?" she tried again, and she took another step, around a bush and slightly uphill. "Hello? It's very dark under the trees, isn't it? Is anyone here?"

"It's not dark at all," a man's voice said from behind her. It didn't help that his fingertips lightly brushed across the back of her neck as he spoke. The touch was soft, warm, and utterly terrifying.

Sara didn't scream, but she did freeze like a trapped rabbit.

"I hope you were looking for me," he said.

"Olympias sent me. Please don't eat me," she said, stupid with total, awful awareness of what was standing behind her.

"Of course not. I'm not that sort of monster," he answered. His voice was surprisingly pleasant, restrained, and polite. "But you're certainly not who I was expecting." Gentle hands on her shoulders turned her easily to face him. "Why would the Hunter send a girl to do an Enforcer's job?"

"I'm not a girl, I'm a—"

"You're a very pretty girl," he interrupted. "I was born in 1936, so the remark is not sexist—to me you are a girl."

"What about the pretty part?" she asked. The words came out before she knew she thought them. Even with mortal vision and in the dark woods she was aware of his height, wide shoulders, and strong, handsome features. He didn't look like he'd been born—but, of course he wouldn't. Had she forgotten for a moment? How very odd.

"Come on," he said. He took Sara by the arm without answering her question and led her deeper into the more isolated wooded part of the park. He broke the silence when they reached a small, littered clearing. "I've been camping out here. Long time since I lived like this."

A break in the trees let in moonlight. Sara couldn't help but look around in consternation at what appeared to be a refuse heap. "Lived like a homeless person? Where do you sleep?"

"Lived off the land," the vampire answered. He did not sound offended at her less than respectful tone. "I sleep in the ground, as it should be. I keep to myself. I am a homeless person," he added.

"A *strig*." A flash of anger blazed through him at the word. Sara felt it as a lick of flame against the fragile defenses of her mind. "Sorry!" She didn't realize that she'd put her hands over her eyes until he took them away.

After a considerable silence while the vampire held her wrists, he said, "You have nothing to fear from me."

He sounded so sad and so very tired that his words brought tears to Sara's eyes. "I—didn't mean to offend you," she told him.

He shook his head. "I'm being sensitive to a word that has no meaning in the real world."

"Real world?" She couldn't help but ask. "How do you define the real world?" She only belatedly recalled that she was here to interview him. She supposed this was as good a way to start the process as any, though she really wanted to know what this vampire stranger thought.

"How do you define the real world, companion to a monster?"

"Companion?"

She must have sounded as offended by that word as he had when she called him a strig. He looked down, and she realized that he was still holding her even as he let her wrists go. "Not a companion, I see that now, but you feel—"

"Attached? I'm Olympias's *slave*."

"I hate that term."

"But it is my reality."

"Really? I'm sorry."

What did a vampire have to feel sorry about? "That's how it is," she said. "Some are born to serve."

"But—that isn't how it should be."

Oh, good lord, he was a hippie do-gooder! Sara wasn't sure if the world could do with more or fewer of them, and here she'd been sent to help make that decision. "Olympias told me about you."

"She told you I wanted to die?"

No. I told her. No need for him to know how Olympias really worked. "She said you were a beatnik with a social conscience."

"The less of that sort of person in the world, the better," he said, with a soft, deep chuckle.

She couldn't make out details of his features, but Sara liked his voice. "It's not for me to decide that sort of thing."

"What? Life and death? Do you think that's really true? Does being a slave—being mortal—absolve you from such responsibility?"

Oh, God, spare me! A philosopher.

"And I can read minds, too. Have a seat," he directed as Sara's mind froze with the panic of knowing she was alone in an isolated spot with a supernatural being that fed on mortal emotions and flesh for sustenance. This being desired the death he couldn't give himself. Who knew what he was capable of—"I wouldn't try to get Olympias angry with me by killing someone she cares for."

His reassuring voice came very close to her ear, and Sara realized that they were seated on the ground and that his arm was around her shoulders. He had said something about sitting, hadn't he? Sara stared into the night as the vampire's warmth shielded her from a cool, humid breeze. After a few minutes it permeated her awareness that she felt safe now, calm, reassured by his presence. He was playing with her head, of course, something only her mistress had a right to do, but Sara appreciated his efforts to put her at ease.

"She shouldn't have sent a mortal," he said when she tilted her head up to look at his shadowed face. "This is not the sort of thing a mortal should have to know about. Mortals need to keep their distance, their innocence."

Sara realized he believed what he said and that he truly was concerned about her mental as well as spiritual well-being. "Why do you want to die?" she came out and asked.

He smiled at her directness. "My name's Andrew, you know. I imagine the Hunter told you that much about me. Let's not be formal right now, shall we—?"

"Sara."

"Nice to meet you, Sara. May we have a brief and productive acquaintance. Now, tell me, where's the Enforcer this evening?"

She'd expected him to ask why Olympias had sent a slave rather than coming herself. She expected him to at least be offended and condescending, if not downright violent, about discussing life and death matters with an underling. "I have no idea where she is," Sara answered honestly. "But the Enforcer is doing something very important," she hastened to add. "Or she'd be here herself."

A snort of laughter greeted this statement. "Don't tell me Olympias has changed since I've been out of town."

"She has more responsibilities than you can imagine." Sara rushed to her mistress's defense.

"Apologies, Sara."

"She wanted me to talk to you first," Sara admitted. "To report my impressions of your—your state of mind."

"To find out if my intentions are really serious."

She craned for a better view of him. How she wished she had at least some of the vampires' night vision. She strained her weak psychic senses to try to read him. She did get the impression of deep despondency from him, of agitation beneath his calm, polite exterior. "Are your intentions serious?"

He sighed. "Of course they are. Do you think I'd go to all this trouble otherwise?"

"I don't know," she answered. "Would you?"

Andrew stood, then helped her to her feet. "Let me walk you back toward civilization." He took her hand and led her back the way they'd come. "I've been living in California and Texas lately," was all he said on the way back to the walking path along the creek. "I'd forgotten how uncomfortably humid the nights here can be."

"I've lived here all my life." Sara was not used to volunteering personal information, and didn't know why she felt the need to fill the deep, dark silence from Andrew with words of her own. "Why do you want to die?" she asked again when they reached the path, where the sound of the traffic and the nearby water somehow made the surroundings seem more safe, more civilized.

"Why?" he repeated her question. There was enough light for her to make out his features now. His smile was sad, and his eyes were haunted. "Why? For one thing, Sara, I'm going insane. Lately I'm being haunted by a ghost." He shrugged. "Spirit of someone I killed, I suppose, though I don't recognize him."

"A ghost?"

Andrew nodded. "It was back in the clearing with us just now. Staring at me. I don't suppose you saw it?"

Sara shook her head. "You saw a ghost? An actual ghost?"

"Not for the first time." He shrugged again. "I told you I was crazy."

"What the hell was that all about?" Mike Falconer asked as he pried himself out of the deep comfort of his chair. He paced for a few agitated moments, then noticed the empty glass and decided that a refill of iced tea was not going to do the trick right now. He went into the kitchen and got a beer, regretting that was the strongest alcohol he let himself have.

He very much wanted a drink, and something for the

blazing headache he'd brought out of the unmonitored Walking session. But he put the beer can down on the kitchen table and forced his thoughts to go back over what he'd seen while roaming outside his body. He'd gone looking for vampires, and what had he found? A couple having a clandestine meeting somewhere in a forest. No, not a forest. There was something familiar about where the couple had been. Falconer was sure it was somewhere he'd been himself, but the location hadn't clicked in his memory yet.

Had he found a vampire? He'd caught bits and pieces of conversation, but nothing definitive. No fangs had been flashed. It was hard to tell if someone was a pale, bloodsucking fiend in the dark if no fangs were flashed and no blood was drawn. He'd caught mental impressions from both the man and the woman and a few words he couldn't remember yet, which was not normal for a Walking experience. Maybe that was proof that they both had some sort of psychic talent. Falconer had received the stronger impression from the male. He was one confused, depressed guy. Was that normal for a vampire?

Falconer was sure that the man was the same person—monster?—he'd seen standing in the water with red eyes and bared fangs when he'd dreamed/Walked the night he'd been attacked. There was something familiar about the man—vampire?—even more than having seen him once before.

The weirdest thing—the impossible thing—was that Falconer was sure the man had been aware of his invisible presence. Last time that had happened, the man had turned into a monster before Falconer's eyes. This time, he'd turned and walked away, carefully making sure the woman was safe.

Did vampires do that?

Chapter 6

"WHAT IS WITH this man?" Olympias complained to the dog trotting along beside her as they headed toward Georgetown. Bitch looked attentive and interested, which was all the job required, while Olympias continued to voice her thoughts. "If I can't find him dreamwalking, how did the girl spot him? Maybe because I'm not in heat. Senses do rev up a few notches when the mating urge hits."

The first thing Olympias had done this evening was follow Sara at a discreet distance until she was certain that her mortal servant was safe with the suicidal vampire. She hadn't been too worried, Andrew had always been a polite kid, a romantic. He was one of Rose's, and Rose raised them right. The truth was, in Olympias's opinion, Rose made a bad habit of taking wimps for lovers, but if that was how Rose liked them, she supposed that was fine. Wimps didn't make very interesting vampires, but from an Enforcer's point of view, interesting vampires weren't all that desirable, either. Maybe breeding the monster out made for a more boring brand of strigoi, but it made for peace and quiet, it made for survival for the entire species in these high-tech, hard-to-hide-in times.

"It makes you want to puke," Olympias observed, remembering an era when being a vampire had been a lot more fun.

There was nothing a girl could sink her fangs and claws into these days that wasn't regulated by the Council and the Laws. Maybe she was a member of that Council and she was likely to vote on the conservative, cautionary side on the rare occasions the Council met to decide how to cope with the modern world. But that didn't mean she liked being forced to hide deeper and deeper in the shadows. She didn't mind that her kind were a minority—predators needed to be in the balance of nature—but being a marginalized minority fighting hard not to become an endangered species was a pain in the butt.

What I need is this bunny's name, Olympias decided as she walked along, her long, quick strides eating up distance. *A phone number. Something concrete and factual, since I can't seem to wrap my mind around his and suck out what I need to know in the nice, old-fashioned, traditional way. What's the use of being one of the few truly powerful, genuine psychics in the world, with long-practiced and -perfected technique, with thousands of hours and years of experience under my belt, when I need a phone book to look up this joker to see whether or not I'm going to let a wet-behind-the-fangs bimbo turn him into a vampire?*

Olympias paused to take a mental breath and patted Bitch on the head. If she gave it some effort, she could find the vampire kid. But the idea of approaching the girl for help after having made such hard-ass pronouncements about the matter was embarrassing, demeaning, and would weaken her standing in a time when she was heading for a showdown with every vampire in the area about their living arrangements. She didn't expect them to take it quietly and didn't yet have a clue where the attack would come from. She didn't know whether a show of superior indifference would cow them into shuffling off in a surly, mumbling heap of resentment. That was the plan, of course, but it was more likely someone was going to challenge her. Olympias didn't want it to come down to her having to kill someone, because, frankly, though it was necessary to clear the nests out of their territories, it wasn't the vampires' fault that the mortal government was spreading farther and farther out of the central city. The Law was clear about vampires living in the capital cities of mortal lands. It could be argued that there were nests in Moscow, but she'd argue that those old Imperialist farts still thought St. Petersburg was the capital of Russia. Olympias's territory was Washington, and she saw the need to keep the city clean of bloodsuckers. At least of the immortal variety. In fact, she'd waited too long to order this move and knew it, even if the nests wouldn't agree.

That was a situation she'd think about later. Right now she wanted to get what should have been a minor vetting job out of the way. She'd decided that the best way—the only way left—was to find the park where she'd stopped the girl from raping her prey.

"This is where you come in, Bitch," she told the eager dog. She rubbed Bitch's ears and passed a mental image of what they were looking for into the animal's mind. "First one to find the scent of the party gets a treat."

Bitch took off instantly. Olympias laughed and kept pace with the hellhound, the pair of them becoming moving shadows passing through the quiet streets of Georgetown. She should have thought of this sooner, for it didn't take long at all before she caught the lingering mental signature of lust, fear, and anger. Within a few blocks she spotted the park, a dark square of trees, grass, and flowerbeds circled by a wrought iron fence and surrounded by narrow streets lined with row houses. Parking in Georgetown was always at a premium, and even though there was little traffic, the narrow streets were jammed with expensive cars, squeezed in nose-to-trunk, taking up every inch of curb.

Before entering the park Olympias noticed a plaque on the fence by the gate. It stated firmly that no animals were allowed inside, a rule Bitch had already disobeyed. The hellhound was already sniffing around a stand of trees. An unnatural chill halted Olympias just inside the gate. The unexpected sensation cast an odd overlay to the fading mental energy already spread across the area. She looked carefully around, searching for the anomaly with all her very sharp senses. She picked up images—no— impressions of images. Faded, indistinct columns of energy—energy that wasn't really there? Images that weren't there but left a residue anyway? Like sensing someone on the darkened side of a mirror? She knew nothing had been there, but that it was a nothing that left its mark. Four or five—entities—intelligences—anti-images scattered all around . . . but not here now.

"Weird," she muttered, while the hairs on the back of her neck rose in reaction. Whatever this nothing was, it was like nothing she'd ever encountered. Considering she'd encountered about every type of psychic and supernatural thing that existed in her more than two thousand years of life, that was saying quite a lot. This made the mystery of her mystery man even stranger, and she didn't like that at all.

It was supposed to be a simple job.

Bitch gave one deep bark. Glowing eyes looked anxiously at her out of the dark.

"Coming," Olympias answered. "Yesterday upon the stair, I saw a man who wasn't there," she said as she moved very carefully toward her dog. "He wasn't there again today." She laughed, remembering a version of the rhyme she'd read somewhere that ended, "I think he's from the CIA."

What she'd come here to do was pick up the man's mental signature and follow it to where he lived. That was what she was still going to do. Once she found him, she'd ask him not at all politely what he knew about the weird things in the park that weren't vampires.

When her pocket rang, Olympias discovered that Sara had thoughtfully tucked her cell phone into her sweatshirt jacket. It was an unlisted number known to one mortal and every Enforcer in the country. The Enforcers were instructed not to use it unless they had a strigoi-threatening emergency on their hands. Indirect forms of communication were so much easier to keep secret than a conversation on a cellular telephone. Enforcers were semiautonomous, very capable, and she was the one who usually called them with instructions. It kept on ringing, and Olympias was tempted not to answer. Olympias didn't want to cope with a national emergency right now. But if Sara was in trouble with Andrew, she'd call for help. That must be why Sara slipped the phone into the jacket.

She pulled out the phone and flipped it open. "What?" The voice was not Sara's. Olympias stood very still and listened. "Memphis?" she asked. "There's an Enforcer in Nashville, but not in Memphis. Right. I see to—hold on, I've got another call on the other line." She hated call waiting and made a mental note to tell Sara to get rid of it as she answered the other call. This caller wasn't Sara, either. "How'd you get this number?" There was the old boys' network, then there was the old girls' network, and the caller was a very old girl indeed. Olympias listened to her for a few moments, dread growing, then said, "Yes, I know about the hotel opening in Las Vegas. Oh. That's not good." She looked around the park. She had no time for bunny hunting right now. "I'll call you back. Right. I don't have your number. Call me back in half an hour, on a landline." She switched to the first caller. "Stay there. I'll call you back."

Olympias switched off the phone and called her dog to her. She had to get home and start the process of putting out a pair of serious fires. She would worry about local emergencies later—which seemed to be happening more and more these days.

"Memory doesn't lie, but it does hallucinate. I hope," Falconer muttered to himself as he made a careful search through the park.

"What?" the friend he'd brought with him asked.

"Nothing." Falconer was looking for a particular tree. Though it was daylight, the place was thick with unnatural shadows, as if it didn't want him to know it was here.

But he knew he was in the right place, though he couldn't explain to his forensic scientist friend that his certainty came from the psychic residue of the Walkers, and not because this was where the attack had to have taken place. The thing was, he shouldn't have forgotten where he'd been attacked. He hadn't suffered any head trauma, and there was no logical excuse for him to have forgotten the existence of a park he passed on his walks all the time. When he'd come to his senses it had been like walking out a long, black tunnel, and he'd found himself standing stupidly in front of the door to his house.

Maybe he should forget the incident and move on, forget the weirdness the Walkers had encountered yesterday, and forget the man who might or might not be a vampire who showed up in visions and dreams when Falconer was looking for something else. Of course, if he were serious about dropping any investigation, he wouldn't have called Russ Krantz from the FBI forensics lab and asked for a private crime scene investigation. Russ was ex-military, and he and Falconer went way back. Tight-assed as the Feds were, Russ hadn't balked at the request, only at the early hour Falconer asked him to meet him. Falconer had placated him by bringing coffee and donuts. Now, as heat built and storm clouds loomed in the early morning sky, the two men ignored curious glances from runners on the park paths and methodically quartered the block-square area.

"Here," Falconer called at the third tree he inspected. "Broken bark," he told Russ when he came trotting up.

"So I see. Stand back," Russ directed, waving Falconer away from the tree.

Falconer stepped back to let his friend work. After a brief inspection of the tree trunk and the ground around it, Russ opened a bag, put on gloves, and took out a selection of equipment. He used tweezers and put things in vials. It was all very arcane to Mike Falconer.

After a few minutes Falconer couldn't contain his impatience anymore. "Well? What have you found?"

"Hair, mostly," Russ answered. "Some fibers. Possibly a tiny amount of blood."

"Evidence," Falconer said, and sighed. He was surprised at how anxious he'd been that there might be no way to prove the reality of what had happened to him. "Good."

"I'll let you know if it's good after I get back to the lab. This is everything." Russ sealed the last bit of evidence and put the container in his bag. "I could bring in some fancy high-tech equipment and go over the area if you like, Mike."

"Neither of our budgets could handle that."

"Not if all you're paying in is coffee and donuts."

"And favors to be returned," Falconer added.

Russ grunted and hefted his bag. He checked his watch. "If you're going to tell me you need this stuff by tonight, you're out of luck."

"Understood." Falconer checked his own watch. He had an appointment in an hour and important meetings the rest of the day. There were no Walking sessions scheduled for the rest of the week, thank goodness. "I wouldn't be home tonight, even if you had anything for me," he told his friend. "I'll be at a party."

Russ canted a bushy eyebrow at Falconer. "Hot date?"

"Only if you consider kissing up to appropriations committee members hot."

The FBI scientist laughed. They strolled toward the

street together. "I thank God regularly that I'm a faceless cog in the bureaucratic wheel. At least I don't have to personally worry about where my funding comes from."

"Lucky bastard. Thanks for the help."

"No problem," Russ answered.

They tossed empty coffee containers into a garbage can. Russ hefted his bag on his shoulder. Falconer did not let himself look nervously over his shoulder at the shadows and ghosts in the park, and they went their separate ways.

The taste of the Irish coffee was good against his tongue, the heat of it spread a comforting warmth. The raincoat he'd folded over the chair next to his was still soaking wet, and his hair was a little damp. Rain poured down outside, the storm clouds covering the city so dark it was hard to tell that it was near the middle of the day. Frequent flashes of lightning lit up the street outside the wide windows at the front of the bar. Bentencourt checked his watch, something that was a habit still more than a necessity. The blood he shared with Rose was changing him. Among those changes was the growing awareness of the exact position of the sun as the earth turned in its rotation.

He loved the taste of her blood, and hated the necessity of having to taste it so rarely. The anticipation was sweet, of course, and the test of his control was good for him. He needed to be disciplined, to remain focused. The threads he held in his hands were only beginning to come together. He had to keep careful watch on each and every intersecting plan. The drives of the body changing and opening up to new and powerful kinds of magic left one distracted to the point of madness. Look at how Cassandra had behaved at lunch the day before, making a fool of herself in front himself and Gavivi, showing her vulnerability.

Poor dear, he thought. There must be some use I can make of her obvious misery.

Someday he would go through that change, but not until he was in control of the world around him. He looked forward to the night he made his first kill and the brief decadence of rebirth that would follow. Once he was a strigoi he would always be in command of the magic, the need.

"Let me go!" he recalled Lora begging last night when Rose stopped her from leaving the house. He had to admit he was impressed that his lethargic little Rose sensed the young vampire's intentions and moved with decisive speed to keep the girl in the house. "I need!" Lora cried.

Rose held her in her arms, rocking her like a loving mother trying to ease the broken heart of a child rather than soothing a monster who ripped them out. "Patience," she urged. "We always need. The hunger bubbles in the mind and whispers all the time—take, Hunt, rape, kill. Fight the hunger, Lora. Be strong, one moment at a time."

"You told me I could have him!"

"You will."

"She hurt me. She wouldn't let me taste him. I stalked him, I claim him. He's my prey!"

"He'll be in your bed soon. You hunted him too close to the Hunter's territory, and that was my fault. I didn't think she'd care. I shouldn't have let you go without consulting with the Hunter. I was wrong."

"You're never wrong," Bentencourt interjected quickly. "The Greek witch doesn't care, except to try to exert control she doesn't deserve. She can't control what goes on inside your nest. The Law says that Lora has a right to take a companion."

"Of course she does," Rose answered, still holding Lora in a grip of steel. Lora moaned and clutched at Rose's shoulders, her claws out, but not piercing flesh that only appeared soft and vulnerable. Rose made Lora look deep into her eyes. "You will have a companion. His blood is yours. Soon."

The constant hunger to Hunt was palpable in both

women. Bentencourt could taste it on the charged air. No matter how well vampires managed to control the dark urges, much of the time it was their weak spot, the place where they could most easily be manipulated. He loved that about them. It made it so easy for him.

Bentencourt smiled at the memory of last night's little drama. Lora certainly would not be granted her wish to take the companion of her choice soon, but perhaps she would have her bunny one way or another. Bentencourt really didn't care what happened to Falconer, as long as Lora's interest in him brought Olympias trouble.

He had plenty of time before he had to leave, especially since he would probably catch a cab instead of walking the ten or twelve blocks to his meeting in this downpour. Time for a pub lunch, and maybe a game of darts if any of the bar's regulars put in an appearance. The place was not too far from the zoo and a metro stop. Too many tourists found their way to the place at lunchtime to sample the excellent beer and simple but genuine Irish fare. Evenings it was different; locals came for the music and gatherings in the back rooms. Several genuine psychics did readings here once or twice a month and taught classes as well. It was a meeting with one of those psychics that had changed his life. He'd ended up holding his own classes as a way of developing his mental abilities and gaining information with the hypnotic and mind-reading skills he discovered he was so gifted with. Bentencourt was not the regular he'd been at one time, but he did miss the evenings holding court in the back rooms.

It was good to indulge in a bit of nostalgia, but Bentencourt wondered why he was really here today. True, this old haunt was not too far from his destination, but he knew there was no such thing as coincidence for mental adepts, only synchronicity. By the time he'd signaled a waitress, given her his lunch order, then turned his attention to the door, he had his answer.

Ah, he thought, *of course.*

Bentencourt raised his hand to get her attention. Grace Avella smiled when she saw him. He noted that she did not look a bit surprised at his presence as she made her way through the mass of small tables to reach his place near the dark paneled wall. She'd been Walking, he concluded, looking for him. He was annoyed with himself for not having felt her. He'd tried such astral projection but hadn't yet figured out how it was done. It was not high on his list of priorities. While the ability to watch the actions of others without detection was useful, he didn't absolutely need it now. Besides, it would develop naturally with other strigoi talents once he'd made the change. He was not paranoid that others could spy on him. He was clever enough to make sure his actions masked his motives, but it was annoying to know that it could be done.

He showed no annoyance when he greeted Grace, and certainly no awareness of how she'd found him. He rose and took her folded umbrella, placing it on top of his raincoat. "What a pleasant surprise," he said as he gallantly rose and pulled out a chair for her. "I've missed our little sessions. You're looking well. Still practicing the exercises we tried out?" She flushed with pleasure at such attention. It was surprising how these old-fashioned gestures disarmed modern women. "I've just ordered lunch. What can I have the waitress get for you?"

"Oh. Nothing. Thank you." She waved away his question with a flustered gesture. "I can't stay. I only stopped by on the off chance . . . well, here you are, and I was hoping to see you."

He gazed upon her with curious delight. "Really? I'm flattered. What can I help you with?" While Grace considered how to word her answer, Bentencourt caught a server's eye and ordered his visitor a cup of hot tea. "To take the chill off from the rain."

"Thanks." She glanced outside. "That's not rain. That might possibly be the apocalypse."

"Oh, no, I'm sure that's not scheduled for several days yet."

She smiled and grew more at ease. "Is it all right if we talk? I don't want to take up too much of your time."

"I do have to be somewhere in about an hour," he answered honestly. He focused his attention completely on her. "But until then, I am all yours."

Grace leaned forward, her elbows on the table and her gaze locked onto his. "I hope you can help me set up an experiment . . . something like the past life regressions we did, but different."

"Go on," he urged. She did. While he listened to her words he also delicately probed her surface thoughts. Within a few moments he knew that Grace and her cohorts could conceivably pose a threat. He also decided how he could use Grace's little group to gain more power among the local vampires and their companions. Quite a delicious opportunity, really.

Sara wasn't quite sure why she turned up at the slaves' usual meeting place when there was no one she was expecting to meet today. She sat in her usual pew within view of her favorite stained glass window. No sunlight flooded in to illuminate the brilliant colors of the glass on this miserable, rainy day, but she liked looking at the window anyway. She felt abandoned, alone, restless, and melancholy and didn't know whether she'd rather have someone to share her feelings with or someone she could give orders to and consult with to give her a sense of purpose.

Gerry was still in Denver. Maggie had sent the invitation to tonight's party by messenger. Caleb was with the White House press corps in New York. Mira was actually on vacation, something Sara would never consider asking Olympias to let her do. Sara had too much to do, and should be in her office catching up right now. So, why was she here? Habit, she supposed. She sighed and took a bite of a very dull cheese sandwich. She wasn't a creature of the night, she was a creature of habit. Besides, she wanted the solitude, which was an odd way of looking at it since the house contained only a dead-to-the-world vampire and a snoring dog and her present surroundings was one of the main tourist attractions in the Washington area. It was so peaceful here, so—

"Tell me, Ms. Czerny, do you come here to pray?"

Her head snapped up at the sound of the mild, amused question. Heart racing, she found herself looking in shock into the eyes of Rose Shilling's latest companion. "Bentencourt," she said, remembering his name. What was he doing here? "Pray?"

His thinning hair was damp, his bland features shadowed by the dim light in the cathedral. He said, "The National Cathedral is more or less nondenominational. Surely there's a shrine somewhere for the old goddess our people worship. Do you pray to her?"

"Our people?" Sara repeated, her wits sluggish. Sara had no idea what he was talking about. Despite hosting services of many faiths the cathedral was actually an Episcopal church, so of course there weren't any shrines dedicated to ancient pagan goddesses on the premises. It took her a few moments to realize that the comment had been meant as a joke and to dutifully smile in response.

A nearby flash of lightning cracked across the sky, and Sara's gaze automatically shifted to watch the sudden eerie glow that lit her favorite window.

"The Space Window," Bentencourt said.

Sara turned back to him and rose from her seat. He was a tall man, and she didn't like the way he'd been looming over her. As thunder rumbled after the lightning she found herself pushing away sudden worry about how Andrew was faring sleeping outdoors in the pouring rain. The companion's presence was the immediate problem, she reminded herself, not a wayward vampire's irregular sleeping arrangements.

"How did you know where to find me?" she asked,

whispering even though the flow of tourists was thin today and there was no one near them.

"Something your associate Gerry said to you when he
left the lunch meeting, about meeting under the rock. He
said it in a way that gave it special significance. At first
I thought he might mean the Hope Diamond at the Smith-
sonian, but that place is always so crowded, and the gem
is displayed at eye level. I could think of only a single
place in Washington where one is actually under a very
significant rock." He gestured to the beautiful, modern-
istic stained glass window in deep reds and blues placed
high in the gothic wall nearby. A small rock was set in
the center of the vibrantly colored glass. "The moon rock
one of the astronauts persuaded the government to donate
to the cathedral." He turned toward the window. "It is
very lovely." He glanced back at her. "It has a special
meaning for you, doesn't it?"

At another time Sara might have found Bentencourt's
friendly curiosity pleasant, but her main emotion right
now was annoyance with Gerry. Gerry was no loose-
lipped fool, but he did have his own agenda. No doubt
he'd decided that Bentencourt was a sensible, reasonable,
forward-thinking person who would be equally reasonable when he was reborn as a strigoi. Gerry would want
to test the waters of his theory about the need to out the
vampires to see if he could find like-minded monsters.
So he'd dropped a hint—and here Bentencourt was.
Damn.

Sara was going to have serious words with Gerry when
he got home. Right now, she smiled at the companion.
"Your guess proved to be quite right." She fought the
urge to demand what he wanted, because a slave must
always be polite to a companion unless given permission
to be otherwise. "How nice to see you so soon," she said
instead. She gestured him toward her favorite pew. "How
can I be of service?"

He declined her invitation with a wave of his hand.

"I've already been away from the office a bit longer than I should."

Of course, he still had a day job. Most companions did. Despite their status in the strigoi community, for the first few years of their association with their vampire lovers a majority of companions were also people who had to deal with normal activities of the mortal world. She noticed that his raincoat was dripping onto the stones of the floor, and it sent a ripple of guilt through her that she was annoyed with someone who'd gone to the trouble of finding her in such awful weather.

"I'm sorry," she told him. "I'd hate to make you late."

"It wouldn't be your fault—may I call you, Sara?" He went on at her nod. "I am the one who sought you out, Sara. I'm sure you're wondering why."

Because Gerry wants you on his team. She swallowed her thought and said, "Something to do with Rose, and the move?"

"Something to do with the proposed relocation, certainly," he answered.

He put his hand on her shoulder. She wasn't used to being touched by anyone but Olympias, and didn't like it. He noticed and took his hand away. She couldn't help the distaste that lingered from his gesture. How odd, that he bothered her today, when she'd rather liked him the first time they'd met. She had no reason to dislike him now; he was being polite and solicitous.

"Yes?" she asked, just to urge him to say his piece so she could get away.

"I couldn't help but notice how the other companions treated you," he said, with the slightest hint of disapproval in his tone and worry in his eyes.

"They can't help their attitude."

"I think they can, but right now is no time to attempt to lecture the other companions on their manners. Right now, the nests are up in arms, and the nest leaders are furious with your mistress. There could be trouble brewing, and the nests having to deal with a surrogate—"

"A slave."

"—rather than the Enforcer herself, can only exacerbate the situation."

"Ain't that the truth," Sara blurted out before she could stop herself. Bentencourt smiled faintly, and she cleared her throat. "I think you judge the situation correctly," she told him. "I take it this is where you come in?"

He bowed slightly, a gesture both courtly and ironic. "You are most perceptive, Sara."

"Thank you."

"But you are not a companion. Pity," he added. "Because you certainly have the—" He stopped himself, and looked away from her for an instant while her heart jumped at his words and she had to fight down a gasp. She didn't know what he meant, and he didn't elaborate when he looked back at her. "I think I might be able to help you," he told her. "If you'll let me?"

"How?" she asked. "With the move?" she added after he stood and looked at her for too long with an expression of deep sadness in his eyes.

"With the move," he said. "For now."

When the nest relocated there would be no later. Which was just as well. Between the encounter with Andrew and this conversation with Bentencourt, she was shaken up enough. She didn't need to be shaken up. Olympias wouldn't like it.

If she noticed.

Sara fought off traitorous thoughts, and asked, "How?"

"I thought I could act as your liaison with the nests," he answered. "It might be more . . . diplomatic that way."

It would also be less humiliating and painful. She turned toward the Space Window, gazed at it while lightning backlit it again, and thought about his suggestion. There were pros, there were cons, she didn't know what Olympias would think.

Finally, she turned back to Bentencourt and said, "I appreciate your thoughtfulness. You're very kind."

He gave a self-depreciating shrug. "Then you'll let me help you?"

Sara gave him a grateful smile. "I will seriously think about it."

"I'm glad." He took a step back. "And I'd better be going now. I'm sure we'll be in touch," he added, before he turned and disappeared into a crowd of tourists milling around the wide main entrance doors of the cathedral.

Chapter 7

"I DON'T WANT to go."

"That's not what you said last night," Sara reminded
Olympias. Honestly, there was nothing worse than a
pouting vampire.

Olympias glanced toward the phone on the bedroom
nightstand. "I didn't have two emergencies last night."

"Maggie thinks it's important you check out this party.
Are Maggie's instincts ever wrong? Besides," Sara
pointed out, "you aren't in Memphis or Las Vegas,
you're here. The Enforcers will do their jobs and report
to you as needed. You might as well go to a party while
you're waiting. It is business."

Sara knew that overseeing the Enforcers was really
about the only part of her job Olympias enjoyed anymore. Maybe her mistress needed to get out into the field
herself. She was a Hunter, after all, a scion of the Nighthawk line. Protecting the strigoi from any detection from
the government and all her other administrative duties
had to be wearing on instincts honed for the kill.

"Besides, you look really hot in that outfit," she added.
"Doesn't she, Bitch?"

At the sound of her name, the hellhound glanced up from the center of the bed, where she was chewing up an old shoe. Bitch probably wasn't impressed by the deceptively simple black dress and beaded bolero jacket, but the tall, elegant Enforcer did look stunning. Sara was an expert with makeup, and her artistry showed off Olympias's angular jawline, high cheekbones, dark eyes, and wide mouth and covered up even the smallest hint of unnatural paleness in the vampire's skin. It took a great deal of work to keep Olympias's naturally curly black hair in its currently short, straight style, but Sara managed to beat it into submission. She took a great deal of pride in how her mistress looked, and tonight Olympias looked damned good.

"No way I'm putting hours into fixing an old bag like you up and letting you stay home."

"It would be a waste," Olympias conceded. She cast a glance toward the full-length mirror and smiled. "Damn, I look good." She looked back at Sara. "If the vanity ever goes away, get someone to rip out my heart, 'cause I won't be me anymore. Thanks. You do good work."

"This is the point where I modestly say that I have a lot to work with."

"This would be that point. But maybe I should stay home. If—"

"No. You need to go. I have it covered." She really, really wanted Olympias out of the house. "You want to go."

Olympias had been complaining about leaving the house since she woke up. Sara had no news about out-of-town problems and had pointed out that no news was good news. Olympias grumbled about this, fumed about being out of the loop and her own frustration at not finishing the job she'd started last night. Despite Olympias's grousing, Sara knew she wouldn't have put up with having Sara fix her face and hair and putting on the dress Sara chose for her if she didn't intend to go to the reception. That was work too, a responsibility no one but

Olympias could carry out. Often enough Olympias brought back information from these affairs that the strigoi needed to head off possible discovery. It really was getting harder to stay undercover in this day and age.

"Your cell phone is in your purse," Sara told Olympias.

"They wouldn't call me on that number tonight."

"No, but I can."

"Right. Don't leave your office. Stick close to the landline. Get hold of me the instant you hear anything."

Sara nodded. That wasn't exactly how she planned to spend her evening, but she would check voice mail regularly. Olympias's word was law, but Sara also had a date. No, not a date. What an odd thought to pass through her head. "About Andrew," she said, not being completely able to commit even a sin of omission against her mistress.

Olympias picked up her small black evening bag. "What about him? Do I have time for a briefing now?"

Sara shook her head. "There's not much to tell. Not yet. We didn't talk in any great detail last night. I really don't know if he's serious or not."

"Are you going to see him again?"

Sara hesitated. "I suppose I should."

"Well, get back to me when you have an opinion." Olympias patted the dog's head and scratched her ears. "We'll go for a run when I get home," she promised Bitch, who went back to work destroying the shoe as soon as Olympias turned away. "Gotta go spy on the spies. Call me."

"I will. Go." *Please.* "Have a good time."

Sara waited, tense and still, almost holding her breath until she was sure Olympias's car was well away from the house. With her mistress gone, Sara grabbed her purse and raincoat and left Bitch alone in the house with only an old shoe for company.

• • •

Grace was too quiet today. Is that a good or bad sign? Falconer wandered through the crowded reception room with most of his thoughts on his staff because he didn't need to keep a whole lot of his attention on the party. Waiters circulated with drinks, a string quartet played discreetly in a corner, people chatted and laughed, and he was aware of it all in much the way he was aware of distant surroundings when he Walked through them during a session.

He knew when to stop and smile, when to look attentive and nod at the right person, but most of his attention was on his staff. *I'm thinking of her as a friend. Worrying about her and not worrying about how any unsanctioned actions she might take could affect the project. Bad sign. Should never have allowed that stupid experiment. Wonder how Russ is coming along with testing the evidence? Should stay away from that, I know it. Bad feeling. Some things man's not meant to know. Don't they say that in horror movies—after the mad scientist lets some monster escape from the lab and destroy downtown Tokyo? I can believe in lab-created monsters—but the other sorts, those are folk legends, primitive fears of cannibal creatures left over deep in the dark part of our monkey brains.*

Speaking of monkeys, that's me. Need to pay attention. He was here as a trained monkey in a dress uniform. It was part of the job, and he'd long ago stopped minding the necessity to be a presence at such get-togethers. He knew that he was a loon, but the important thing for the project was that he didn't look like one. He looked like a steady, serious person. The uniform fit well on his tall, wide-shouldered frame, he was told he had a pleasant speaking voice, he still had all his hair, and the gray at his temples supposedly made him distinguished looking. His hands were huge and his nose was crooked from being broken in a long-ago fight. He was a big, ugly Mick, but such features showed him to be a manly man and not some airy fairy New Age—loon.

People weren't supposed to know what he was, but they did. He wasn't supposed to know the secrets of other black ops personnel, but he did. They all used their talents, mental and technological, to spy on each other, especially around this time of year when they were jockeying for funding.

There were about fifty to sixty people in the room, a larger gathering than Falconer expected, since the appropriations committee being wined, dined, and wheedled controlled funding to black ops and highly classified programs. The irony was that no one was allowed to ask anyone else "How's business?" in such a setting, and no one was allowed to answer if they were asked. In fact, anyone who asked any such questions would be immediately escorted out and would end up having long conversations with faceless men in windowless rooms. People who needed millions of dollars were socializing with people who controlled the millions they needed, and no one was allowed to talk about it. It was all very silly, but someone had decided that putting a social face on the spooks—and loons—helped in the funding process.

"Me," Falconer said as he reached a buffet table, "I'm here for the food."

What I'd really like to do is kill something, Olympias thought. *Or—*

As she took a drink from a passing tray, Olympias noticed that her nails were significantly longer than they should be, almost to the length of mating claws. This would not do, even though she knew that there were those in the room who thought—even fervently hoped—that she was a dominatrix.

If only they knew.

And she was almost tempted to show the ones who wanted her just what she could make them do. Wouldn't that be a fun way to finish the evening? But there'd be a press conference tomorrow, and media analysis, and spin doctors as well as real doctors for these folk to deal with. *But at least I'd have some fun.*

Take a deep breath, girl, have some champagne. You're not here to play games. Too bad. Maybe she needed to Hunt. She didn't need to often, but maybe that was it. It was more likely that she was twitchy with boredom from reading the surface secrets of some of the dullest, yet most paranoid minds she'd come across for a while. Maggie had been right about this being the party for Olympias to attend this week. Sara had been right not to let her blow it off just because she had other crises in other parts of the country. The cell phone in her small black evening bag hadn't rung once, but she didn't discount that her twitchy nerves were caused by waiting for the phone to ring.

It was a good thing she was here, but the people were so banal and unpleasant, despite smiling faces, polite tones, and nice, but conservative clothes—not unlike ninety percent of the mortal and immortal populations. Her search through the bureaucrats' heads had turned up a few juicy, useful secrets, but mostly she'd found fear and envy, vice, ambition, and greed, all of it far too career focused. Wouldn't the world be better off without a few of them?

No Hunting! she ordered herself. *Be good.*

Enforcers always had to be good. It wasn't fair. It also resulted in one occasionally going quite mad and causing far more trouble than any average vampire could manage. Mad Enforcers were what she had Istvan for. Her smile widened. It might be fun, being Hunted by Istvan. She knew she could outthink him. Could she outfight him?

Olympias shook her head, chasing away the pleasant fantasy that had momentarily replaced her boredom. Boredom was a big problem with vampires, too, and a concentrated dose like this was enough to make one twitchy. She sipped champagne. It was good champagne. Not as good as blood of course, but champagne was for celebrations, blood was for when you were horny. She couldn't recall the last time she'd had anything to celebrate, and she certainly wasn't—

"Whoa!" She spun around, and the big guy in the dress uniform caught her attention with the force of a shock wave. The strength of his mental energy pulsed for less than a second, powerful shields slipping for a moment and quickly masking his talent once more. No one noticed, no one felt it but her.

Her breath caught, and her drink tumbled from numb fingers, shattering glass and sending a spray of golden wine across the floor and her shoes. People stared, and she swore and walked away from the mess with the disdain of a queen who was used to being cleaned up after. Besides, she had bigger fish to fry than worrying about having just called attention to herself and ruining a four hundred dollar pair of shoes.

He was too far across the crowded room to have noticed her accident, though he might have noticed her noticing his mental slip. She guessed not, since his head and shoulders remained bent as he spoke to a woman much shorter than he was, while Olympias stalked toward him. People moved out of her way, unconsciously recognizing the predator among them.

Falconer had nearly jumped out of his skin when the congresswoman said, "So, you work for the Walker Project."

The moment of lost composure passed without her noticing. Though the top of his head nearly popped off, his smile stayed in place, and he bent forward to say to her quietly, "That is my current assignment."

Her eyes took on an eager glitter. "What's it like?"

Closet New Ager, he decided, or closet hippie who was new enough to Washington to still think she could help save the world. "I'm not at liberty to discuss the project at the moment."

"I'm new on the appropriations committee, and I know I'm ignoring the pretense. What's it like? What am I thinking right now?"

"That you really wish you didn't have to strain your neck to look at me," Falconer guessed.

"I think she's thinking she should go to the little girls' room."

"Yes," said the congresswoman in a vacant, faraway voice. "I do. Excuse me."

Falconer had already forgotten her by the time he turned to face the other woman. It was just as well, as the tall woman he faced was the sort to take up a man's full attention. She was—

"Tall," she supplied for him. "At least you won't have to hunch over to talk to me." She smiled, it dazzled. There was amusement in it, but not a hint of gentleness. No softness about her ageless, sharp-featured beauty, either. Her dress was simple, severe, showing off a lean body that was utterly female. Black suited her.

"And I can bench press a tank," she said, guessing his thoughts as he blatantly looked her over.

Was there anyone else in the room? There had been a moment ago, hadn't there? There was something familiar in her voice. "Who are you?" he asked, giving in to the impulse to touch her. His fingers brushed her shoulder, that was all, but the sensation was electric. She felt it as well, he knew because the expression in her dark eyes shifted, her focus on him sharpening. The intensity was almost painful. She was a dangerous woman. Very dangerous. She made his blood sing. He smiled, no stranger to danger, up for the challenge. "My name's Mike. Who are you?"

"Do you really want to know?"

He shrugged. "It's only fair. You know my name."

The man had magnificent shoulders, wide enough to block out the sun—were it shining. She remembered the fire of the sun. There was an echo of that fire sparking between her and the mortal soldier. "Olympias," she told him.

He tilted his head to one side, intrigued. "*The* Olympias?" he countered.

"The one and only."

"I am impressed."

She touched her throat, coyly. "You've heard of me?"

"Oh, yes. I've heard of you. Alexander the Great's mother. Philip of Macedon's queen."

He knew his history, but a career officer would know all the battles of two of the most famous generals of the ancient world—her world. He would not know of her battles, but at least he'd heard of her. "Points for not saying 'wife.'" She inclined her head graciously. "Ours was a political arrangement."

"History records the relationship differently."

"History lies."

"Aren't you a little—"

"Young to be the former queen of Macedon?"

"I was going to say tall."

"We grew Amazons in Epirus."

"Really?"

"Yes. That's something else lost to history, that Amazons were real. I was born in Epirus."

"I remember reading that in the history books. The historical sources never mentioned you being tall."

"Alexander took after his Macedonian father, I'm afraid. He was a short little shit."

"But a magnificent general."

"I've never liked soldiers much."

She looked him over, from head to toe, taking in the well-tailored uniform on his rangy, wide-shouldered frame, his wide, thin-lipped mouth, the narrow, intense blue eyes. She liked everything she saw but the uniform, and his presence at a party full of black ops personnel. This man would not be here if he weren't deeply involved in some super secret covert military operation. Not good. Not good at all. There was an air of incredible intelligence about him, a certain scholarly gentleness about him that was belied by the long, slightly crooked nose. He was a warrior, all right, a deceptively calm one. A warrior that thought, a man involved in a highly classified operation, and a powerful psychic. This was a very dangerous man, and she wanted him badly. There was also something familiar about him.

Where had she seen him before?

"Good goddess," she murmured an instant later. "It's the bunny!"

"I'm glad you decided to come."

Damn! Sara hadn't meant to say that. Not like that. Not looking into Andrew's eyes across the short distance of the small round table outside the Dupont Circle coffee shop. The words weren't meant to sound—needy. Personal.

It was a noisier than usual night in the circle area, mostly because of the ragged guy standing at the entrance of P Street shouting and screaming and begging God for mercy. Drug addicts, crazy people, and drunks acting out were a common enough sight in any big city; one grew numb too quickly to the sights, sounds, and smells of the city's flotsam. So common, people stopped noticing the effort they made not to see them.

The only people paying the crazy man any attention were the cops trying to herd him into their car. The flashing lights of the squad car parked diagonally across P Street added a certain gritty ambience to the popular area. There were tourists around—there were always tourists around—but Dupont Circle was very much a local hangout. It had been her hangout back when she was just out of school, with a new job, new friends, her first apartment.

Everything was different now, but she still liked to come here, liked the energy of this place at night. She liked to watch the chess players over by the fountain and to shop at Kramerbooks late at night. She could usually count on feeling connected to the above world when she came here—except that she'd made the mistake of asking a vampire to meet her here, which let the spooky world she now lived in bleed into the world where she was no longer quite at home. Odd as it seemed, glancing at sullen, sad Andrew, she didn't think the choice of meeting place had been a mistake.

Andrew remained silent, though his gaze never left hers. She took a sip of coffee and decided to start over. "I'm glad you realize that there's much more I need to learn about you before I can report to my mistress." *There. That sounded professional. Distanced. This was not a date. This was an interview with a vampire*—oh, lord, she hadn't thought that, had she?

In an effort to regroup, she picked up the cell phone sitting beside her coffee cup and pressed the button that dialed the stored voice mail number. There weren't any messages, thank goodness.

"Why do you keep doing that?" Andrew asked when she put the phone back down. "I don't like those things," he added. "Doesn't anyone want to be—out of touch—anymore?"

"These young people and all their gadgets," Sara added, with a disgusted shake of her head. "Why in my day—what was your day, anyway?" She knew something of his history from Olympias, but wanted to hear it from him. For her report.

"I notice you haven't answered my question."

"Are you going to answer mine?"

"Fair enough. You first."

She spun the phone around with her finger. "I am doing my mistress's bidding."

"Always a convenient answer."

"She's waiting for an important call."

"She can't check her own messages?"

"She doesn't—" Sara waved away Andrew's question. She didn't dare tell even a suicidal vampire that she was out without permission. "I answered you. Now it's your turn."

He took a sip of coffee and made a face. "It's cold. The coffee." He looked around. "The night. Life."

Sara rested her elbows on the plastic tabletop. "Are you always so dramatic?"

"I'm attempting to impress you with my—"

"Whining?"

He reached across the table to take her hand. "Whatever irritates you enough to get me killed is fine with me."

Sara looked around furtively, not sure if she was more worried about his words, or the touch of his fingers grasping hers. He had large, long-fingered hands. She'd noticed that about him the night before. Strong hands. Of course they were strong; he was a vampire. Nobody on the busy street was paying them any attention. There were a lot of couples around, and their attention was intensely focused on each other, being private in a very public place. The crazy guy was still shouting in the middle of the street, and music spilled out of the coffee shop, along with the white noise of many conversations and a great deal of cigarette smoke.

She should take her hand away, but she didn't. "You still haven't answered my question."

He looked puzzled. "I don't even remember it."

She glanced at the cell phone lying next to their twined hands, aware that it represented contact with the rest of the world, and her duty to the Nighthawk who owned her. "Why do you—want to be alone?"

Vampires were not hermits; they were psychic creatures, full of all sorts of cravings that required the presence of others to fulfill. Even strigs, the loners that lived outside the nests, sought out contact. Maybe more than other vampires, come to think of it. They Hunted more, feeding on the emotional rush of bringing death; they took more slaves for the pleasure of domination. They weren't civilized, they risked their immortality by ignoring the Laws, but they weren't alone. She understood what it was to be alone.

"You have it all," she said, spilling her thoughts before he could answer. "I have nothing. I stand on the threshold of your world, knowing I can never fully come inside. I press my nose against the glass and see all you have—

power, eternity, community, traditions, history. You are history. You walk through it and own it—"

"We're above history," he interrupted. "We do nothing. We aren't allowed to do anything."

She might have been more heartened if he'd sounded bitter or disgusted, but he sounded bored. Why did it matter to her that he sounded tired—and that he wanted to die?

"You think you're the one who is alone, Sara?"

"I think I'm not what you are."

"I think you've made a wise choice not to be what I am. I'm not complaining that I wasn't given the choice," he went on. "It's a little late to complain about that now. My bloodmother was—is—quite nice by our standards. She never put me through the hell some companions endure, didn't think I needed to pay that price for immortality. Immortality." He sighed. "I'm about to sound sorry for myself. This is your only warning. Get out now."

Sara laughed. She didn't suppose it was appropriate, but she couldn't help it. She supposed finding a suicidal vampire charming was odd, but what about her life wasn't? "I think I'm strong enough to stick around."

"Well, you've been warned." Andrew glanced toward the shouting man in the center of the street. Another cop car had arrived on the scene, along with an EMT vehicle. "Excuse me a moment, Sara."

Then he was gone.

She didn't know what other people saw, but she was aware of shadows, and a flicker of speed. The man in the street stopped shouting and walked calmly toward the waiting medics, a smile on his bearded face. A moment later Sara's hair was stirred by a brief, gentle breeze, like a soft caress of fingers sifting through it. Then Andrew was sitting across from her once more.

She glanced toward the street and back to Andrew. "He's going quietly. What did you do?"

"Told him he wanted to go. It only took a touch of telepathy to calm him down."

"Oh. He's psychic?"

Andrew nodded. "Any mortal like us could go that route, use drugs to keep the voices out of our heads."

The psychically gifted with no natural shielding, he meant. The lucky ones were found by vampires before they cracked, but there were no vampires in the city limits of Washington to find this lost soul. "How sad."

Another nod. "Finally figured out that the poor guy was sensing our presence, and it freaked him. Didn't take but a whisper to get him calmed down enough to get him at least a little help. No saving him, though." Andrew's sadness returned in a dark rush that nearly overwhelmed Sara.

"It was good of you to do what you could."

He looked her in the eyes. "That's another of my problems."

She couldn't breathe for a moment, not until he looked away. Sara drew a shaky breath. Her heart raced. "What is—your problem?"

Andrew rose and offered her his hand. "Let's go for a walk."

She almost forgot her cell phone on the table, but Andrew scooped it up and handed it to her. "Wouldn't want to get you in trouble with your boss."

She thought she was already in trouble. She knew what his other problem was. Andrew was nice. She wasn't going to bring it up; it must be terribly embarrassing for him. She did want to know how a nice man had become a vampire, and how he'd stayed that way, and why that contributed to a death wish when there was so much good he could do with the powers his psychic talent had let him be reborn with.

She almost slipped and asked, How'd a nice man like you become a vampire? simply for the awkward having-something-to-say-facetiousness of it as he led her toward a crosswalk. Instead, she asked, "Where do you want to walk to?"

He seemed both eager and nervous when he answered,

"Do you like Georgetown?" He stopped as they reached the sidewalk on Dupont Circle. "What am I thinking? That's too far for a mortal to walk, isn't it?" He turned toward busy traffic moving around the Circle.

"Georgetown?" she asked as he hailed a cab. "Why?"

"I used to live there. Think I'd like to see if my wife's house is still there," he added as a cab came to a halt in front of them.

"Wife? You have a wife?" She heard her voice go up into a silly, outraged squeak.

A hand on her elbow urged her forward. She got in and slid to the other side of the backseat. As Andrew got in beside her, he added, "I told you I was from around here."

Chapter 8

"I HAVEN'T BROUGHT anyone home for a while."

"You didn't bring me," Olympias pointed out. "I drove." She found his being diffident as they stood at the top of the steps of his townhouse rather adorable. She hadn't expected a big, confident sort like him to go all shy on her. She liked being surprised, it happened so rarely.

The touch of his hand on her elbow as he ushered her toward his front door was delicate, his attitude civilized, even slightly embarrassed. She felt his thoughts that it was rather silly and odd for a man his age to be indulging in a one-night stand. But he wanted her all right. His thoughts were civilized, but his emotions were a storm of lust. It wasn't anything she'd done to him. Chemistry rather than telepathy was involved here. It pleased her to know that his desire came from within himself. He wanted her. It pleased her, flattered her, disarmed her, even.

And she certainly wanted him. His aura, his touch, even the sound of his voice, sizzled through her. It was a pleasantly refreshing sensation for a jaded old bird like her. It was a mortal kind of desire, this wanting of his flesh for purposes other than feasting. She missed mortal sensation. All this living at an acutely psychic level wore one down sometimes.

"This is fun," she said and kissed him again. They'd been making out pretty heavily at every stoplight on the way over, and she and the soldier boy were as disheveled as they were hot and bothered. She'd taken him outside for a little tête-à-tête for Lora's sake. She meant to mind-rape the poor bastard and go about her business. Instead he'd touched her, a simple brush of his fingers against her cheek and throat, their gazes had met—and they'd ended up here.

"This is no way for grown-ups to act," he answered when she stopped kissing him long enough to let him catch his breath. His hands made more of a mess of her dress while he added, "Maybe we better get in off the street before the neighbors notice."

"They won't notice," she assured him as he turned away long enough to unlock the door. "But let's get horizontal somewhere comfortable." Simple passion this might be, but she'd never done it in doorways. Queens and vampires learned to watch their backs. Never do anything distracting in a place where you might be vulnerable.

His picking her up and spinning them into the front hall like a pair of newlyweds crossing a threshold caught her totally by surprise. The gesture caught her even more off guard than his almost immortal speed. She was surprised by the house as well when he put her down in the front hall. The only light he turned on lit the staircase at the end of the narrow hallway. Her colonel had called the place home. His presence permeated it, soul, spirit, and dreams, and had for a long time. This was not some place he'd leased for the duration of a tour of duty. "You were born here."

He didn't seem surprised by what she'd said. "I've lived here on and off my whole life," he answered.

Interesting.

"Maybe this would be a good time for introductions," he added, putting his arm around her shoulders and urging her toward the stairs.

"You know who I am," she said. "Mike—"

"Falconer."

Even more interesting.

"Really?"

"It's not an uncommon name."

"I have heard it a couple of times recently."

"Really? Where?"

She almost stopped this little escapade right then, but he touched her cheek with the back of his hand, all the while giving her a sweet, curious smile that sent a fresh jolt of heat through her jaded senses. Instead she gave a throaty, sexy chuckle, and said, "Never mind."

She slipped her arm around his waist and pulled him up the stairs.

"I shouldn't be saying this, but—your blood smells really great, you know?"

"Uh—thanks." Sara did not know what to think of Andrew's words. On the one hand no one had ever said that to her before. On the other hand, no vampire should pay her such a compliment, and not only because it wasn't true. If she had a third hand, she might consider the ramifications of someone on the not exactly empty Georgetown street overhearing them. There were lights on in most of the townhouses they passed, lots of traffic in the street, but she supposed they were private enough. Being overheard was fine for him—Andrew was planning on exiting this mortal and immortal coil.

"I know you have an arrangement with the Hunter," he went on. "But I wanted you to know. Sorry."

He was being far too gentlemanly in calling what she had with Olympias an arrangement. She wasn't sure what she resented more at this moment, the truth, or Andrew's kindness in disguising it. He did not look deathly pale when they stopped to stand beneath the glow of a street-lamp. He was such an attractive young man, even with his unfashionably long hair and brooding expression. His eyes were large and dark, quite thickly fringed with long lashes. She felt magic when she looked into them. There didn't seem to be anything particularly otherworldly about him. He seemed like such a nice man, though he talked about blood, her blood, as though it were a sweet perfume.

"That's all right," she said. "I—"

"The world is very strange, I know," he interrupted, catching her thoughts.

"Our world—"

"Your world." His expression turned harsh, bitter. "I'm out of here as soon as it can be arranged."

"I—"

"You can't imagine why anyone would want to die, can you?"

"Will you let me get a word in?" She should have fear, or at least cautious respect for him, he was a vampire, but Sara found herself wanting to stomp her foot in frustration, preferably on top of one of his grimy athletic shoes.

He looked like he was about to say something, then he smiled and put a finger over his lips instead.

Fine. Good. He was going to let her get in a few words. But what did she want to say, and why was it important that she talk to this suicidal vampire?

Why do you want to know why, you mean?

Telepathy is cheating. It's still talking. Out of my head! she ordered. Frankly, there was nothing deep and dark and tortured about his touch in her mind. She felt gentleness, amusement—fondness? For who? Her? He didn't feel insane. She grabbed Andrew by the arm and tugged him deeper into the darkness. He could pull shadows around him. She needed to rely on the tall bushes in front of one of the houses to provide them with more cover from the lights of passing traffic.

She pulled him closer, grabbing him by the front of his shirt this time. "First off, bub, I'm not a vampire, never going to be one—so stop referring to our world when you talk to me. I work for a vampire, and believe me, from the outside I am painfully aware of all the advantages your kind have over my kind. You have amazing powers. You have immortality. You have the power of life and death over us measly little mortal creatures. You could rule the world if you bloody well wanted to. You can have all the wealth and power and slaves and worshipers you—"

"You called me 'bub.' "

"Did I? Who cares? Don't interrupt me in mid—"

"Diatribe," Andrew finished, annoyingly.

"Tirade," she corrected.

"Whatever you say, sister."

"Sister?"

Andrew smiled. She knew the sight of mating fangs even when she only caught a faint glimpse of them in the night.

"Well!" she said, and tried to back away. His hands were on her waist, and his eyes looked compellingly into hers. He wasn't letting her go anywhere, and she didn't really want to.

She knew this was getting them nowhere, but she hadn't felt so alive in years. She realized how close they were to each other, and how close they were to something happening between them. She'd never felt her blood race like this, never felt the air sizzle and crackle in a way that made her hair stand on end and sensitized her skin in a way that intimately caressed her even though she knew she wasn't being touched. She'd never felt this flare of insatiable hunger, not even the one time Olympias had—

"You don't belong to her," Andrew said.

She did. "I do." What difference did it make to him anyway? "You're the one who wants to die," she added. "Do you want to take me with you?"

"Of course not. I—want to take you."

His last words came out slowly, full of diffidence and embarrassment. She absorbed his emotions, keeping herself from blurting out that she wanted him as well.

Andrew sighed, said, "Come on," and then he pulled her deeper into the shadows. They ended up on a bench deep in a mansion's back garden. His hands and mouth were all over her. It was wonderful and frightening at once. Sara only barely managed to keep her hands off of him. She couldn't help but respond to a long, deep kiss, but she didn't move. His weight covered her and the heat of his body permeated her; his touch roused even more heat, but Sara dug her nails into her palms and didn't move. She didn't realize she'd drawn blood until he slowly opened her fists and touched his tongue to the crescent cuts in her palms.

"Perfume," he whispered as he tasted each droplet of blood. "Like roses."

An orgasm shivered through her, along with an image of blood red roses. She felt him absorbing her emotions, and didn't care, knowing he took only what she'd let him arouse in her. Was this anywhere near what it was like to be a companion?

The thought hit her so hard she started to cry. Andrew knew her pain as well, and took it, sucked it up with as much fervor as he had her pleasure.

"Parasite," she heard herself whisper. "Monster."

"Yes," he whispered back. He kept caressing her. "Do you want it to stop?"

No. Of course she didn't. "I don't make personal choices." Because she was having trouble controlling her breathing, the words didn't come out as coherently as she'd have liked, but she knew Andrew understood her anyway.

He moved away from her, helped her to sit up, then sat with his head lowered and his hands clasped tightly on his knees. "Stupid," he said. "It's all so stupid." Sara didn't say anything, and after the silence dragged out for a long time, he finally looked at her. "The world I've lived in for the last fifty years is so utterly stupid—useless, farcically ridiculous. There is nothing right about this world. Nothing sane. I don't even think we rate as well-adapted parasites. Are we allowed to invent, to create? No. What has any vampire ever done for the world we live off of? There's a rumor that says we invented all-night convenience stores. What sort of legacy is that?"

"You can't draw attention yourselves. It isn't s—"

"Safe? Who cares? Why must we live a life without risk or challenge?"

"Because your—species—would be destroyed if—"

"Who cares? We serve no purpose." He sighed. "I serve no purpose."

The bitterness in his voice twisted her heart. She put a hand tentatively on his arm; his muscles were as tense as steel. "You obey the Laws." She felt like a fool parroting such words. What sort of comfort was that?

He stared into the night. She didn't think he was aware she was there. "I'd be in the Rock and Roll Hall of Fame by now if Rose hadn't wanted me. I'd have accomplished something. My wife wouldn't have died thinking her husband abandoned her. My son would have had something to remember. I would have had a life."

That stung. "You have immortality," Sara snapped.

"Never asked for it. Don't want it."

"Well, you've got it, so you might as well enjoy it!"

"Enjoy—" His hands suddenly gripped her shoulders. The pain was excruciating. His angry face was suddenly too close to hers. "My immortality should have been the son I never got to know, didn't help raise, couldn't love but from a distance. I think he's dead now. Don't know if seeing him is driving me crazy, or if I'm seeing him because I'm already crazy."

He pushed her away and was up off the bench pacing before she saw him move. She crossed her arms over her breasts to massage her aching shoulders. Part of her wanted to get up and run, but he'd tasted her blood, which could make her prey in several different ways. More than fear of how this natural hunter would respond should she try to escape held her in place. A thread of sympathy bound her to the restless vampire in front of her. She couldn't deny that the strong curiosity to know him, know about him, know what drove him that had formed at their first meeting grew stronger with every passing moment they were together.

"How can you see your son if he's dead? How can you even have a son?"

He swung around sharply to face her. "I wasn't always a vampire, you know."

"I know you were Rose Shilling's companion back in—what?—the fifties?"

"And sixties. Rose took her time draining the mortality out of me. She's—" He glanced up at the night sky. "I used to think of her as sweet. Even after the devotion we infuse into our companions wore off I thought she was the nicest person I ever met." He laughed bitterly. "I went Hunting with the woman, watched her change into a creature that kills and consumes mortal beings. She took me Hunting to change me, and I've killed since. I want to do it all the time. It's not the killing of mortals that I mind so much. There are plenty of mortals that need killing. It's the wanting to Hunt that eats away at you. Until you've fought this constant hunger—Rose put that hunger in me."

"You control the hunger. So does Rose."

"At least she doesn't Hunt often. She's not a woman of strong appetites. She's not all that interested in sex, either. She didn't want me in her bed every night—at least she let me have a little bit of a life. I think she only makes companions because she sees it as her duty under the Law. Not every vampire takes companions, you know?"

"Olympias isn't interested," she heard herself admit easily, when her duty was to keep silent on any information about her mistress. Somehow, she couldn't manage to feel any guilt for this minor bit of treason.

"Good for her," Andrew answered. "I've heard that there's this irresistible urge to make other vampires but— some do it every few decades, some every few centuries, some never reproduce. No matter how few there are of us, there's still too many."

"How can you say that?"

"Cause I am one, darlin'."

"That doesn't give you the right to—"

"If I had it in me to be an Enforcer, I'd go that route rather than trying to get an Enforcer to rip my heart out."

"It's a biological change, isn't it? Some kind of genetic mutation?"

"More like a magical mutation, I think. The rest of us are helpless against what we are. We can't kill each other or ourselves. I did try—at least I tried to think about thinking about doing it. Made me sick—helped make me crazy. So I turned to the Laws . . . like a good little strigoi. I figure the best I can do is contribute a few meals to somebody who can destroy us. We should die. It's a good thing the population's so small. I'm glad that the mortality rate among fledglings is so high—bet you didn't know that, did you?"

She did, she was the one conducting the vampire census. One reason nests existed was to nurse newborn vampires through the crucial months or years it took them to regain their senses. Not all nest leaders were as careful and concerned about this difficult task as they should be. Even in the caring nests, not every fledgling adapted to the difficult physical and mental changes required to become a full-fledged vampire. Despite her knowledge, this time Sara only shrugged.

"I've made a vampire, back when I was still living in California. I performed the spells while he made his first kill. That makes me a bloodsire, I guess, but I've never had a companion," he went on. "He probably lived. The nest that took him in was strong. It was a nest I had to leave, even though this man and I had never been lovers.

I've had nightmares ever since. That's what started this downhill slide. That's when the loneliness started eating away at me. And I did it as a favor, thinking I was doing a good thing for a man who deserved a second chance." He gestured toward the sky. "As if vampires can do good. All I did was create another vampire."

Sara figured this was no time to say that she didn't see anything wrong with that. She'd certainly lost control—of her emotions, of the situation, of the conversation—if she'd ever had control of any of it. "Sit down," she told him.

She patted the spot beside her on the bench. She figured they were both surprised when he sat down. She was certainly surprised at the shared comfort that came when he put his arm around her and she relaxed automatically against him. Silence reigned for a few minutes, but the tension drained out of it quickly enough. She tried to sort out just where the conversation had veered off and how to bring it back on track.

"Your son," she said finally. "Tell me about your son."

"Maybe it's painful to talk about."

"Maybe you need to talk about it."

"Maybe I do. I can't seem to shut up when I'm around you. Why is it I trust you, Sara?"

Maybe because I am nothing and no one.

"I don't think so."

"Stop reading my mind."

"Stop feeling sorry for yourself. That's my gig this evening."

"At least you know it. Your son?" she inquired, before he could answer that he was willing to give her a turn—because she knew that was exactly what he was going to say.

"I was already Rose's companion when my son was conceived."

Her skepticism meter went nearly off the scales. "Oh, really?"

He ignored her tone. "I told you Rose was a little—lax. She let me fool around on her."

"You shouldn't have been able to."

He shrugged, and she felt it all along her body. "I'm a musician. Rose knew what musicians are like. She's not the jealous type."

Vampires were always the jealous type—or so Sara had been led to believe. "This sounds very—blasphemous."

"It happened, sweetheart. I was there."

"Fooling around on your mistress?"

"With my wife."

This statement curtailed Sara's outrage somewhat, or if it didn't curtail it, at least her outrage was smothered by consternation. "Weird," she said.

"Tell me about it."

"Tell me."

"I met my wife in college. I didn't want to go to college, but my diplomat father insisted. I was glad I went, when I met her. She was from right here in Georgetown. That's why I'm always drawn back here, I think. One of the reasons I applied directly to Olympias was to get a chance to come home to die."

"I—see."

"I spent most of my vampire years in Los Angeles and Austin, but I've always thought of this as home." He made a sweeping gesture that took in the whole city. "I think my wife's family'd been in Washington since the place was built. Her dad was in the military—my kid took after his granddad." Andrew shook his head. "But then, I wasn't there."

"You were one of the original hippies, I take it?"

"Definitely. I clashed a lot with my wife's father. But he decided that I was from a 'good' family and that I'd eventually straighten up and give up playing music in beatnik clubs." He chuckled. "I did move off the folk circuit—but never mind my aborted career. We'd been married nearly two years when Rose put the bite on me.

Of course that changed everything—but I kept trying to get home."

Sara's heart ached for Andrew. He must have loved his wife very much to be able to fight off the blind devotion that came with sharing blood with a vampire. She wanted to kiss it and make it all better. But it had happened a long time ago, and she had no right. Besides, he was in the wrong. She tried with all her might to believe that he was the one who had no right to cheat on his vampire mistress. Even if Rose was a silly woman who hadn't known how to appreciate him. If Sara had been in Rose's place she would have tied this wandering minstrel to her bed if she'd had to.

"What an interesting idea."

Sara blinked in surprise at his picking up her thought, but didn't have the grace to be embarrassed. "Out of my head," she ordered the vampire, making a shooing motion. "Go on."

"I'm beginning to think you'd look fetching in dominatrix gear."

Sara refrained from voicing the thought that came to her. If he caught it, he gave no indication. It amazed her how the man—vampire—could be so angrily glum one moment, and so cheerfully teasing the next. The way he treated her, and let her treat him, was also amazing. "Your son," she urged.

"Michael. Michael Andrew Falconer, born July 15, 1960, died—sometime recently, I think. I was Rose's creature when he was conceived. It's worried me that somehow I passed along some psychic shit to him, but I don't know. I'll never know. I saw him as much as I could when he was little. I tried to keep track of him from a distance as he grew up, but the time came when Rose had to change me. The transition from fledgling to sane strigoi took a couple of years. I was sent to California. I vaguely remember a long car trip. I adjusted to being what I am, was even happy with my life. When I finally got around to checking on my kid, I found out he'd followed his grandfather into the service. Found out my wife had cancer. If she'd had the least bit of psychic ability I might have been able to help her, but she had no part of the curse that got me into my current lifestyle. So I went on with my life until the depression hit a couple years ago." He shrugged. "Been going downhill ever since."

Sara kept her concentration on his son. "How do you know he's dead? Did you read an obituary or—?"

"I've seen him."

Okay, maybe Andrew was as crazy as he claimed to be. "Seen him?"

"His ghost."

"Ghost?"

"You believe in vampires, don't you?"

"Only because I know some personally."

"Werewolves? Demons?"

"But—"

"But you don't believe in ghosts? We've discussed my seeing them before, remember?"

They had, hadn't they? Had it only been last night? She nodded. "In the park."

"Yes. I told you I didn't recognize who I saw. It took me a while to realize it after the first time I saw it, but now I know who the specter has to be. Vampires lie a lot, Sara. Please remember that."

It was something they did for their own protection. "Are you lying now?"

"No."

The word could easily have been a lie. She had to remember that he was seeking permission to die. Why not lie to a mere slave if it advanced his scheme to get himself eaten by the slave's mistress? Why not make out with the slave to rouse her mistress's anger? He had nothing to lose, and what happened to a slave didn't matter. "Bastard."

She felt his surprise at her suddenly turning wary and angry. If that surprise turned to anger she might be in for a hell of a bad time. And it would be her own fault. What sane person knowingly let herself be alone with a vampire? She hadn't told Olympias where she was going to be—she was even disobeying a direct order to be here. She'd even forgotten her duty to monitor the phone for messages Olympias was waiting for.

All because she was attracted to someone? How could that have happened?

"I am such an idiot," she muttered.

"Where are you going?" he asked when she got up from the bench.

"Home," she said. "If you'll let me."

"If . . ."

She waited with her back to him, and her shoulders hunched tensely. Then his hand was beneath her elbow, his sadness engulfed her. He guided her in dense silence, thick as a cold winter fog, back through the garden and onto the sidewalk fronting the narrow Georgetown street. The cold fog stayed wrapped around her, even after he hailed a cab, helped her into it, and closed the door without saying good-bye. Odd, how she wanted him to say good-bye.

At least she had the presence of mind to give the driver her address, and she took out her cell phone to check for messages as the cab pulled out into the street.

He had the most gorgeous back Olympias had ever seen, perfectly muscled, wide at the shoulders and beautifully tapered down to a narrow waist and lovely little flat buttocks. Oh, yes, Lora's bunny was very nice from the rear, she thought as she stood across the bedroom and watched him finish undressing. He stood in front of light gold drapes covering tall windows. The contrast of the gold material enhanced his fair coloring.

Lora was going to hate her when she found out Olympias had him first—but, Lora hated her anyway, and Olympias didn't care. It wasn't as if she was going to bite the boy. She'd fuck his brains out, but he'd still be a virgin in the morning.

She smiled with anticipation and took a step forward. He turned as she moved, and she saw his eyes widen with surprised pleasure. She'd shed her clothing much quicker than he had. His appreciation permeated his emotions as well as his expression, and showed in his physiology as well. His skin was flushed, his breathing sharp, and the man was hard. She moved to him and showed her pleasure at his appreciation with her touch. His chest was only lightly furred, and his belly nicely flat. His was a mature body, strong and fit, and sensitive to arousing touch. Exploring warm flesh and taut muscle was a treat. Her own arousal grew as she absorbed the building waves of pleasure she brought him.

It was Mike that moved them to the bed, lay her down and took a long, languid time slowly exploring her from the top of her head to the tip of her toes. He seemed to know instinctively how arousing she found fingers stroking her scalp and through her hair to be. He took his time to tease his tongue around the pearl and diamond studs she'd forgotten to take out of her earlobes.

He was, quite simply, a superb and considerate lover, taking pleasure from giving pleasure. Even if he had not been the most psychically gifted mortal she'd ever met, but only a mere mortal, Olympias would still have delighted in the experience. That he was gifted as well as giving made the pleasure purer, sharper, enough to strongly tempt her to draw blood and move their lovemaking to an even deeper level.

She managed to control the impulse, though she had to fight to do so.

Lost in sensation, she scratched his back when he entered her, drawing the faintest scent of blood welling below the surface of his skin. The slight pain blended into his pleasure, driving him higher. Their lovemaking grew fiercer after that, her reactions feeding his, and he drove harder into her, with her urging on the quickening pace of his thrusts.

Sharing an orgasm with him was the first memorable moment of the new century, and she murmured, "Thank you," when she came.

That's worth repeating, was Olympias's first coherent thought as she emerged from lovely, blissful exhaustion. It had been a long time since someone had made her feel like a woman—since she'd let someone make love to her, she reminded herself. The sex had been a mutual, consensual, activity, but only because she'd allowed it to happen that way. *And why do I feel the need to remind myself I'm really in charge?* A deep yawn spoiled what would have been an ironic smile. *Aren't I a little old to need to remind myself that I'm not really vulnerable?*

Mike was a warm, dozing weight on top of her, totally relaxed, oblivious to the presence of the monster in his bed. She liked it that way and stroked fingers gently through his short, light brown hair, willing him to cover her flesh with his for a while yet. He was sweaty, but she liked the masculine, musky scent of him.

There I go with that monster crap again. Being a ruthless, selfish, hard-hearted bitch doesn't necessarily make me a monster. I gave up believing in strigoi propaganda, she reminded herself. She sighed, remembering that she no longer believed in many of the Laws she enforced, and added cynical to her list of her own faults.

She really was tempted to wake him up and do it all over again. It was hours until dawn, and holding him made her horny.

She thought it might be nice to bite him, keep him as a boy toy she could visit once in a while. No need to go so far as to make him a companion, of course. Just feed him a drop of magic elixir and own him for the rest of his natural life. That was her preferred mode of operation, though she hadn't taken a sex slave in centuries. Of course, this bunny was not slave material, too much talent for that. He'd understand quickly enough that there was more he could be. He wouldn't crave companion status the way slaves like Gerry and Sara did, he'd demand it as his right. And companionship was—

Exactly what Lora wanted with Colonel Michael Falconer.

"How'd I manage to forget that?" she whispered, and chuckled, knowing that Mike himself had erased her memory of everything but the way his touch brought her to life. Fortunately she'd only forgotten for a few minutes. "Shh . . ." she murmured when he stirred and began to lift his head. She stroked his cheek, where a faint trace of stubble tickled her palm.

His head shifted to pillow on her breasts, and her fingers went back to stroking his hair, while she stared at the ceiling and tried to decide what to do about him. She could easily break his neck, Olympias supposed, which would deny the pleasure of his company from herself and Lora both. It was easy, but what possible good would it do? She could keep him for herself, or she could give him to Lora. Lora did have first claim, she should be fair about that.

Why?

Because I'm off the idea of having companions, she reminded herself. Companions went away. At least slaves merely died, one could mourn their mortal passing and not have to answer the phone to find out how happy they were with new lovers and new adventures. Goddess, but that grew old!

All right, then, Lora could have him.

Except, Olympias remembered, she still didn't know exactly what top secret thing it was Colonel Falconer did for a living. She still needed to figure out his connection with the ghosts she'd seen in the park last night. She was certain that there was a connection. Until she found out everything there was to know about Falconer she couldn't make any decision at all.

And what better way to find out his ghostly ties than right now while he was completely relaxed, with all his defenses down? All she needed to do was slip inside his pretty little head and ransack his mind while he was sleeping. All she needed to do was close her eyes.

"Excuse me, but don't I know you from somewhere?"

"No," the tall woman answered, looking deeply into his eyes. "No, you don't."

Falconer looked around in disgust. He was back in the damned park. Couldn't he escape from the crazy memories of the place?

"What happened here?"

"You know." He turned to look at her closely. Dark as the night was here under the trees he could see her clearly. Dark hair, dark eyes, pale skin, strong, stubborn jaw. "You were here. It was you."

Her look flashed fire that sent a bolt of pain through his head. "It wasn't me. You don't remember me. Who are you? Who are the ghosts?"

He took Olympias into his arms. "How could any man forget you?"

"That's flattering, but—"

Falconer awoke with a start, a headache, and with the terrifying realization that he was being held down, pinioned in a steel embrace. "Hel—" he started to shout.

"Mike?" a woman's voice whispered in his ear. "What's the matter?"

Falconer realized he wasn't fully awake and worked hard to bring the world back into perspective. He was being held, wasn't he? He'd—brought a woman—home. That was it. She was in his bed, holding him. Comforting him from a nightmare?

He managed to get his panting breath under control enough to gasp, " 'S okay. I'm—" He opened his eyes and blinked a few times. He must have gone to sleep as soon as they—the lights were still on and—

He became aware of warm, naked flesh pressed to his, helping to chase both loneliness and confusion away. He was in his room, in his home, and the woman with him was Olympias. "I can't remember your last name," he said, the first inane words that came to him spilling out of his mouth.

"That's because I didn't tell you my last name," she answered with gentle amusement. "We're both in a secretive business," she added.

He remembered now, they'd met at the appropriations party. They both lived in the world of spooks and classified information. "I was having a bad dream," he confessed to her. "I don't remember what now."

"It's better to ignore the nightmares," she advised.

He wanted to tell her that he normally did his dreaming while he was wide awake. But that was classified. He couldn't tell her anything. She'd understand that.

"If you want to talk, I'm willing to listen," she said.

Falconer eased away from her and turned onto his back. She'd caught his thought, hadn't she? Of course she was psychic. It made sense, in the way they'd come together, in the way they'd been so in tune when they made love. Whatever agency she worked with was involved in some form of psychic research. It was possible she'd made sure to meet him to find out about the Walker Project. It was possible they'd come together because they were alike. Why they'd met didn't matter.

"I want to make love to you again," he told her.

Soft fingers brushed his cheeks. "I imagine you'll get the chance."

He turned his head to look at her. She was sitting on the side of the bed. He might have reached out, but he sensed she was already far away from him. "But not now," he said. She stood and began to dress as he spoke. He sat up and watched her, mesmerized by the grace of her movements. He considered it, but did not try to persuade her. He knew that she would not stay the night. "You're going."

"I have to. I'm not a morning person," she told him after she slipped her short black dress over her head. "It would not be possible for me to drive home during early rush hour."

He looked her over from her tousled hair to the spike-heeled black pumps she'd just put on. Her makeup was wrecked. It made her look quite the wanton, and younger than the sophisticated woman he'd brought home. He did not want to let her go, but could not summon even the simple word *stay*. He almost felt as if she willed him to silence. She did blow him a kiss, and he could have sworn he felt her lips brush his.

"I know where you live," she told him. "So there's no need for you to ask for my number. See you soon," she promised. She turned to the door, and was gone.

Falconer went to sleep almost thinking it had all been a dream.

Chapter 9

SHE WANTED TO see Andrew again. Sara knew that by the time she got home, even though she'd been furious, hurt, and feeling like a fool when she left him. It was wrong to want to see him again, stupid, she didn't know what she was thinking, but she still wanted to see him again. She sat down on the hall stairs, with the dog's head in her lap, and fought the urge to cry after she checked for phone messages. Crying was not an acceptable way for either a grown woman or Olympias's chief slave to act.

"This is all wrong." When Bitch lifted her huge head off Sara's lap to look at her, Sara went on. "My life was so much less complicated a few days ago—dissension among staff, tension with the local vampires, emergencies from around the country—easy stuff. What am I going to do now?"

Bitch cocked her head as though she was listening. For an instant Sara almost thought she saw a glimmer of sympathy in the hellhound's big brown eyes. More than likely Bitch was thinking about chasing bunnies, getting a treat, or simply wanted out. Sara rubbed the animal's velvety ears, but Bitch turned away from her and sprang to her feet. A moment later the door opened and Bitch bounded down the hall to greet Olympias as she entered the house.

"Down!" Olympias shouted at the dog.

Sara ran forward to grab Bitch by the collar and pull her away from Olympias. "Sorry." Olympias leaned against the door, her head tilted back. She was even paler than normal for a vampire, her face drawn and weary. "What happened to you?" Sara asked. "You look terrible."

Olympias mumbled something that might have been, "Barely made it out." Then she took a deep breath and looked at Sara. Was that fear in her dark eyes? She was definitely shaken. "What happened?" She blinked, then ran a hand through her hair. "I had a great time. Until the last few minutes."

"Did someone attack you?"

"Not consciously."

"What happened? You were only supposed to go to a party."

"I met Lora's bunny at the party, and survived the experience—just."

"But—"

"I have the headache of the century. Don't ask how."

"How?"

Olympias glared, but she answered. "I tried to have a quiet little talk with him from inside his head. Unfortunately, he has very, very strong shields. *I* was too relaxed. I didn't want to hurt him. I barely got out of his bedroom without letting him know how strongly I reacted to his defenses. Damn near vamped out on him."

"Bedroom?" Sara asked. "What were you doing in his bedroom?"

Olympias moved past Sara and the hellhound, toward the kitchen, her steps dragging. Sara followed. Olympias took a seat at the kitchen table and dropped her head into her hands. "I need a cup of coffee."

Sara hurried to get a pot going. She cast furtive glances at Olympias as she did so. Her mistress looked very shaken up. Sara knew it wasn't kind, but she nursed the hope that Olympias was too upset to ask her how her evening had gone.

"Coffee's on," she announced, turning to give her full attention to her mistress. "What else can I do?"

Bitch was leaning against Olympias's thigh, while the Enforcer absentmindedly stroked her sleek black fur. She stared at the white tile surface of the kitchen table, but didn't looked up at Sara's question. "A posset of opium mixed in warm wine would be nice."

"How about aspirin?"

Olympias shook her head. "The pain will pass when I go to sleep." She checked the clock on the microwave. "Damn! At least half an hour before I pass out. I vaguely remember driving back from Georgetown. Not even sure where I parked the car."

"I'll check on it," Sara assured her. Sara took the pot from under the still brewing coffee machine and poured a cup of coffee, while hot liquid sizzled down on the hot plate. "Here."

"Thanks." Olympias drank down the strong, hot coffee in a couple of gulps.

"Anything else?"

"No—wait." She glanced up. "Any calls?"

"Two."

"You didn't—"

"Call you with messages? No need. The report from Memphis is that they're making it look like what the cops noticed is a group of white supremacists rather than a nest with too many companions and slaves. The nest is slipping quietly away. Crisis over. Law enforcement gets to bask in the glow of having disbanded a group of neo-Nazis, while the media has a field day being outraged about how could it happen in their fine city. Nobody gets caught, nobody gets killed. No mention of vampires, even in the tabloids." Sara was glad the voice mail messages she'd listened to and deleted as soon as she got home had been concise and detailed.

"Good. One crisis down. How about Las Vegas?"

"No word from Vegas, yet. Second call was a heads-up from Marguerite out in Portland. She's heard a rumor that someone out there has taken a prison warden as a companion. She said, and I quote, 'the implications could be interesting.' "

"Using a prison as a Hunting ground could indeed be interesting." Olympias yawned. "I'm sure Marguerite can handle it. Anything else?"

"Not tonight." Sara desperately hoped Olympias didn't remember Andrew.

Olympias rose from the table. "You heard any rumors about ghosts in Georgetown?"

Sara jumped. "Ghosts? Have you seen a ghost?" She barely caught herself from saying 'too.'

Olympias's expression almost worked its way up to curious. "Have you?"

"No." At least she didn't have to lie to her mistress. Could she lie to her mistress? She didn't offer the information that Andrew had seen a ghost. She supposed it was wrong not to tell Olympias, but Sara wanted her mistress to forget about the suicidal vampire.

"Never mind," Olympias said as she rubbed her forehead. "You look for the car. I'm taking my headache to bed. To think the girl thought she was up to taking him as a bunny," Sara heard her mistress mutter as Olympias left the room.

"Glad to have you back, Gerry."

He took a seat beside her in the pew near the center of the nave. "Good to be back," her fellow slave answered. "I stopped by the house. You weren't there."

"Obviously."

"What are you doing here at three in the afternoon?"

"Wanted some open space."

Gerry looked up at the vast space of carved stone and

bright stained glass of the cathedral to the high ceiling overhead. "Pretty roomy, I guess." He looked at Sara again. "I've wondered if you ever consciously realize why you spend so much time in a church?"

"I am not trying to atone for any sins." *Not usually. And define sin.* She hadn't slept, she was very cranky, and even worse, very confused. *Did thinking about Andrew constantly constitute disloyalty, or maybe even a sin? Was Olympias a goddess or—what?*

"You're hiding from a vampire," he explained. "Hoping God will protect you from evil."

Stupid idea. She gave him an impatient look. "I thought I was avoiding walking the dog."

"That's a pretty good reason too. But why a church?"

"Why a duck?"

"What?"

It seemed Gerry had never heard of the Marx Brothers, and Sara didn't feel like enlightening him now. "Never mind. How was Denver?"

"Still surrounded by mountains."

"You know what I mean."

"Do you know that Denver has one of the highest vampire populations in the country?"

"Of course."

"I wonder why. You think it's the weather? Proximity to the slopes?"

"I wonder why you care."

"You are so testy this afternoon."

"And you are so bright and perky I want to slap you silly."

"Did you ever meet someone who just being around them put you in a good mood?"

Yes. And he wants to die. "I have no idea what you mean."

"I mean I ran into Roger Bentencourt out in the garden. We sat and talked for a while. He's very stimulating to be around."

Sara sat up sharply and looked around. "What's Bentencourt doing here?"

"He's waiting to talk to you. He's waiting now, I mean. When we ran into each other I asked him to wait to talk to you in private first. He was cool with that."

Gerry was quite pleased with himself. "You mean you tested a companion to see if he'd let a creature he has every right to order around get ahead of him in line?"

Gerry crossed his arms. "Yeah. Got away with it, too. He's a very civilized man. He's going to make a very nice addition to the vampire population. We need more fresh blood like him."

"I wish you wouldn't use that term. And I wish you'd leave him alone."

"You're still being cranky. I didn't go to him, Sara. And it's *you* he wants to speak with."

"Why does Bentencourt want to talk to me?" She vaguely wondered if she should rush out to the garden and beg the companion's forgiveness for not attending to him immediately. This was accompanied by the stronger impulse to say screw it, which was the one she went with. "Let him wait. I need you to tell me how it went in Denver."

"I didn't find the nest. I didn't find the coin."

"Oh, great. Is this another crisis she's going to have to deal with? Doesn't Olympias have enough on her hands?" Then again, anything that kept her mind off Andrew . . .

"Does she have crises? Has something happened while I've been gone?"

Sara was thoroughly annoyed at Gerry's eager curiosity, and instantly suspicious. What had he and Bentencourt been talking about? Not that Gerry wasn't a devoted slave to Olympias, or Bentencourt anything but a devoted companion to Rose who was concerned that his mistress's household was being displaced from their home. She told herself she was being paranoid for no reason, but snapped at Gerry anyway when she demanded, "Did you find out anything?"

Gerry slumped back in his seat. "You are no fun today, Sara Czerny. And before you snap at me again, here's my report. Seems a couple of slackers from the Brotherhood of Reivers decided to take over a Denver nest. A body ended up being found by the Denver police. The nest fled to Chicago—where Ariel believes at least one of the old dudes became snack food for this guy named Istvan."

"Believes?"

"Istvan told him he was taking over the case; everything else Ariel found out via rumor. The Denver Enforcer heard these rumors from Ariel. I assume Ariel assumed Istvan would tell Olympias. I heard it from a slave of the Denver Enforcer."

"So Istvan has the coin Olympias asked about?"

"Apparently. Maybe he collects them."

"Then maybe Olympias's intuition about the missing coin is wrong." She couldn't be right all the time. Sara tried, and failed, to be guilty over the disloyal thought. "Istvan solves problems."

"Permanently." Gerry looked at his watch. He glanced toward the side door nearest the herb garden. "I don't think you should keep Bentencourt waiting any longer. He *is* a companion."

"And you're a—"

"Don't swear in church."

"I wish you would go away."

"Happy to," he said, and got up and walked out.

Sara almost followed him to apologize for being so short with him, but instead she sighed with utter exhaustion, tilted her head toward the ceiling, and closed her eyes. *The sun poured down on her, dappled through the thick trees. The stream rushed by only a few inches from where she sat, glinting silver in the light. The hand holding hers was large and warm, but very pale. She said, "You'll burn if you aren't careful."*

Andrew laughed and kissed her temple. "We're safe in here."

"We?" She felt safe, but knew she wasn't. "I shouldn't be here."

"You shouldn't be anywhere else. You've been a prisoner too long."

"I'm not a prisoner. I'm—"

"I'm sorry to disturb you, Ms. Czerny," Bentencourt whispered, his mouth very near her ear, "but we don't have much time to talk."

Sara sat up with a start. Bentencourt's hand on her shoulder was the only thing that kept her from jumping to her feet. Panic gripped her for a moment, until she remembered where she was. She looked around wildly, seeing only carved stone and wood and acres of jewel-toned glass.

"Please don't have a heart attack," Bentencourt said. "I don't know how I would explain my frightening you to death to your mistress."

She looked at the bland-featured companion. "You didn't frighten me."

He smiled. "I'm glad to hear it, Sara." He stood and put his hand under her elbow. "The gardens are beautiful today. Let's talk outside."

People were watching them. She noticed one of the docents coming their way. She smiled wanly and waved for the cathedral volunteer to return to the tour group he'd left. He nodded and turned back. She let Bentencourt guide her outside into brilliant sunlight. She couldn't help but think of Andrew when the warmth of the afternoon light touched her face. What an awful time to have it bad for someone, she thought. Then she turned her attention to Bentencourt.

"Down here," he said, and led her to a bench set in a shaded alcove. The scent of lavender perfumed the warm air, the stone of the bench cool to the touch. "Refreshing here, isn't it?" Bentencourt asked after they were seated. "It should help revive you."

His solicitousness did have a soothing effect, even though she resented pity from anyone. She said, "Thanks," though it took a huge effort.

He gave her a few moments, then asked, "Feeling better?"

Of course she wasn't feeling better! She was in love with the wrong vampire for goodness's sake—and goodness certainly had nothing to do with it! "Fine," she answered. "I haven't had much sleep recently. Guess it caught up with me."

"You're very conscientious in Olympias's service. It's bound to catch up with you. Someone should tell your mistress to take better care of you."

"Are you going to bell that cat?" The words came out of her mouth before she could stop them. "I mean—"

"No need to explain to me. You're human," he said. "All us humans feel frustration with our bosses upon occasion. Our peculiar circumstances don't make us less human."

"No," Sara agreed. "I suppose not." She thought he put way too much energy into being supportive, but she focused her whole attention on Bentencourt and was very polite. She even dredged up a smile. "I'm sorry for taking up your time. I'll be happy to help you in any way I can. No, wait," she said, remembering something before he could reply. "There is something you can help me with. Maybe. At least—"

"Yes?"

"Rose." She wasn't sure how to put it, or even where the idea came from, other than a sense of desperation and time running short on being able to save Andrew from himself. "There's a young man—vampire—one of your mistress's bloodchildren. He wants to commit suicide. Maybe she could talk to him."

Bentencourt lost his perpetually imperturbable look for a moment, but when his usual concerned calm returned, he asked, "Suicidal? I don't understand."

Sara hastened to explain the rules under which vampires were allowed to end their lives, and concluded, "I'm sure he isn't really sure he wants to do this. I need—I need to tell Olympias what he really wants."

"*She* doesn't want to kill him? For the thrill of the chase?"

"Only if he really wants to. I don't think—no, I shouldn't say that. I don't *really* know what he wants." She only knew what she wanted and couldn't have. Still, she could accept that she could never be with him as long as he went on with his life. She'd have a certain kind of happiness if Andrew decided to live. She'd be happy for him, at least. "Could you ask Rose to talk to him? Please?"

"Certainly," Bentencourt answered, with a definitive nod. "Olympias shouldn't have burdened you with this. Never send a mortal to do a vampire's job, I say."

Maybe that was what was wrong with her. Maybe Bentencourt was right and her mistress had asked too much of her this time. She almost grasped Bentencourt's hands in gratitude. "Thank you. I appreciate your doing this. Andrew is camping out in Rock Creek Park. I'm sure Rose will be able to find him. I really can't thank you enough for the help."

"It will be Rose you'll need to thank. Speaking of my beloved, that's why I'm here."

"Of course."

"Rose is very upset about this abrupt order to vacate her home of over two centuries. Do you think that Olympias would be willing to meet with her to discuss the necessity of our nest vacating our home? Will you relay this request to your mistress?"

"Yes, of course." Sara realized that Rose must require the old-fashioned formality of using diplomatic channels rather than picking up the phone.

"Good. And you'll let me know what Olympias says."

Again, Sara answered, "Of course." She began to stand up to leave, but he put out a hand to stop her. "Something else?"

"There is a friend of mine who is waiting for an answer from Olympias on a very personal, intimate matter. Perhaps you know what I mean."

Sara had to think about it for a few moments before she said, "The bunny?"

"I was trying to be subtle, Sara."

"Sorry. You know how to contact the vampire who wants him?"

"I am acting as go-between in this matter, yes."

Why wasn't this guy working for Olympias? He seemed to have more of a handle on what was going on locally than anyone else. There weren't supposed to be any vampires locally, which was the big problem they were trying to solve. Olympias didn't have the time to keep tabs on them. That was the point in making them move. Olympias had said she'd check on the mortal, and had taken the time last night to find the man. And come home with a headache from doing her duty as a local Enforcer. Not that the surrounding nests appreciated that she did work for them.

"She did make contact with him, I believe," Sara answered.

"Has Olympias made up her mind about whether my friend can have him as a companion?"

"I—don't think so." Sara recalled mention of a bedroom in connection with the mortal. Bentencourt did not look satisfied with this equivocating. What was the last thing Olympias had said on the subject? Something about the young vampire not being able to control the mortal in question? "I think she has concerns about your friend's ability to handle the relationship."

Bentencourt chuckled. "Believe me, Sara, once you taste your lover's blood, there's nothing you want more than to please your vampire lover. If you ever get the chance to know that ecstasy you'll truly understand about who *handles* the relationship." He touched her hand. Sara fought hard not to jerk angrily away, but she knew he felt her stiffen. "What do I tell my friend?"

"To wait, of course." Sara got up off the bench. "The decision is for the Nighthawk to make," she added, knowing that she sounded portentous. She still held her head up proudly and walked stiffly away, no matter how silly she supposed she looked to the companion left sitting on the bench.

Did he ask for her number? Falconer couldn't remember. He stared out his office window, almost painfully aware that there were a lot of things about last night he didn't remember. Considering how very precise his memory was, the lack of it was very disturbing. He had an important assignment ahead of him, he needed to be calm and focused.

Unfortunately, he barely remembered stumbling into the Walker Project headquarters this morning. He vividly recalled the sex. He remembered that he hadn't discovered her last name. He remembered her beautiful, thick black hair, and her night-dark eyes. He remembered the heat of her mouth against his and the feel of small breasts and hard nipples.

The woman was like nothing he'd ever known in bed. Their coming together had been like nothing he'd ever known. Every touch and taste and move was brand-new, wildly exciting, yet the act had also carried the comfort of long-time lovers coming home to each other. He wondered if she'd felt it too, the connection that ran like a deep, ancient river through blood, muscle, bone, and spirit.

Or, maybe he hadn't gotten laid for a long time and he'd imagined it all in the euphoria of finally getting a woman into bed.

He smiled faintly as he lifted the first cup of morning coffee to his lips. He was almost glad of the cynicism, for he'd learned that wearing a protective shell in matters of the heart was by far the safest way of dealing with them. There'd been women, there'd been a wife, and their thoughts, feelings, and needs always came to grind against his mind and work their way inside to where he didn't know what was him and what was them. Had he ever been truly, soul-deep in love with any of them, perhaps it would not have mattered. He'd never had a soul mate.

Perhaps now . . .

Oh, please!

He put the cup down on the desktop hard enough to slop hot coffee over his hand. "Damn!"

The door opened as he shouted. "You're not in a very good mood this morning," Sela said, her large frame filling the doorway. "And it's only going to get worse."

"What's Grace done now?" was his first reaction. Followed by, "Did anyone ever teach you to knock?"

"Not part of my civil service training. And why are you suspicious of Grace?"

"Call it a feeling."

She grinned. "A man of your abilities should never doubt his feelings."

"We're trained to be observers," he reminded Sela.

"Then why are you in here feeling, when you should be in the conference room or with your controller, observing?"

Good question, but then, Sela's empathic and telepathic talents were nearly as finely honed as her skills in navigating the intricacies of the government's bureaucratic structure. The cynical part of his mind pushed away fond thoughts and sensual memories. Business was business, and protecting turf was a big part of business here in the Capital. He needed to find out if Olympias was a potential friend, enemy, or rival, even while at the same time thinking they might have some kind of future as lovers. There was personal, and there was business. Falconer could operate on both levels. Sela was the one he called on for sensitive assignments, looking into areas that might affect the project's security or funding.

"Her name is Olympias," he answered Sela. "We met at last night's party."

A wicked glint appeared in Sela's dark eyes. "She took you home and had her way with you."

Falconer did not dispute her intuition. "She is a very high-level psychic, I think."

"You think?"

"I couldn't completely read her. She couldn't completely read me." He tapped his forehead. "I'm not sure we did it on purpose, but we danced a little in here. I don't know what either of us learned. I need to know who she works for, and I don't think I can be objective about it. Find out who she is. Go Walking through some government offices if you have to."

Sela brightened considerably at the prospect of doing a little interdepartmental snooping, but she still asked, "Why?"

He smiled. "I want to ask her for another date."

"You could have just gotten her phone number."

"What's the use of having the resources of a government agency to call upon, if I can't abuse the power? Now," he said, getting up from behind his desk, "tell me what Grace is up to."

"She invited us over to her place last night for a practice session."

"Practice?" Falconer asked suspiciously. "Is she trying to adapt past life regression for Walking?"

"How'd you guess?"

"I am psychic, you know."

"I've heard that somewhere."

"Is that what she's up to?"

"Did you really think she'd give up after one failed session? If we hadn't all seen the same thing, she would have considered it a stupid idea and given up on it. But we did see the same place, the same images, crazy and unbelievable as those images were. Something real happened. You really think our Gracie is going to give up until she figures out what happened and how to refine Regressive Observation into a way to objectively look into the past?"

"Regressive Observation?"

"That's what she calls it. Apparently she got some pointers from her friend who does past life regressions and—"

"She discussed what happened with a civilian?"

"Jeremy, Donald, and I *are* civilians, Colonel Falconer," Sela answered, a little huffy. "If you mean did she discuss details with an outsider, of course not. She got pointers on a hypnosis technique, then she invited her fellow *civilian* coworkers to her apartment for a little get-together."

"You practice Walking outside secured areas?"

"No. We had pizza. We did discuss researching methods of psychic time travel. A field of endeavor, which, as you know, has no connection to the mission statement and activities of the Walker Project."

"If there's no connection, why are we having this conversation?"

"Because I think that what Grace is thinking about trying could be very dangerous."

"Messing around with any type of astral projection is dangerous. It requires controls, procedures, safety nets. It probably shouldn't be done at all. We do it all the time, but there's a possibility it's driving us all crazy." Seeing vampires, for example, that was evidence that Walking was taking its toll.

"Now you tell us."

He did not appreciate Sela's sarcasm. "You knew the job was dangerous when you took it."

"Why are you talking in comic book this morning, Mike?"

"Probably because we're discussing Grace."

"I know you care about her."

"Enough so that I don't want to see her—or any of you—end up in a padded room. That is where the things we do can lead, especially if we do it on our own, outside of laboratory conditions." He eyed Sela suspiciously.

"Tell me you aren't involved in any psychic time traveling schemes."

She let out a bark of laughter. "After seeing vampires last time? I don't think so. Donald and Jeremy, though . . ." She shrugged. "Donald's young and enthusiastic. Jeremy's ambitious to prove he's the government's hottest psychic. Grace just wants to learn new stuff. Her enthusiasm could drive the other two into experimenting with her. You will nip it in the bud, I trust."

Falconer nodded decisively. "Count on it."

"Right now?"

He glanced at his watch. "No. I'm due to Walk through an African embassy before a Delta Force team goes in to rescue hostages. They've been told they're getting their intel from someone on the inside, and that someone is me."

Sela sighed. "All right, all right, I get it. We do important work providing information that can save American lives. I'll let you get to it." She turned back toward the door, but couldn't resist a parting shot. "I'll be spying on our own government programs if you need me."

Olympias tapped Mike on the shoulder as he stepped into the gray mist and said, "Nice way to run an intelligence op."

He whirled, sending the mist around him swirling into a small funnel cloud. "What are you doing here?" he demanded, stepping through the tornado he'd created.

"Here is certainly a subjective term, isn't it?"

He spun slowly around, becoming fully aware that they were not exactly anywhere. His face did not show concern, and he certainly wasn't afraid, but there was a hardness about him as he came to face her again. He was a warrior prepared for battle, and Olympias found this attitude far more attractive than she wanted to admit. She'd sworn off military types long ago, but a woman from a time when everyone carried sharpened blades couldn't help but respond to the combination of steely purpose and testosterone.

"How did you do this?"

"I have my little ways. Don't worry, being connected like this won't last long. Cool it," she advised. "I'm not going to bite you." She gestured, stirring the fog.

"Where are we?"

"On neutral ground," she answered. "The link you have to your body isn't severed, but you can't see it right now."

"How?"

"We call it dreamriding or dreamwalking."

"We?"

"Let's not discuss how or where we're having this conversation, Mike."

Corporeal they were not. She was asleep in her bed, with the dog snoring next to her. She supposed he was sitting or lying in an office or lab somewhere in the Washington area. She didn't know his physical location, since it was his spirit she'd gone looking for this morning. After a long search, feeling her way in deep darkness, she came upon a silver thread of light, and followed it.

She'd found Mike Falconer wandering around a darkened mansion that reeked with the concentrated essences of fear and tension. She realized that he was consciously projecting his consciousness, using it to spy on someone. The intense emotions might have drawn her attention if she hadn't discovered something very significant while following him as closely as his shadow through the rooms and halls of the faraway house.

Olympias had really discovered two significant things. One was that she enjoyed being near the distilled spiritual core of the person who wore the body of Michael Falconer. This came as no surprise and didn't bear talking about during this meeting she'd arranged here in limbo. Perhaps it was not wise to step into his awareness and let her presence be known, but she had a few ques-

tions about the second thing she'd discovered, so she let
him become aware of her presence after he finished his
job.

"You're the ghost," she said.

"Not unless you've killed me, I'm not. Then you'd be
dead, too," he added.

"The party line is that we aren't dead, just different."

"We?"

"Never mind. You won't remember this conversation
anyway." Olympias was relatively certain she had complete control of the situation. She'd managed to slip into
the deepest part of his awareness while his attention was
elsewhere. She wanted him to confirm what she thought
was going on. Then she would go away and decide what
to do about him, and what was obviously a government-
run psychic spook program.

She moved very close to him. She cupped his face in
her hands and let him try to get away from her. After a
few moments of being unable to budge, he became very
still, staring furiously into her eyes.

"I saw ghosts when I went back to the park the other
night. The ghosts of five people. They weren't ghosts at
all, were they? What I saw was a residual image from
whatever it is you do. You left similar but fainter images
all over the building back there. What is it you do?"

She'd asked the question with all the ability to bend
another psychic's will that was at an ancient Nighthawk's command. It still took quite a mental struggle
before Falconer answered her.

"Walking," he said. "We call it Walking."

"You went walking in the park?"

"Yes, but not in the usual way. One of my team devised
an experiment to try to find out what happened to me in
the park. We attempted to Walk back in time."

"And what did you see when you Walked back in
time?"

"Vampires," he answered promptly.

"Thought so." Shit. She stared very deeply into his

eyes, going deeper still into his mind. "But you don't believe in vampires, do you." The words were a command, not a question.

His answer was automatic and sincere. "Of course not!"

"You won't let anyone else on your staff believe in them, either."

"Of course not," he answered again. "That would be too dangerous."

Olympias found that to be a very interesting answer, but she didn't question it. Instead, she kissed Michael Falconer very thoroughly, spirit to spirit, building a fire of passion between them. She left him with only feelings of desire and pleasure when he thought of her, building up emotions she found already simmering in his mind. She left him the gift of their sharing mutual pleasure and wiped every other memory and suspicion from his head.

She did the best she could do, then she let him go, surprised at her own reluctance to return to her own empty bed.

Chapter 10

ROGER BENTENCOURT PULLED into the carriage house that had long ago been converted into a garage behind Rose's home, switched off the engine, and sat in the car, composing himself before going inside. He had planned to return home before sunset, to greet Rose in her bed when she awoke, but rush hour traffic had spoiled his plan for private time with his vampire lover. He always felt better when he was with Rose, even though he was painfully aware the peace she brought him was all a result of being allowed to share her blood and body. He made himself sneer at his automatic devotion, but he couldn't deny the soothing properties of being with Rose. She was beautiful, he very much appreciated her body, though he valued her malleability more. Everyone needed some form of stress relief, his happened to be a silly old vampire.

There were four bays in the large old garage. The household had three cars, and Bentencourt noticed that all three vehicles were in the garage. That meant Alec was home. Bentencourt permitted himself a sigh, but didn't let it bother him. Alec was an annoyance, but really only a minor hindrance to the way Bentencourt ran the nest. Fortunately, Alec was greedy, self-involved, and clueless about the true nature of power. Alec would have made a perfect guest on one of those who-wants-to-be-rich-and-famous television game shows. He liked thinking that he knew everything and that making money was the fast, easy way to power.

Alec, like most of the strigoi population, was deeply brainwashed into ignoring their powers, and their superiority to mortals. Bentencourt saw no reason to enlighten the vampire population to their own slavery, not when it came in handy in his own plans to rise to power.

Bentencourt forced down his contempt for Alec. It would not show when he entered the house. He would try to avoid Alec, but he would smile when he next encountered the male vampire, and politely offer Alec another bit of financial advice that would send Alec scurrying out of town once more.

Alec was easy to deal with. Bentencourt's real annoyance was that his plans were not going as swiftly as he'd hoped they would once he'd set Lora on Falconer. He wasn't used to being impatient, yet he had to keep reminding himself that it had only been a few days since his scheme had been set in motion. It wasn't as if the plan was set in stone, or was on a precise timetable. He had to use what there was to work with, find and make opportunities, and be flexible. The basic plan was to take Olympias down and set Rose up as the senior nest leader in the area. It had to appear as though the vampires of Washington had united to overthrow a rogue who abused the Laws of the Blood from her position as an Enforcer and temporarily replaced her with a just, Law-abiding nest leader until the Council could sort things out.

He would be the power behind Rose before and during this period of uncertainty, and he would infiltrate all the other nests with his allies and supporters. Once he ruled the local vampires, they could then quietly infiltrate every branch and bureau of the government with a small army of slaves he'd persuade his friends were necessary for their own protection from the powerful mortals. He'd always known the Council would send another Enforcer after the coup, but by the time the newcomer settled into the job, Bentencourt would have his moles in place. It would be better if the slaves belonged to him rather than to vampires he influenced, but he had to work with the tools that came to hand for the next few years. The point was to have an organization already in place once he came into his full powers. Start from scratch now, and his rise to power when he made the change would be swift enough to take the Council off guard.

Then—good riddance to the antiquated, outdated, totally ridiculous Strigoi Council. Though he would rather conquer at the head of an army, as he had done in the past life when he had been Philip of Macedon, he would still rule the world. This time the late Philip's vicious bitch of a wife would not stand in his way. Olympias would not stop him.

Olympias herself had given him ammunition to use against her when she ordered the nests to evacuate their homes. He wished his plan to seduce Sara Czerny were going faster, but the slave was feeding him some useful information. Perhaps she wasn't the type for subtle manipulation, not that he thought his overtures had been particularly subtle. She didn't seem to pick up on his hints that her psychic ability was strong enough for her to become a companion, and that he was offering her the chance to be *his* companion once he became a vampire. Perhaps the loyal little slave needed to be presented with evidence of how Olympias had lied to her. Or perhaps Sara had become infatuated with this suicidal vampire she'd told him about and wanted to become this newcomer's companion.

"Silly fool," Bentencourt murmured. He got out of the car and headed with measured steps through the garden and toward the house.

He knew full well that Sara was going to belong to

him. Olympias would be disposed of, but Sara was invaluable. Sara was the most powerful Enforcer in the country's chief of staff. Sara quite literally knew where all the bodies were buried. Sara knew everything there was to know about every nest, strig and, most importantly, every Enforcer in the country. Sara controlled all the slaves already working within the government. Bentencourt *needed* Sara, and he was going to have her. All he needed to do was make her hate Olympias and love him, even before they shared any bloodbond. He wanted her to gladly betray Olympias for him. It appeared this Andrew person might need to be gotten out of the way first, but Bentencourt believed he might have a use for a suicidal vampire.

His frustrations left him as he smiled at this thought. Of course, there was some information he needed first, to see if the scheme was at all viable. Fortunately, he already needed to have a conversation with the one person he knew that took a devoted interest in strigoi history, rumor, and gossip. He truly did value Lora as a member of Rose's nest. He thought he might even miss her when she was gone.

There were voices raised inside. He stopped to listen in the hallway outside Rose's sitting room. Shouting was not a sound Bentencourt was used to in this house, but he liked it. Dissent was what the plan was all about. The loudest voice belonged to Alec.

"We can't pack up and leave!" he shouted. "Our lives are here."

"I know that far better than you," Rose countered.

"My livelihood is here. I have investments, business interests."

"I have deep roots here. I'm in pain, Alec."

"We all have roots here. Every nest, even the strigs."

"We don't talk about them in this house."

"Maybe we could use their help."

"Don't tell me you know how to contact that sort of—creature?"

Alec hesitated, then admitted, "I've got a couple working occasional jobs for me."

Rose's voice rose. "I forbid it!"

"This is no time to be prejudiced, Rose. We all need to stand together this time. Have you called anyone?"

"Called?"

"Nests. We need to get the nests together. At least you nest leaders need to meet and discuss what you can do. They look up to you."

"Well, I—"

Bentencourt smiled and walked away. It looked like Alec was taking on one of his jobs for him. It seems the household's male vampire wasn't as much of a liability as Bentencourt previously thought. Bentencourt knew the further he could distance himself from responsibility for future events the safer he would be. The point was to gain power by covert means. Misdirection was key. *Thank you, Alec, for your greed, it makes you one of my cat's-paws without my actually having to recruit you. Thank you, indeed.*

There was a spring in his step as he went up the stairs, but he put on a grave, sympathetic air as he knocked on Lora's door, then went in without waiting for her to answer it.

"Well?" she demanded the moment he walked in. "What did she say?"

The girl was in heat, there was no denying it, and growing mindless with it. Lora needed some kind of release. A Hunt might calm her down, or a violent confrontation to channel off the pent-up energy. Rose could have done something about it. She could have at least given Lora a sound thrashing, or chained her up in one of the outbuildings to keep her from being a danger to herself or the neighbors. But, at his urging, Rose hesitated to interfere. After all, he'd assured his mistress, why hurt or confine the girl when Olympias was bound to decide quickly. Lora had the right to take a companion and to enjoy the release of all her pent-up lust when the time came. How could Olympias keep the girl from her chosen lover unless she was turning into a territorial dictator? Olympias had allowed Rose to take him as a companion, hadn't she? And he'd lived and worked in the heart of the city at the time.

When Bentencourt failed to answer Lora instantly, she grabbed him by the shoulders and tossed him across her room. He hit a wall, slid down it to his knees, then hurriedly got up and turned to face her as she slammed the door.

"Good evening," he offered, holding his hands up defensively before him.

"Well?" she demanded again.

Being alone in a room with a crazed vampire was not a safe thing for a mortal, but Bentencourt would not let himself be afraid. They were emotion eaters as well as blood drinkers. It increased your life expectancy to remain calm around a vampire. "Sit down," he urged, his voice and manner projecting soothing concern. "You know I'm here to help you. You have to be calmer before we can talk. We need to talk, Lora." He used all his hypnotic psychic skill to reach her, pacify her, get her to focus on him.

Finally, Lora did sit, perching nervously on the end of her bed. Her gaze was fixed on him. "You know something," she said. "Tell me."

He leaned against the wall, his palms resting on the flower-patterned wallpaper. "In a moment, my dear. In a moment."

"You want something from me first!" she snapped back.

"Yes," he admitted, giving her a warm, encouraging smile. "You can help me. Your helping me against Olympias helps us both."

"I hate her!"

"With good reason. You're a vampire, I am a mere mortal. You know a great deal I do not. I need your expertise."

She responded to the flattery. "Are you asking nicely?"

"I always ask you nicely. You know I care for you, Lora."

She nodded. "You're the only one who does—until I have my own companion."

He kept his tone soothing, as smooth as honey, and his emotions were full of affection, unshielded, letting her drink them in. "I want to help you get him. I know how much you need him."

"What do you need to know?"

"You told me a few days ago, and I quote, *'Nighthawks don't all turn out Hunters. I think there's some kind of change they have to go through. Like getting made into a queen bee or something.'* You said that Rose and the bitch are of the same bloodline. How do you know?"

Lora ran a hand nervously through her short brown hair. "I used to live in Portland. I was a companion to vampire in Marguerite's nest. A vampire was brought to her who was going through the change into a Nighthawk. I remember Marguerite saying that Jimmy Bluecorn had done it again. That he never turned into a monster's monster himself, but a lot of his kids did. I guess this Bluecorn is the original hippie. He's one of the really old ones, into peace and love and justice and crap like that. Marguerite thought he made it to America even before Columbus."

"You're kidding."

"Just telling you the Portland Enforcer's theory. She obviously didn't care for the guy."

"Why?"

"He can't keep his fangs in his mouth. Has a companion almost all the time. Marguerite mentioned that Rose was one of Jimmy Bluecorn's bloodchildren when she was looking for a nest for me to live in after I made the change. She said that the ones that don't turn Enforcer are generally pretty tame. She was certainly right about that."

"Indeed. We lead a quiet life."

"I hate it here."

Bentencourt had let his curiosity draw him off track. That was not like him, but he stored the information away. Everything he learned about strigoi culture was valuable. "And how is this Jimmy Bluecorn connected to our Rose?"

"His portrait's hanging in her bedroom." She laughed harshly. "That's who's looking over your shoulder when you're making love."

Bentencourt noticed that his hands were suddenly fisted at his sides, but he clamped down on the jealous rage. Jealousy was a natural part of being a companion and had nothing to do with his real emotions. His love for Rose was nothing more than a chronic disease he'd learned to live with, a by-product of ambition, really. Someday soon he would be cured of it and totally free. In the meantime, he coped as best he could, acknowledged the false feelings, then put them aside and went on.

"And how is this Jimmy connected to the Greek bitch?"

"Same dude made her and Rose into vampires, centuries apart, I'd guess. Don't think he was involved in turning Olympias Nighthawk, but his blood gave her the mutation or whatever. Rose and Olympias are related. They're bloodsisters. Rose knows it. Don't know if Olympias knows or cares, but Rose knows, and she hates Olympias because of it."

"How does Rose know?" If anyone among the strigoi kept genealogy records, he hadn't found evidence of it. Pity his sources were so far rather limited. This kind of important information would be the sort of thing Sara might know. She was going to be so useful to have under his control.

"I don't know!" Lora answered. "I just overheard her muttering to the portrait about it once when I was passing by her bedroom and the door was open."

"So Rose *could* become an Enforcer?"

"If the mood ever hits her, sure."

"And how does one become an Enforcer?"

"I think you have to *join* the Enforcers. I think strig Nighthawks are hunted down by packs of Enforcers; at least that's the rumor I heard. I can't imagine a Nighthawk who isn't an Enforcer. The only thing scarier than a vampire, at least when they let us act like vampires, is a Nighthawk. Can you imagine a Nighthawk that doesn't live by any rules?"

Yes, he could. In fact, it took a great deal of effort not to grin fiendishly at the idea. "If Rose can become a Nighthawk—"

"She is a Nighthawk, but she isn't a *changed* one."

"Does that mean I become a Nighthawk when I'm a vampire?"

Lora shrugged. "Yeah. Sure. This conversation is boring. What about *me?* I want my bunny!"

"Just a few more questions. Please, Lora, this is important. The answers you give me might even help things become more interesting around here. I got off track, and I'm sorry. What I need to know is *how* one becomes a *changed* Nighthawk? What triggers the recessive gene?" Could it be triggered in Rose?

"I don't know the details." She made a disgusted face. "I know that to change, the Nighthawk has to kill and consume another vampire."

This was the answer he'd been hoping for. It looked like there might be more than one use for this suicidal vampire Sara had told him about. "Thank you," he said, genuinely sincere for once. He came to sit beside Lora on the bed. Such proximity could prove dangerous, but he felt the need to appear at his most sympathetic and fatherly—to be *there* for her. "Now I have to give you some bad news," he told her. "Temporary bad news, at least. I'm sure we can find a way to change Olympias's mind. I'm sure Rose will intercede on your behalf—"

"Intercede?" Lora shot to her feet, faster than his eyes

could register. She looked down at him, quivering with rage, eyes full of pain. "What are you talking about? Olympias said 'no' didn't she? The bitch said I couldn't have the man I love!" Bentencourt didn't answer, and Lora whirled away to pound on a wall. "Damn her! Damn her!"

"My sentiments exactly," he murmured.

Lora turned back to him. "She can't do this to me!"

"She is the Enforcer of the City, my dear. Of course she can—"

"She can't. I won't let her. I won't let her have him!"

With this last shout, Lora was gone. Out of her room. He caught only a blur of motion as she sped away. He saw the bedroom door open, heard the front door slam a moment later, and knew that Lora was out of the house, on her way to Georgetown. On her way to make trouble for Olympias. He smiled. All that really mattered was trouble for Olympias.

His frustrations of the day melted away, as it looked to be shaping up into a very productive evening.

"You know what I'm in the mood for?" Olympias asked Sara as she wandered into the office a little after sunset.

Sara had heard her mistress running the shower upstairs a few minutes before and turned around from her computer screen now to see Olympias dressed in a T-shirt from the National Zoo and a faded pair of jeans that were wearing out at the knees. Sara made a mental note to throw out the jeans when Olympias wasn't looking.

"What?" she asked.

Olympias leaned against the doorjamb, and the huge black dog leaned against her. "Cheesecake. No, I don't expect you to run out and get me some," she added when Sara started to get up. "I'll stop somewhere when I go out tonight."

"You're going out?" There were times when Olympias didn't leave the house for weeks except for late night runs with Bitch. That Olympias had attended two social functions within a few days was one of the many odd aspects of this week. Sara looked her mistress over critically. "Dressed like that? Do I need to tell you to change clothes?"

Olympias ignored her sarcasm while she rubbed the dog's head. "I plan to drop in on a friend. Sorry, Bitch, you have to stay home."

"You don't have friends."

"He won't care what I'm wearing." Sara's words registered after Olympias spoke. "I do have friends," she responded. She looked thoughtful. "Somewhere." She touched a finger to her square chin. "I think."

Olympias's words registered on Sara. "What he? I mean, which *he*? You have a he?" For a moment the wild notion that Olympias was interested in Andrew flitted through Sara's mind, then she remembered that last night Olympias had made contact with the mortal Lora wanted. How could she have forgotten, when Bentencourt had asked her about the situation only a few hours before? Because she was thinking too much about Andrew, she supposed.

"I don't have a *he*. I have yet another complication," Olympias told her.

"Lora's prospective companion?"

Olympias nodded.

"What could be complicated about him?" Then Sara sighed and answered her own question. "Don't tell me, he works for some super secret government intelligence agency. Otherwise, it's not likely you would have met him at last night's party."

Olympias smiled proudly at her, and a warm glow permeated Sara's being at the attention. It didn't make her feel as warm as a look from Andrew did, and she found that less disturbing than she should have. Olympias's affection had always been a distant thing, the kind regard of a goddess. Right now she smiled back at the goddess, more interested in the conversation than mooning over another vampire.

"You said last night that he gave you a headache," Sara recalled. "So the spook is psychic—of course, Lora wouldn't want him if he wasn't psychic." Olympias nodded at that. "Is he a psychic spook?" Olympias nodded again. Sara made a face. "I thought we managed to discredit that sort of thing with the distance viewing scandal."

"Bureaucracies," Olympias complained. "I don't think it's possible to keep a stupid idea from proliferating once a government department latches onto it. I managed to get into Mike's head today—finally. I learned a few things from the way he subconsciously blocked me last night and managed to sneak past his defenses, dreamwalking into his assignment while he was working."

"And his work is . . . ?" Sara prodded.

"Providing very accurate intelligence data." She rubbed the back of her neck before going back to petting the dog. "I'm going to have another talk with him, but I need you to find out all you can about Air Force Colonel Michael Falconer and something called Walking."

Sara came to her feet when she heard the name. "Falconer?"

"You recognize the name."

Sara very carefully kept calm and focused, not letting her emotions spill over into her work mode. She'd never tried to hide anything from her mistress before, but found it surprisingly easy. "The suicidal vampire is named Andrew Falconer."

Olympias nodded. "My suspicion is that Mike was born after his father became a companion. Fortunately, not after he became a vampire. That would make things way too complicated."

"You can have kids after you become a vampire?"

"I certainly couldn't, thank the gods. The son I had as a mortal caused enough problems. Fortunately, ninety-nine percent of vampires can't reproduce in the mortal way. The ones that can . . ." Olympias smiled, and there

was something fond and reminiscent about it. She held a
hand up to forestall more questions. "I doubt Andrew
passed any vampire gifts on to his mortal offspring. What
I think is that the Falconers must simply be a very psychic family. I should have found out more about this
Walking thing while I was in Mike's head today, but he
tired me out last night." She laughed. "In more ways than
one. What I did discover is that the type of astral projection they perform leaves a psychic residue, a kind of
ghost image. That's what I picked up when I thought I
saw ghosts in the park."

"You saw ghosts in a park?"

"Didn't I tell you about that?"

"I've heard you use the word *ghost* in the last couple
of days, but you didn't explain."

"Why didn't I?"

"Possibly because the Las Vegas and Memphis situations came up?" Sara suggested. She was thinking about
Andrew and how she had to get to him to tell him about
his son, but she forced herself to stick to business. The
sooner the evening briefing was over with, the sooner
Olympias would be out of the house. "Memphis is taken
care of," she reminded her mistress. She prayed that
Olympias didn't bring up Andrew. Sara certainly wasn't
going to bring up any other subject on her own.

"Anything on Las Vegas?"

"Possibly peripherally. There was a report on CNN
about a new hotel having to be evacuated. There weren't
a lot of details."

Olympias considered this for a moment, then chuckled.
"For now I'm going to consider that the situation is in
hand. If you hear anything, let me know."

She started to turn away, and Sara almost let her go,
but the habit of duty got the better of her earnest longing
to be rid of her mistress for the evening. "Where will you
be?"

"First I'm stopping somewhere in Adams Morgan for
gyros and cheesecake. Then I'm heading over to Mike's."

"Fine," Sara said. She didn't remind Olympias to take her phone. She pointed at Bitch and ordered, "You mind the fort," as soon as Olympias was gone. The hellhound ignored her, lay down across the doorway, and started licking one of her paws. Sara started to step over her, but the phone rang. She almost didn't answer it, but on the second ring, Sara gritted her teeth and grabbed the cordless phone out of its cradle. "Yes?"

"Ms. Czerny? Sara?"

"Yes, Roger?" she asked, recognizing the companion's voice, even though she had never heard him sound agitated before. "Are you all right?"

"I'm fine. Rose is fine. However, there's a bit of a problem with Lora. You should tell your mistress that Lora is on her way to Falconer's house right now. She's going to do something rash."

"I see," Sara answered. She didn't know what she was going to do. *She* had no idea where Falconer lived, or even where Olympias was at the moment. She'd said she was heading to Adams Morgan; it was a busy, lively area of the city. Vampires moved fast; Olympias was probably already eating dinner in one of a dozen neighborhood bistros. Sara cursed herself. She should be on top of this! She didn't let any of her own concern show when she answered the companion. "Olympias is aware of the situation. Thank you," she added, and hung up the phone.

Sara didn't know what Olympias would do. She didn't know if Lora's taking Falconer was a good or bad thing. She had never felt so out of the loop. But it did occur to her that there was one person who desperately did need to be brought into the loop. Mike Falconer was Andrew's son. Part of what was driving Andrew to suicide was desperation about what had happened to his son. Andrew at least deserved to know what was happening, and she was going to tell him.

"Hey, Sela," Falconer spoke into the phone. "Tell me what you've got."

"Maybe I should use telepathy," the voice on the other end of the line said. "It'd be more secure."

Falconer sat back in the deep leather chair in his home office and crossed his long legs. A glass full of amber ale rested on the table beside him, and there was a book in his lap. He wore sweat pants and no shirt, and was feeling more relaxed than he had in days. "I'm not in the mood for telepathy tonight. Mundane suits me fine."

"You're no fun."

The Walking session this afternoon had been harder than usual. The actual Walk itself hadn't been so bad, but he'd had trouble returning to full awareness of his body's physical surroundings afterward. There was a part of him that thought he *ought* to be disturbed at the slow reentry to the corporeal world, but he felt like he'd had a mini vacation instead. He'd been in a cloudy, peaceful place. It hadn't been SOP, but he'd come back feeling fine and still been able to give a full, detailed report on his mission.

"I am so fun," he told Sela.

She gave a deep, wicked chuckle. "Then maybe I should come over and give you my info on Ms. Olympias in person."

Falconer sat up a little straighter. Memories blazed through him at the mention of her name. "What have you got?" he asked, mind all business, but body reacting another way entirely. How could he want someone so much at the sound of a name?

"Not much," Sela answered. "But it's a beginning. Seems Olympias's name was put on the guest list to your party at the request of a lobbyist named Maggie Donner. This Donner is with—"

The crash of shattering glass from the window behind him drowned out the rest of Sela's words. Falconer dropped the phone as he sprang out of the chair. As he whirled to face the broken window, a young woman rose up off the floor, dusting shards of glass off her clothes and shaking it out of her short brown hair.

"What the hell—!"

She looked at him with a hungry, possessive gaze, and smiled a horrible, bright smile. Fangs gleamed in the room's mellow lamplight, and her eyes gleamed, without any trick of the light.

"I've come back for you," she said, stepping forward, glass crunching beneath her feet. She licked a drop of blood from a small cut above her lip.

Falconer's stomach heaved at the gesture. For a second, Falconer stared unbelieving at the creature who'd invaded his house. She was beautiful and hideous. She aimed lust at him like a weapon. It beat at his senses, and he felt her calling to him, trying to reach deep into his mind and make him think it was he who craved her.

He shook his head wildly and looked around for a weapon.

He knew that a silent security alarm had been tripped when the window broke and was alerting the nearest police station. He heard Sela's voice faintly shouting from the phone lying on the chair. He knew that this invader didn't care about such mundane precautions as alarm systems and witnesses. This was a monster out of nightmares. His nightmares. Impossible, and very real. He remembered her face, and the other one. It hadn't been a dream. It was all too real, and happening again. She wanted him. Her hunger was terrifying.

"The vampires in the park are real," he said loudly, hoping Sela would hear as he backed toward the door. "This one—and Olympias."

Chapter 11

THE FIRST THING he did was throw the beer into her face, then the beer glass. She only laughed. Then he grabbed the lamp. He wished it was a cross, but the base was wood; maybe he could somehow use it as a stake. The room was plunged into semidarkness, lit now only by moonlight coming in from the broken window and the glow of the computer screen.

As he backed toward the door, lamp held before him like a shield, the vampire looked around the room. "We have got to redecorate this place. You've been living alone too long, darling."

Darling? Wasn't she supposed to be talking about sucking his blood and damning his eternal soul? How'd she get in here? Didn't vampires have to be invited in? Or was that just in the movies?

"I don't know if I'll let you stay here, or have you move in with me, but I'll decide on living arrangements later." She smiled, and when she did, her fangs seemed to grow even longer. He definitely had the impression she wanted him to look at the sharp, elongated incisors, as though doing so was equated somehow with him staring at her naked boobs. She wanted him to look at her boobs, too. He could feel her wanting him to want her. Her thoughts pawed at him, the ephemeral touch obscenely possessive.

This talk of domesticity was equally obscene and made him cold with dread. "Get out of here," he demanded. "Get away from me."

"You don't love me yet," she pouted, coming toward him. "That's ungrateful—after I've sent you so many dreams of me. Don't you remember my touch on your mind?"

He remembered a feeling of unease, the occasional sense of being stalked that he'd dismissed as Walking-induced paranoia. He did remember being chased by her—now he remembered it, though Olympias had gone out of her way to make him forget it. Olympias was one of them. A vampire. Like the Audrey Hepburn look-alike with fangs he was facing. Like the male one he had seen dreaming and Walking.

Olympias was a vampire.

He could almost ignore the threat before him as his mind tried to wrap itself around the anger, sense of betrayal, and fascination that fact caused him. Fascination, not fear. What that said about him, and about Olympias, he didn't know.

What he did know was that he had to get away from this vampire before he could worry about what anything else might mean.

He backed into the wall near the door and flipped on the overhead light. Any tiny hope he had that the bright light might somehow stun her vanished when she laughed. Her mouth was beautiful when she laughed. Her smile was stunning. He stared at it, and for a brief instant, he almost smiled back.

Falconer took his eyes off the vampire's mouth and studied the rest of the intruder's face carefully, though he instinctively avoided looking into her eyes. He *knew* he could be caught by the hypnotic force of her gaze if their eyes met, though he didn't know how he knew. Another old movie myth, maybe. She was beautiful, delicate and dark haired, skin as fine as alabaster. Incredibly beautiful. Magically beautiful. The unearthly beauty was something she wore, something she'd put on, like makeup.

"Olympias hasn't bothered to try to impress me."

He said it as he reached for the doorknob. The next thing he knew, his wrist was broken, and he was screaming.

The vampire held him up by his broken wrist and slapped him so hard he thought his head might come off. "Don't talk about her! Say her name again, and I'll rip your tongue out." A moment after she made the threat she laughed. "I've got too much use for your tongue, sweetheart, but I'll rip something off. Maybe I'll start with your toes. Can't think of any use for your toes." She stepped hard on his foot and pressed herself against him. "Except maybe to go dancing."

Her desire called to him, with the heat of her body and the heat of her thoughts. She was in heat, he realized through the haze of pain. She was literally suffering from a need to mate, and she'd chosen him for her partner. The knowledge was sickening, her need suffocating. He wanted nothing to do with her.

But if she bit him . . . if she bit him, he *knew* he'd want her then. They controlled you by taking your blood, infected the ones they made their lovers. He knew that. Didn't know how he knew. Maybe from Olympias. Maybe from something he'd heard as a—

—heard as a kid.

The almost memory dissipated like smoke as the vampire reached for his crotch.

That was when he hit her with the lamp. As hard as he could. And he was not a weak man.

Of course the blow only served to make her angrier. "Bastard!" She wrenched the lamp out of his hand, then threw him across the room. Falconer hit the desk, felt his back crack against the computer. He fell forward onto the floor. He caught himself on his hands, and nearly passed out from the shock of pain as his weight came down on the broken wrist. He collapsed face first onto the rug and almost didn't notice when the heavy computer screen crashed down on his back.

The vampire kicked the screen off him, then began kicking him. "You want her! I can smell her on you, you cheating bastard! You're mine. Mine!"

Every sentence was punctuated with a kick. Into his ribs. His head. Falconer tried to roll away, and she followed him, still raving. Still kicking. He finally managed to grab her ankle with his good hand, and pull. Instead of knocking her off her feet, it only made her laugh. She shook him off like she would an annoying insect, laughed, and dragged him to his feet once more.

She propped him up against a wall, put her face very close to his, held up a hand adorned with sharp claws, and whispered, the words a dark caress, "Now I'm going to make it hurt."

And she did.

What penetrated the pain after a long bout of agony was another voice. It was a deep voice, but a woman's voice all the same. She was full of anger that was as cold as his attacker's mad fury was full of heat. He heard words, but they rasped against his psychic senses like a blade being drawn. He couldn't help but smile when he heard her, though he tasted blood.

What Olympias said was, "Get away from him, you bitch."

"What the hell is that?"

"Exactly—she's a *hell*hound. Haven't you ever seen one before?"

"What the hell's a hellhound?"

Obviously, Andrew had not seen anything like Bitch before she and the huge dog came crashing through the bushes to his campsite. It frequently amazed Sara how

ignorant many vampires were about their own history and
culture. Maybe because she wasn't a vampire she found
the subject more fascinating than those who actually
lived the life. "Some people simply don't appreciate what
they have."

"What?"

"Never mind. We don't have time to talk. We have to
go."

"Go? Go where?" Andrew grabbed her by the shoulders when she turned to hurry back toward the walking
path. He spun Sara back to face him. Bitch growled, but
didn't lunge. Andrew's expression was full of trepidation.
"What's going on? Has Olympias decided to kill me?"

"You think she'd send me for that? This is about your
son," Sara hurried to explain. "Do you want to see him
alive or not? No, he isn't dead," she hastened to inform
the melancholy vampire. "But he might be if we don't
hurry. At least, I think they're going to have a cat fight
over him, and who knows how he's going to end up."

"They? Who are they? Who's him?"

Sara didn't think Andrew realized he was shaking her.
Bitch growled again, and he stopped. "Mike Falconer.
He's the bunny—excuse me, the mortal Lora's after, only
Olympias wants him too, only I don't think she really
realizes that that's her problem and it doesn't have anything to do with why Lora can't have him, because
there's politics and secret military stuff involved, and
Olympias can't allow vampires to be discovered by secret
military stuff. You see."

"I have no idea what you're talking about."

"Neither do I. Except that I found out this evening that
your son is alive. You haven't been seeing his ghost, but
a psychic projection that's—"

"Secret military stuff?"

"Yes. He's psychic."

"I know. He's my kid."

"Which is why Lora wants him."

"Because he's my kid?"

"Because he's psychic." She tugged at his arm. "Come on. Lora's going to bite him tonight. That is, if we or Olympias don't stop her. My money's on Olympias, but if she doesn't get there first—I don't know what we're going to do. Because I brought Bitch to track Olympias, and if Olympias doesn't get to your son's house first, I don't know how we're going to find him."

"My son's house. My son." Andrew sighed, closed his eyes for a moment, as though he was savoring the words. Then he looked at Sara again and asked, "Does he live in Georgetown?"

"Yes. At least she mentioned driving back from Georgetown last night."

"Then we don't need your—" He glanced warily at Bitch, who sat on her haunches with her tongue lolling out. "—hellhound. I know exactly where my son lives." He grabbed her by the wrist. "Let's go."

"He's mine! You can't have him."

"No one belongs to anyone in this territory unless I say so." Olympias looked down at Falconer, who'd slid down the wall, leaving a trail of his own blood on the wallpaper after Lora had whirled away from him to face Olympias. "Doesn't look like there's much left to fight over." She knew the scent of all that virgin blood excited Lora. Olympias had to fight against the rush of desire herself. Olympias was glad she had at least arrived before Lora'd marked him for herself. Olympias hadn't felt this sort of blood arousal in years, and she licked her lips.

The gesture was unconscious, and it infuriated Lora. "You've slept with him, haven't you? You've slept with him!"

"Yes."

"How could you? You knew he was mine!"

"I hadn't said he was yours."

"He's mine!" The girl's shout was deafening. She quivered with rage and bloodlust, and other lust as well.

She was crying. Her claws were covered in the man's blood, and she was crying.

This child was not sane. Olympias tried to tamp down her own anger and the desire that swirled around her. She wanted to believe she was responding to the girl's projected emotions, but she had to admit that her desire for Falconer was her own. She didn't have to explain anything to Lora, *she* was the Enforcer.

Maybe it was some tiny hint of guilt that the girl had seen him first that made her say, "Calm down. I didn't take a drop. Get over it. And get out of my way," she added, gesturing for the girl to move aside. Another thing she hated to admit, she wanted to get to Mike Falconer to see how badly he was injured, not to finish off the job Lora had started. She cared for this mortal. "Damn it."

"Damn you!" Lora stayed planted between Olympias and Falconer. She held her fully extended claws up before Olympias, and her fangs were now Hunting length.

Olympias was not impressed. She'd given the kid a chance. One chance was fair. Anything more was weakness. Olympias showed her own claws as she stepped forward.

Mike lifted his head when she moved, focused a dazed gaze on her, and croaked out, "Olympias."

She couldn't help but smile. The stubborn dear. "You're a tough one, Mike."

"Bitch!"

"That's my dog."

"How could you? I hate you!"

Olympias expected Lora to respond by attacking her; instead Lora lunged toward Mike.

"If I can't have him—"

Olympias's claws sank into Lora's back before the girl could finish the sentence or do any further harm to Mike Falconer. "You can't."

She tossed Lora across the room, heard wood splinter as Lora crashed against the doorframe.

Instead of taking the hint, Lora rebounded quickly, and

leapt over Olympias, still trying to get at Falconer. The girl was totally in Hunter mode, focused on ripping mortal prey to shreds. She needed flesh now, not mating blood.

Olympias grabbed Lora by the arm and whirled the young vampire to face her. "Goddess damn it," Olympias said, and ripped Lora's chest open.

Lora screamed as her heart was torn out, but the sound didn't mask the wail of police sirens outside. Olympias glared toward the street entrance of the house as she squeezed the still-beating heart in her bloody hand. This night was not going as she'd planned.

"I hate when this happens," she said to Mike, who was trying to sit up, with very little success.

Someone was pounding on the front door now, and there was shouting outside as well as the continuing sound of sirens. The residents of Georgetown liked privacy and a low crime rate. The Georgetown police generally showed up at any call in significant numbers to impress upon the wealthy neighborhoods that they were capable of handling anything. Olympias knew they couldn't handle her, but supposed she shouldn't be found here with a corpse on her shoulder and a heart in her hand. She glanced toward the broken window and dark backyard beyond. She'd come in by jumping through the open bedroom window on the second floor.

She looked at the injured man, but didn't have time for sloppy sentiment. "Gotta go. We'll talk later. Try not to die," she advised the human. "Don't discuss this incident with anyone," she added before she jumped out the window with Lora's corpse. "Because that will prove fatal."

She might have blown him a kiss in leaving, but she remembered what she was holding in time. While she might have been incompetent this evening, she was never gross. So she bounded out the window and disappeared into the night instead.

•   •   •

"We're too late."

Sara put her hand on Andrew's arm. "No we're not."

Andrew shook her off and pointed toward the emergency medical vehicle blocking the narrow brick street outside the house. "Then explain what that's doing there."

Sara glanced up at him and sighed. He was being dramatic and unreasonable. She couldn't blame Andrew. After all, in a very short space of time he'd heard that his son was alive, rushed here with Sara, carrying her most of the way. Bitch had raced happily beside them, eyes glowing, and scaring the bejesus out of everyone they passed. They'd arrived in front of the Falconer house with pedestrians' screams ringing in their ears at the same time as the cops, the ambulance, and the crowd. Bitch had sniffed the air, barked once, and disappeared. This was just as well, as the huge dog tended to draw attention. Drawing attention would not be good. In Andrew's high-strung state, attention from mortals might set off his Hunting instincts.

"The medics are here to take him to the hospital," she said patiently. She was used to being patient with vampires. It helped keep them from going on rampages. "You already heard the officer tell his neighbors that Colonel Falconer was injured, but alive."

"What if he's been bitten? Do you think I want my son to go through the same thing I did? Without any choice?"

Sara looked around anxiously, worried they'd be overheard. There were too many people, too many lights. She'd noticed one or two of the neighbors glance their way, suspicious of strangers. Andrew was scruffy, and she was disheveled. This was not the sort of neighborhood where street people wandered freely. She'd stared hard back at the neighbors, getting them to look away out of force of will, but if Andrew insisted on talking crazy, even in whispers, attention wasn't going to stay off them for long.

She jerked a thumb toward the deserted shadows, and they moved away from the crowd in front of the house. "He can't have been bitten," she said once they were out of the crowd. "He was found alone in the house. No strigoi would leave a new companion alone. He's been injured. Maybe he fought off the one who wanted him. Olympias said he was a strong psychic. Lora's a young vampire. He's been injured, but he's whole." She clutched at Andrew's shoulders. "He's alive, and he's going to be all right," she reassured him.

Her words drew a faint smile from the vampire. He stopped staring toward the ambulance and turned his warm gaze on her. "You're right. He's all right. When I concentrate I can hear his heartbeat. He's in pain, but he's strong." Andrew brushed a strand of hair off her forehead and planted a brief kiss on it.

She blinked, and her toes curled. "What was that for?"

"The ghosts are gone. You drove them away, Sara," he told her. "You are amazing."

"No I'm not."

"You gave me my son back." He chuckled, the sound a low sweet rumble. "You gave me my life back."

His words set off a small nova inside her. How could a creature of the dark fill her with so much light? This could not be good, but it was so very right. Their beings touched, twined—it must almost be what it was like to be a companion. She tried to misunderstand what he was saying, looking into his eyes the whole time. "You don't want to die anymore?"

"I'm not going to die," he answered. He snagged an arm around her waist and pulled her close. "I still might be in trouble with Olympias."

"Protecting your son from becoming an unwilling companion?"

"That might be part of the problem."

This was bad. Very bad. Why did she feel so good? It was staring into his eyes, wasn't it? He was a vampire. They had powers. "Part?" she asked.

He smiled. And she thought something inane about whether those were fangs in his pocket or if he was just happy to see her . . . except that fangs . . . were beautiful. His were. Gleaming. Sharp. Sexy.

"Come back to the park with me."

It was a request. It was her choice. If she did it was probably going to get them both killed. "All right."

At least she'd die happy.

"Please, Roger, I'd rather be alone now." Rose sighed wearily. "I have so much I need to think about."

"I understand," Bentencourt answered, but he closed the bedroom door and came silently across the thick carpet toward the bed, despite having been told to go away. Rose was sitting on the bed, her back propped up by a thick pile of pillows. There was a book open in her hand, an old, leather-bound diary she frequently reread.

He settled down beside her and took her hands in his. "I don't want to add to your burden, Rose. Talk it out, if you want. You know I'm a good listener."

She sighed again. "I'm not a leader. I've never been very good at being a leader."

"People come to you for help. They believe you can lead. I know you can, but you have to believe it yourself."

She smiled wanly. "You're sweet to say so, but I know my limitations. I'm not strong."

He chuckled. It was a deep, rich, *loving* sound. "You're a vampire, and a nest leader. The first vampire made in this land. You're a part of the land. There's strength in that." He took the book out of her lap and set it aside. "Your strength is rooted in the past, but you're strong here and now."

"Alec made phone calls. He was right, I think, to call the other nests, but . . ." She sighed again.

The sound was irritating, but Bentencourt took it as a good sign. "They want to have a meeting?" he asked gently. "They want you to lead them? As they should. It is your rightful place."

"I don't want to be a leader."

"No good leader ever wants the position fate thrusts on them. Doing what you have to do, what has to be done, that's what makes a good leader. You have a sense of what is right for the community. You must act on your instincts."

That drew a faint smile from her. "Darling, if I acted on my instincts—"

"You'd be a queen among vampires."

"Oh, no. We don't do that sort of thing—set up personal kingdoms and all."

"Really?" He projected as much concerned puzzlement as he could. "Perhaps I've gotten the wrong impression from the way the Greek woman behaves. She's set up a fief, but she's hardly behaved like a leader." He spoke his next words with all the earnestness he could command. "You're the leader the nests need. You're the one to set things right."

"I—don't know."

"Listen to what the nest leaders have to say," he advised. "You'll have to seriously consider acting for them if they prefer you to Olympias."

"Perhaps I will have to talk to Olympias—as the voice of consensus," she added.

"You'll do the right thing." He felt her reluctance melting a little in the face of his belief in her. "I love you," he told her, twisting the simple truth to his purpose. "You are a good person."

She waved a hand dismissively. "I'm a vampire, Roger."

"A just person, then."

She didn't try to deny it, was quite flattered, really, to be held up as a paragon of vampire virtues. Virtues that were all weaknesses as far as he was concerned, but what were the virtues and weaknesses of others, but tools for him to use. Whatever he could bend to his purposes, he would. Right now, he used a soft brush of his lips across hers to draw Rose's attention further to himself. He deepened the kiss, and let himself adore her for a while. It was easy to do, and made her feel better. Made her more trusting and dependent as well. When he had her aroused just enough, he made slow, gentle, worshipful love to her. He craved the taste of her blood and the heightened excitement that came when her fangs sank into his flesh, but he did not ask for the completion of blood exchange. It was the best way to show his loyalty to her, a proof that he loved her and wanted to stay with her as long as possible. It garnered more trust from her without his having to say a word. It was good to be able to manipulate on the subconscious level when there was a psychic involved.

After they'd made love, he held her close for a while, keenly aware of the passage of time. "Feeling better?" he asked her after an appropriate number of minutes had passed.

"Feeling delicious," Rose answered. "Not that any of our problems have gone away."

"I know." He stroked her hair. "Doing what I can do. I'm here for you." He sighed. "But—"

Rose raised her head to look at him. "I don't like the sound of that."

"There's more to this crisis than you know," he said slowly. "More you should know if you're going to speak for the nests. There's some things I've found out—from talking to other companions and dealing with the Greek's chief slave—that poor girl has the gift to be a companion, by the way, but Olympias chooses to enslave her instead—never mind. I know that's not anyone's affair."

"It is Olympias's choice," Rose answered. "Though it shows the sort of person she is. She's a wasteful, arrogant creature, and always has been. What more do you need to tell me?" She sounded irritated. "I really hate the thought of going to sleep with her on my mind."

"I'm sorry. If you'd rather wait until—"

"No. The meeting's tomorrow night. Tell me now."

"There is a companion in one of the nests in need of rebirth. Olympias has done nothing to arrange a Hunt to deal with this."

"I've heard about that."

"Forgive me. Of course you have. You've been in contact with the nest leaders." He sighed.

"There's more," she prompted. "What?"

"This does concern you in a way, which is why I think you should know. Andrew Falconer was once a lover of yours, wasn't he?"

"Of course he was." She smiled as she picked up his feeling. "No need for you to be jealous, we were lovers decades ago."

"But you still have fond feelings for him. I can tell."

"As I'll have for you when you leave my bed. What about Andrew?"

"Olympias's slave talked to me about him. She told me that Andrew petitioned the Enforcer of the City for permission to die, and Olympias has completely ignored him."

Rose sat up. "Andrew wants to die? How sad. But if that's what he wants—"

"He's sought out the proper person to fulfill his wish under the Law, but she hasn't made the time to pencil him in on her schedule," Bentencourt told her.

Rose shook her head, and her gaze went to the portrait over the mantel. "She's ignoring her duty. I don't believe it." Another shake of her head. "Yes I do. What does the creature do with her time?"

"Apparently she's pursuing the same mortal Lora has requested as a companion."

Her attention swung totally back to Bentencourt. "What?"

"Her slave makes excuses, but that is a slave's duty. I believe Lora is in danger from Olympias." He glanced at the clock on the nightstand. At the same time Rose glanced out the window. Now that he was certain that there was no time for Rose to do anything about it, he added his last piece of information. "Lora went out this evening, and hasn't returned. I fear she might have set herself on a collision course with Olympias."

"You think Olympias is going to kill one of my nest-lings?"

He said, "Let's hope not." But the truth was, he certainly hoped so. Even if things didn't work out as he hoped, he'd certainly given Rose enough worries to chew on while she lay helpless during the long day.

"Sara!" Olympias called as she entered the house. Bitch barely had time to make it through the door before Olympias slammed it closed. "Sara!" she called again, and dumped the body on the hall floor.

Her legs still ached, but the long leaps she'd taken to put as much distance between herself and the crime scene would pay off. Olympias knew that the police would be troubled by finding such a short trail of blood outside Falconer's house, and the crime lab would be puzzled by the anomalies found in those drops of blood, but nothing would come of the investigation.

Bitch had joined her at some point during the flight. The dog joined her now as Olympias sat down on the stairs. The dog sat on her foot and leaned heavily against her. Olympias rubbed the animal's ears. She could feel that the house was empty. "Sara!" she called out anyway.

Where had the girl gotten to? She was supposed to be here when she was needed. Olympias stared glumly at Lora. "To help bury the body."

Why did I kill her? She wondered. *Killing's easy. I should have—*

"Admit it."

All right.

I killed her because I was jealous. Also—Mike was hurt, and that infuriated me.

"If she hadn't gone for him . . ."

If, if, if. Deal with what is.

"I botched everything. Acted like the greenest Enforcer out there." Made it personal rather than justice. What was the matter with her? Mike Falconer, she supposed. Damn it. She always screwed up when she let herself care for someone.

Speaking of caring—Olympias lifted her head and shouted again. "Sara!"

Chapter 12

"HANG IN THERE, Mike, you're going to be okay."

If that was so, why didn't he feel like he was going to be okay? The excitedly cheerful voice belonged to Grace Avella. He was horizontal, which was not a good sign. He was in the hospital, wasn't he? It smelled like a hospital, antiseptic, over-air-conditioned air. He didn't remember the trip to the hospital, but he did remember how he'd gotten here. "Shit."

"Oh, good. You're awake."

He should have kept his mouth shut. Falconer opened his eyes. Grace stood over the bed. The expression on her pretty young face flitted from concern to curiosity to anger and back again so fast that it made him dizzy. He closed his eyes again, but when he did he became aware of a sensation that resembled someone knocking on his head like it was a door. He wasn't interested in letting anyone into his mind right now. To ignore the would-be intruder, Falconer turned his attention back to Grace.

"I'm awake."

"You don't look so good."

He didn't bother replying that he obviously didn't feel

so good. Some memories came back of various medical types poking needles into him and waking him up throughout the night to tell him things when he would much rather have been unconscious than informed. He knew he'd been given a transfusion, that he had broken ribs and several bones in his wrist were also broken. He was lucky his back wasn't broken—it only hurt like hell. They'd stitched up the deep cuts they believed were from his being mauled by an animal, and were running tests to see if he had rabies. He didn't think you could get rabies from vampires, but hadn't mentioned this to the medical staff.

"The police want to talk to you," Grace said after silence drew out for a while. "They've got an officer waiting outside."

"How'd you get in?"

She grinned. "How'd you think? Nobody noticed me 'cause I didn't want them to." She wiggled her fingers and made woo-woo noises. "This psychic stuff can come in handy."

"I thought I taught you to use your powers only for good."

"I'm good."

He grunted and pressed the button that raised the hospital bed to a sitting position. He noticed that the second bed in the room was empty and that the sun was shining outside the large window. His room overlooked a parking lot. How cheery. He was not currently in pain, which meant he must be pretty well medicated. His mind was clear enough, though. "Why's there a cop outside?"

"They want to know what attacked you. Georgetown is jittery. There was a very large dog spotted in your neighborhood last night. And the media is speculating—as the media is wont to do."

"Mmm. Anybody from the office waiting to see me?"

"I'm from the office."

He raised an eyebrow sarcastically. It hurt. "Anyone who outranks me?"

She shook her head. "We've got it covered."

Falconer didn't like the sound of that, but let her go on without commenting.

"Sela explained to them how she was on the phone with you when it happened. The official story is that she heard someone break in. She said the intruder sounded surprised to find anyone at home. The intruder had what sounded like a large dog with them. From what she heard it sounded like a burglary that went bad rather than some sort of security breach."

"And they believed her."

"She only uses her powers for good, Mike. Or for you. We all work for you before we work for the Project. Except maybe Jeremy, but he wants to be in on exposing the existence of vampires for the sake of his career, so he's hanging with us for the moment."

Oh, God, vampires. Why had he told Sela about the vampire? Because he hadn't expected to live for much longer after the vampire chick broke in, he supposed. Which had been a stupid excuse to involve his people in a dangerous situation.

"I don't want to talk about vampires," he told Grace.

Grace looked at him sternly. "Are you going to pretend that they don't exist?"

"Yes."

"Why? For the safety of the team?"

"Yes."

"We saw them when we went Walking, Mike."

"Linear anomaly."

"Bullshit. Walking is accurate. Just because we didn't want to believe in what we saw, doesn't mean it wasn't real."

"We're all loons," he answered. "We had a mass hallucination."

"That hallucination put you in the hospital."

"I was attacked by a burglar with a large dog. Sela says so."

"Your FBI friend called. He said the lab tests turned

up some weird shit. You want to tell me what he was talking about?"

"No."

She was not deterred by his stubborn refusal to tell her all about it—and let her help. "We're going to find them," she declared. "The Walkers aren't the only psychics in Washington, you know. We can get help."

"No help. No taking this out of the group."

"It's already beyond the group. In fact, it has nothing to do with the project, or the government. This is humanity versus monsters. We can stop them."

He remembered the one that had attacked him. He was a big man, and he knew how to fight. The vampire had been a small, fine-boned woman, and she'd tossed him around like she would a doll. And Olympias—Olympias had tossed the other vampire around with even more ease, and then she'd—

Ripped his attacker open with her bare hands and—

"Mike! Mike! Are you going to throw up? Do you want me to call a nurse?"

He blinked, and came back from the dizzy edge of nausea. "Stay out of this." Her expression remained stubborn. She didn't recognize that he wasn't giving an order; he was begging her. Right now he knew there was nothing he could do to stop her. "We'll discuss it when I'm out of here," he said. "Please don't do anything until then."

Grace backed away from the bed. "We will discuss it," she said.

It wasn't a promise not to do anything. He knew he wasn't going to get one. "Fine," he said. "Thanks for stopping by. Don't let the cop see you leave." Someone was knocking on his head again. "I really need to get some sleep."

He really did.

"Even injured you are one hard head to crack into."

"I really wish you'd knock."

"I've been knocking for an hour. Pretty girl, your vis-

itor. She looked familiar. What's her name?"

"You don't think I'm going to tell you anything about her, do you?"

"She seems to believe in vampires."

"Lots of people believe in vampires."

"And vampires believe in them until they get them to believe otherwise."

"I'm not sure that made sense."

"It seems a great many vampires believe in you. You Falconers draw attention to yourselves."

"Animal magnetism?"

"Hot blood and sexy minds."

"Falconers? Why the plural?"

"Long story. Vampires have lots of long stories. We don't like to share them. With you I'm willing to make an exception."

"Do you find this floating bodiless in space conversation as disconcerting as I do?"

"You want to go somewhere for coffee?"

"Sure."

The next instant he was in the Afterwards Café, sitting across a table from Olympias. There were people sitting at tables all around them, all of them immersed in reading books and drinking coffee. No one was in the least aware of their presence.

"We're not really here, are we?" he asked the pale woman on the other side of the table.

"Of course not. You're on drugs, I'm comatose, we're dreaming together. Which means the coffee is free, and it's always fresh. Would you like to know the history of coffee?" she asked.

"I'd rather know what you are." He noticed that they were both wearing black turtlenecks and slacks. She was wearing sunglasses. He experimented with the dream imagery, and his clothes changed into his uniform.

Olympias took off her dark glasses and looked him over critically. "Impressive. You learned that sort of control in the Walker Project?"

He picked up a large white mug of steaming coffee and took a sip. It was fresh, delicious, and scalding hot, but it didn't burn his mouth. "The point of an information exchange," he reminded her, "is to exchange information. What are you?"

"Sorry for what happened."

"We both know what I mean. You saved me from the vampire chick. Twice. Why?"

"Don't flatter yourself, doll. I was doing my job."

"Which makes you, what? A vampire cop?"

She nodded. "Enforcer of the City, or Hunter of the City, as they say out on the left coast. Some of the other titles include Nighthawk, Daughter of the Nighthawk Line, and Goddess Chosen. Then there's the really old names for what I am—Tytan, Bubo—very few remember those. What I do boils down to being a vampire who protects."

"You protect humans from vampires?"

"Don't look so hopeful. I'm not a protector of your world; I'm a protector of mine. Most of the time I protect vampires from mortals. And vampires from each other, and other supramortal beings."

"Supramortal?"

"It's a word I just made up. It's very hard to define what demons and werewolves and fairies and all that other trash is. Pests, mostly. Mortals are the most dangerous. I spend every waking—and most of my sleeping—moments keeping vampires from being discovered by mortals. A thankless job, I might add. It's not even an elected post. I was appointed. I had no interest in coming to America, but the Council decided I was the best one for the job—meaning that they wanted me out of town—" She took a deep breath. "Am I boring you? 'Cause I'm boring me."

"You're fascinating. What town?"

"Prague, of course, just after the Great War. Though if you've ever faced a Mongol horde you might not consider what happened during World War I all that im-

pressive. The center of strigoi power has moved quite a bit over the centuries," she explained. "To Warsaw and Budapest among other places. The one thing movies get right is that many vampires speak with Eastern European accents. The ones that don't are second-class citizens, believe me."

"Why are you telling me all this? Planning to make me forget it when we're done?" He took a sip of delicious imaginary coffee. "If you have a need to talk to someone, you should seek professional help. I'm not a therapist."

She smiled. He watched carefully, but could detect not the slightest hint of fang in her dentition. Of course, they weren't exactly in the real world. If a newbie at this like him could manipulate his appearance, Olympias could probably make herself look like a talking giraffe if she wanted to. Or the sexiest woman in the world.

"I don't need special effects to do that," she said.

Falconer shook a finger at her. "You're reading my mind."

"Where do you think we are at the moment?"

"Sharing our minds," he answered. He looked around the phantom coffee bar. "You're not doing this without my help."

"You're guessing." She paused to drink her own coffee before adding, "A good guess."

"Why are we talking?" he asked. "Why are you bothering to tell me vampire history?"

Olympias folded her hands on top of the table. She turned a very direct gaze on him. Nothing but earnestness shone out of her dark eyes. He wondered how many centuries she'd had to practice that open look. "I'm being sincere," she responded to his cynicism. "Not my normal attitude at all."

"What's your normal attitude?"

She laughed. And the next thing he knew Falconer was seated across the table from a creature that did not resemble a vampire at all. He was tempted to scream, jump out of the chair, and run away. He asked the multiple-

*fanged monster across the table, "You want another cup
of coffee?" He studied the creature's sharply pointed
muzzle. "And maybe a straw?"*

The monster threw back its head and laughed, then
became Olympias again. "He doesn't mind my having a
bad fang day. Goddess, I think I'm in love."

He already knew he was, which he supposed was sick,
disgusting, and perverted. "Should I thank you for saving
me?" he asked. "Why did you save me? For yourself?"
he guessed. Hoped? That was sick.

"You flatter yourself."

"You're blushing."

"I am too sophisticated to blush." She touched her
cheeks. "Hmm. How odd that a reaction that I can consciously control doesn't cooperate in here."

"Maybe because you have to tell the truth inside your
head."

"People lie to themselves all the time. Even people like
us."

"Loons and mons—creatures of the night?"

"People who have their roots in the underneath world.
Your roots are with my kind, Mike. You may be mortal
at the moment, but your dad is not."

"My father is dead," he answered, deliberately stubborn, and filled with the usual anger. "I hope he is. He
abandoned my mother, and I don't want to talk—"

"But you do want to talk about it. To know what happened. We're telling the truth in here, Michael."

"Speaking of truth." He changed the subject. "Are you
really the Olympias? Did you kill Philip of Macedon?"

"Not personally, no. I didn't get my hands bloody back
in my mortal days. Missed out on a lot of fun that way."

"You murdered your husband?"

"I arranged the assassination of a political rival who
had arranged to have my son and me murdered." She
shrugged. "I got there first. In the end—" Another shrug.
"Alexander didn't live to see the results of the changes
he brought to the world. I did, and I don't really like the*

consequences. Andrew Falconer didn't desert his family," she went on, her direct gaze focused intently on him again. She made him listen. "What happened to your father is what nearly happened to you last night. A vampire took him as a lover, without bothering to ask if he wanted to be her lover. When you become a vampire's lover, you eventually become a vampire. Before he became a vampire, and left town, he left a little something with his wife. You."

He heard what she said, wanted to disbelieve it, but couldn't. The news should have been devastating. Maybe it would be later. Right now, he focused on one of the things she'd told him. "Left town. Could my father have returned recently? I saw a vampire—Walking or dreaming, I'm not sure which—this was even before the attack in the park. Was that my father?"

"I have no idea."

"Yes, you do."

She shook her head. "Andrew is in town. I don't know if you saw him. Maybe. You've got some weird gifts. This Walking stuff has to stop, by the way."

Ah, so they'd gotten to the real reason she'd intruded on his mind again. "Are you asking me nicely? Ordering me? Somehow going to use my father against me if we don't disband the project?"

Olympias sipped a fresh cup of coffee. Then looked at him over the rim of the cup. "The ground your people are treading is very dangerous, Mike. You have to decide whether you want them to live or die."

"Damn you!"

He rose angrily to his feet, but Olympias was gone by the time he was out of his chair. Then the room disappeared, then the world turned to gray fog. Falconer turned around and around, growing dizzier and dizzier. He felt like he was being poured down a drain. Fortunately, after that, everything went black.

• • •

"Thanks for seeing me."

Bentencourt had some trouble keeping his smile as benign as usual, as he basked in Grace's nervous excitement. She looked delicious, there was no other word for it. If he'd had fangs he'd have been all over her the instant she walked in the door of the Irish bar. Such a feast was not on his plate just yet, but anticipating his glorious future brought the smile that was so hard to keep curious and friendly.

He had a lunch appointment with several other people, but had arrived early on an intuition that something interesting would turn up. A cell phone call from Grace the moment he arrived at the pub turned out to be the answer to his intuition. She'd sounded excited, and he'd told her to meet him at the usual place. It turned out she was already on the way, and joined him within a minute of his being seated.

Grace was always interesting, young, vital, and full of life. If all went well, that life would be ending soon, but the knowledge that her blood would be drained for the sake of his cause both pleased and amused him. His plan was coming together swiftly. Olympias would soon be defeated, and thanks to recent discoveries, he could arrange for her to die sooner than his original plan had called for. It was hard to keep from becoming positively giddy with anticipation. He couldn't afford to let himself be this way. This was the most dangerous time, while he pulled all the strings at once, wove them together into the final pattern that would bring the bitch down.

He made himself relax. He made himself focus his full attention on the young woman opposite him. He did not bask in the triumph of watching her eyes widen and her expression go dreamy with the usual reaction his full regard had on people. "How can I help you?" he asked her. *What can you do for me*, he thought.

She glanced from side to side, and kept her voice low as she spoke. "I have a feeling you aren't going to be as surprised as most people would be about what I'm going to tell you."

"You're going to tell me about vampires," he said, cutting to the chase.

Grace sat back in her chair, looking deflated. "Yeah."

"Didn't you think I wouldn't experiment a bit on my own after we discussed techniques for linear astral projection?"

She accepted his excuse for the knowledge easily. "So you found them too."

He nodded. "I did. I wasn't really surprised." He pointed between her and himself. "People with special talents like ours exist. It's actually something of a relief to realize that we aren't freaks—and that the supernatural world that logic and science has denied has refused to go away because no one is supposed to believe in it anymore. It's probably safer for us that our gifts and powers are derided as nonexistent by the establishment. Think how the government could exploit us if it knew about us."

She gave him a hard look, and for a moment he thought he might have gone a bit too far, since Grace had carefully never mentioned her involvement with a government agency to him. What he knew about her had been picked up telepathically. Right now, he sent mental commands to her to obey any suggestion he made and ignore any suspicions he might arouse.

Fortunately, her attention was firmly set on the subject she'd come to discuss. "The world might not know about them, but we do. What are we going to do about them?"

He appeared to give the subject some thought, while Grace watched him with growing impatience. "I suggest observation might be the first step," he said finally.

"We have observed them."

"We have—"

"Physically observed them."

Grace shook her head. She looked quite scared. "One of them attacked a friend of mine. He's in the hospital."

"Really?" Bentencourt was genuinely intrigued. "I'm happy your friend is alive. What happened?"

"Mike doesn't want to talk about the details. He doesn't want to put the rest of us in danger."

"Knowing that vampires exists puts you in danger," Bentencourt answered. "I'm sure your friend is concerned for your safety, but I think silence is more dangerous than taking a proactive approach."

"Exactly what I think. But I'm not sure how to go about hunting them."

"Perhaps knowing how your friend survived the incident would help."

She nodded. "All I know is what another friend heard. She was on the phone to Mike when the vampire broke into his house. I guess that puts the myth that vampires need to be invited in to rest, 'cause Sela heard a window break, and then Mike told her the vampire was there. There was a fight, and Mike got beaten. Sela says she heard him screaming, and Mike's not the screaming type. The craziest part is that it sounded to Sela like a second vampire showed up, another female."

"The first vampire was a woman?"

"Didn't I mention that? It sounded like the first female vampire wanted to bite Mike, but that the second female that showed up didn't want the first one to have him. I could see fighting over Mike," she added. "He's not exactly handsome, but he's got this whole macho but soft-spoken gentle but tough as nails thing going on that I personally find irresistible. If he was ten or fifteen years younger I would have jumped him myself, but . . ." Grace took a deep breath and gave Bentencourt an apologetic look. "That's not telling you about the vampires, is it?"

"Fascinating as your description of this Mike is, no."

"Sorry. Remember that what Sela thinks happened came from listening on the phone, so her context isn't exactly perfect."

"I understand."

"She thinks she heard the second vampire kill the one

who attacked Mike. The police didn't find any vampire bodies when they showed up, just Mike, all beaten and clawed. I guess he isn't as badly hurt as he looks, but he looks terrible. Do you think the second vampire took the body of the first one with her?"

"It would be logical that vampires wouldn't want any evidence of their existence to be found."

"That makes sense. I think this pair must have been the ones we observed when we tried Walking backwards. They fought over Mike that time, too."

"No doubt."

"Maybe they're the only ones around."

"I doubt that."

"Me too. Besides, even if one of them killed the other one, that's still one vampire too many."

"I quite agree."

"Guess we have to find and somehow kill her."

Bentencourt could barely contain his pleasure. From what Grace said, his plan had worked exactly as he'd set it up. Olympias had killed Lora. He would now make sure that the rest of the area's vampires were outraged at the violation of Lora's rights, and at her vicious murder. *Bravo, Lora, you've served your purpose. Time for Grace to serve hers.*

"If I were to find a way to physically observe vampires, would you and your colleagues be interested in joining me?"

Grace didn't look happy, but she slowly nodded. "We do have to do something. I know that. I was all gung-ho about it at first. But the more I think about facing vampires—"

"You won't have to face them alone." He gave her a reassuring smile. "We'll observe them, figure out how to kill them, then develop a safe strategy for destroying them."

"Find out where they sleep in the daytime, you mean? Attack them when they're helpless?"

"Precisely."

"Couldn't we trace them down by Wal—astral projection?"

"I certainly think you should try that method. I'm going to try looking for their waking whereabouts. I'll call you if anything turns up."

"Me too."

"I'm afraid I can't talk any more right now," he apologized. Bentencourt stood. He took Grace's hand and helped her rise, then he gave her a quick, reassuring hug. "All will be well," he promised. "Remember, we are the good guys."

She smiled. "Right. Thanks for the help."

He nodded, and she turned to make her way through the growing lunch crowd. He remained expectantly standing, his gaze on the door. While he watched her go, he called one of the numbers on his cell phone's speed dial, but once again got no answer from Sara Czerny. He left a message, then decided to call Sara's assistant, Gerry, after his next meeting. He'd let the slave run his errands. *It's about time I stopped doing all the work,* Bentencourt decided.

A moment after Grace exited, his fellow companions entered. Dark, lovely Gavivi looked as elegant as ever. Cassandra looked even more strung out than she had at their last meeting a few days before. She slammed the door hard behind her as if to emphasize her mood. Bentencourt almost sighed wearily at the thought of how difficult getting his points across to the blood-hungry companion was going to be. Patience, he told himself. There wasn't much time, and he had to be convincing.

"I think," he said, once he had his fellow companions settled and a rare steak and bottle of whiskey in front of Cassandra, "that the time has come for us to do what we can to help bring those we love into the modern world. Even more importantly, we need to do what we can to help them against that bitch Olympias. Olympias is a threat to our lovers, to our nests. I've discovered so much that is going on that she's kept hidden from us." Gavivi looked skeptical, but interested. Cassandra glared at him fiercely. He wasn't sure whether he was getting through to her, but he put all his power into telling her, "You need to make a kill. There is a group of mortals that are a danger to the nests. With your help . . ." He flicked a glance at Gavivi before he went on. "With your help— when you tell your lovers what I'm about to tell you— all the nests of the city will Hunt tonight."

"The nests are meeting to discuss moving," Gavivi pointed out.

"They need to discuss much more," Bentencourt told the other companion. "There's very real danger from the so-called Enforcer. She can be stopped. We can keep our homes. We can keep our lovers safe. One vampire has already died." He felt how that knowledge shook them. He spoke to them slowly, drawing them in with all the intensity at his command. "Help me," he pleaded with the companions. "And no one we love will die."

If ever there was a time when Sara wanted to roll over in bed, nudge her lover, and ask, "You awake?" this was it. Only, it was the middle of the day, so of course he wasn't awake, leaving her to think deep, worried thoughts all by herself. Things could be worse, she knew, and would be, later. At least for now her body was sated and her blood sang with the new power and joy of belonging and being complete. And there was a roof over her head. She'd managed to persuade Andrew to check into a hotel rather than share their first night as lovers in a sleeping bag in Rock Creek Park. Considering that there might not be a second night as lovers if Olympias was really pissed off about Andrew's presumption and Sara's betrayal, Sara wanted to make the most of the moment.

The sex had been glorious, the sharing of blood indescribable, and there had been room service, champagne, and clean sheets in a suite that had a balcony with a view of the well-lit cathedral up on its rounded hilltop.

There had been talk as well, though she hadn't let Andrew talk about their future together. Even in the throes of passion, Sara had a pretty good handle on the numerous ways she and her vampire lover might not have a future.

Even now, staring at the ceiling and being nudged by guilt and the call of responsibility, Sara didn't regret a moment of what had happened. Even if Olympias decided to tear her limb from limb, she'd die happy—screaming, but happy. She was a companion. More than that, she'd made the choice. She loved Andrew, and had loved him before his fangs sank into her flesh, before he'd opened his own flesh and offered his sacred blood for her to drink her fill. There had been no rape, no unwilling possession. This was pure. This was perfect.

"This is maudlin and disgusting," she said, propping herself up on an elbow to look down on the sweet face of her sleeping lover. "But you're not awake to hear or see me, so I'm going to gloat and wallow for as long as I like." She bent down and kissed his lips, then his throat, and further down his bare chest. That he didn't respond didn't make the worship any less gratifying for her. She loved him, and knew he knew it. But even she could not kiss a sleeping statue for very long, no matter how perfect Andrew's body was.

Eventually Sara got up and took a shower. She meant to come back to bed when she was done, to cuddle up beside Andrew and sleep the day away in anticipation of their lovemaking when night finally came. Habit, however, overrode intentions, at least to the extent that she pulled her cellular phone out of her pants pocket and stood looking at it for a while, fighting the impulse to call home and at least leave a message for Olympias when her mistress woke up.

Which would be a stupid thing to do, wouldn't it? Would it? Should she face her mistress, or run away with Andrew? Should she rely on Andrew to handle it? She should, shouldn't she? He was the master, she was the companion. He would protect her and make everything all right, wouldn't he? Her heart told her yes, but her heart was pumping his blood and the magic that made her his; of course her heart couldn't help but say stupid things like that. Sara's head told her it was up to her to do something to save them both. But what?

Maybe she should call Olympias. Maybe she should at least check her messages. She finished dressing, went out on the balcony, and listened to her messages. There were four. Two from Bentencourt, two from Gerry. "Gerry," she murmured, staring off into the distance, seeing the cathedral in the near distance. Maybe he was there now, waiting for her. Would she ever go back there to meet with the other slaves under the Space Window again? She'd miss it. She'd hated being a slave, but she'd *liked* her job. Andrew offered her love, a future if they lived to see it, but hooking up with him certainly screwed her career.

Maybe not. Maybe if she just talked to Olympias . . .

"Maybe I should just commit suicide . . ." Her mistress was going to be so pissed. Vampires were territorial, possessive.

And Olympias had betrayed her, lied to her. Sara was hurt and furious at the Enforcer. A part of her wanted to forget about Olympias and get on with her new life. A small part of her wanted to somehow return to that life, to make some kind of peace and accommodation with her old mistress. A part of her still loved Olympias, though she tried to beat that part down to merely liking her boss.

Whatever her tangled up feelings, Sara knew she had to do something, and before Andrew woke up, did the manly, chivalrous thing, and made the decision for her. She hoped she was doing the right thing, put her faith in Gerry's gung-ho belief in the necessity of changing vampire culture, and dialed his number.

Chapter 13

THERE HADN'T BEEN any problem with the hospital when Falconer decided to leave after he woke up. He told the police detective he didn't remember anything that had happened. He was glad the police took an interest, if only because it meant the military that ran the Walker Project would lay low for security's sake and wait for him to brief them after the cops lost interest in the case. The policeman told him they thought his attacker had been a burglar with a vicious dog. He'd agreed that made the most sense, then he got dressed and checked himself out.

No one said, you're a seriously injured man in need of care and observation. Instead they'd given him some pain pills and sent him on his way. He figured the staff was happy not to have to deal with the insurance hassles of even one more night of Falconer's taking up a hospital bed. He was glad they'd taken him to a civilian hospital rather than a military one, which might not have been so easy to get out of.

He took a cab home, and the first thing he did when he got there was get a beer out of the fridge. Then he ripped the yellow crime scene tape off his office doorway, went into the wrecked, bloodstained room, sat down, washed down a couple of the pain pills with the beer, and tried to figure out what was real and what he'd imagined. He even tried coming up with a few logical explanations.

Looking around, all Falconer could think for a while was, *This is very weird.*

Possibly it was the combination of alcohol and pills, and possibly it was because traditional logic didn't make any sense, but it didn't take him long to come to the conclusion that it was the weird stuff that was real. Reality was that his dad was a vampire, his girlfriend was something sort of like a vampire—only *more* so—and he was a psychic loon who ran a government secret psychic loon shop. What he needed was another beer.

"Sort of girlfriend," he muttered as he went back to the kitchen.

She'd saved him twice, and they had slept together, and she'd invaded his mind on at least two occasions. Did that mean they were going steady? Had he thanked Olympias for the times she'd saved him? Should he be grateful or offended because she hadn't bitten him? Should he be packing his bags and getting out of town now that he knew that the woman he was attracted to was a vampire? Was she attracted to him, or was he being unsophisticated and sloppily romantic when she had some pragmatic scheme in mind? They'd talked a lot, but what did he really know?

He knew his dad was a vampire.

Was that true?

Falconer took the second beer into the living room, where he had to put it down before he picked up a silver-framed photo of his parents. Mom was dead, Dad was the living dead. "What a family," he murmured.

He remembered the good-looking man in the picture, but really hadn't thought about him in years. He never saw any resemblance to Andrew Falconer when he looked in the mirror, hadn't inherited even a tiny bit of the man's musical talent. He hadn't listened to the recordings since he was a kid, but he remembered that the man had been quite a musician. Mom said so. Mom said that his father had loved them and must be dead because he'd disappeared, and Andrew wouldn't disappear without saying good-bye. Falconer had never believed in her wishful thinking, but now he began to believe she'd been right all along.

Sometime today, sitting in a coffee shop inside his own head, he'd felt a powerful surge of anger at the mention of his father. Right now he wasn't angry, confused and curious, but not angry.

Then again, maybe he ought to be angry—for his mother, and for the father that had been made into a vampire against his will. Maybe his father needed him. Maybe that was why he'd seen him—if the vampire he'd seen had been his father. Falconer studied the old photo closely. Was this man also the vampire he'd seen?

Had Olympias told him the truth about anything?

Even with the pain pills, his broken wrist still hurt. He didn't notice the cuts and bruises so much, but the wrist was bad. He put down the photo and picked up the beer. Whether it helped numb anything or not, it felt cold and good going down.

He needed to do something. Maybe he should find the man in the photo. Maybe, but all he wanted to do was be with Olympias. "I need to talk to her." It was an excuse made to an empty room. It disturbed him that he was reduced to talking to himself. It was bad enough he was a loon. There was no reason to become an eccentric one. He did need to talk to the vampire queen. She was a threat to his people and his project. To hell with the project, it was the people he cared about. His loons.

Maybe if he reported all he knew to his superiors . . .

And he knew exactly, what? Olympias had implied the existence of all sorts of 'supramortal' critters during their interior dialogue. He'd never seen any evidence that there

was anything weirder in the world than extremely psychic humans until a few days ago, and he'd been involved in the loon corps for over a decade. Training told
him he should report the existence of these supramortals,
that their existence could pose a threat . . . but Olympias
seemed to think it was the mortals that posed the greatest
threat.

Falconer shook his head. He didn't know what to think
or do. He needed to confront Olympias. Find out what
she intended to do. Talk to her and—

She has claws, a sudden ache in his side reminded him.
Super human strength; the ache in his wrist was evidence
of that. Big nasty teeth.

But she didn't do this to me, he remembered. Besides,
never mind the aches in his body, there was a different
ache in his soul, some sort of combination of loneliness
and yearning and recognition. He knew it wasn't wise,
knew he might have to kill her, but such complications
didn't stop him from needing her.

"Olympias," Falconer said, and closed his eyes to go
Walking.

Maybe it was the combination of the pain pills and
beer. Maybe it was because he needed physical rather
than ephemeral contact. For whatever reason it didn't
work, and Falconer gave up within a few seconds.

How was he supposed to contact her if he couldn't—
"Damn! I am an idiot!"

He found a phone and called Sela. "I feel fine," he told
her after her initial burst of concern. "I'm good. I'm
home. No, I don't want to see anyone yet. If they're at
Grace's tell them to stay there. I'll be in touch. I have to
check something out first. You know the woman we were
talking about when we were interrupted last night? Yes.
I know what I told you about her. Forget I said it. You
had information about her. Do you have an address? Yes,
of her lair." He memorized the street and number as Sela
told him. Then, to avoid any more questions, he hung up
on her.

• • •

"Sara! You're not Sara," Olympias said after flinging open the door. She frowned up at the big man whose shoulders blocked the view of the yard and the street beyond. The sun hadn't been down long. "Sara wouldn't use the doorbell. What am I thinking? I'm not thinking. That's the problem. I'm barely awake, and she still isn't home. I should have sensed it was you. You look terrible. What are you doing out of the hospital?"

"I heal fast," Falconer answered. "Nice dog," he added, as she stepped back and let him into the house.

"She's nice until I tell her not to be. That's Bitch."

"Charming name. I think we've met." He touched his throat with his good hand while Bitch padded forward to press her big head into his crotch for a proper greeting sniff. Olympias admired that Falconer managed not to flinch. Bitch liked everybody until she was told not to, so it was no surprise when she pressed her head against Mike's hand. Fortunately, it was the hand that wasn't bandaged, and he automatically began scratching the beast's furry head. "Soft as velvet," he said. "Can I sit down?" he added. He swayed on his feet. "Before I fall down."

"Sure." She took his arm and led him to the office at the back of the house. "Sara's office," she told him after he settled in the office chair. Olympias spread her arms out to take in the computer and file cabinets, the shredder, the fax machine, and all the other paraphernalia of the modern world. "I have no clue what most of this stuff does. I need Sara." She waved her arm. "I'm helpless. By the way, how did you find me?"

He glanced around. "I have my own—Sara. She's your assistant, right? Is she a vampire, too?"

"Not if I can help it. Everybody needs a Sara. She's not here." Olympias tapped her head. "Even worse, she's not here." She leveled her gaze on Mike. "Do you know what it feels like to lose someone you care for?"

"My father," he answered without hesitation.

"You were what, four? I've got a few thousand years on you. It doesn't get any better with time. I miss everyone I lose, and I miss them all the time. It's too soon to lose her, but I know I have. If she's dead there's going to be hell to pay. If she isn't—there's going to be hell to pay. You have no idea who or what I'm talking about, do you?"

"I have—a small idea."

He looked at her with a calmness that was quite disconcerting. What was worse, there was a sort of pitiless compassion in his emotions that might have calmed and soothed her if she'd let it. He didn't judge her, but there was also a strong sense that he wouldn't put up with any bullshit from her either. And he'd called Bitch a nice dog even after what had happened the night they met, which was another strong point in his favor. If she got him to leave her life soon maybe she wouldn't miss him—except that she'd missed him even while she spent most of day dreamseeking the missing Sara.

"Maybe I've been thinking too much about other situations to concentrate properly."

"What other situations?"

"Secret situations." She'd lost track of things the last few days. And Sara had been distracted. Olympias saw that now.

"Me?"

Olympias settled down on the floor, her legs crossed and her back against the wall. Bitch flopped down beside her and rolled over in hopes of a belly scritch. She rubbed the hellhound's stomach. "You are not the most important problem on my plate right now," she informed Falconer. "Though I suppose I should explain to a nest leader about killing one of her nestlings."

He looked both appalled and curious for a moment before he said, "I suppose that's the polite thing to do."

"Technically, I don't have to explain my actions to anyone, but Rose—Oh, great, I forgot I need to talk to Rose about—never mind. As you can see, I've forgotten more important things than disbanding your crew before they get in deeper trouble. There's always more stuff going on around here than a sane person can deal with. If only I had Sara here to remind me of what I'm—"

"Like what?" he questioned. "What sorts of things do you have to handle?"

"Every damn vampire emergency."

"Such as?"

She wished she didn't find his interest charming. She had no business telling Falconer anything, but she answered. "Such as right now I suspect there's a dragon loose in Las Vegas."

"That's not around here."

"And it wouldn't be my problem if the Enforcer of Las Vegas wasn't missing." She waved her free hand to keep him from inquiring further. "Drop it, before I have to bite you, kill you, or give you brain damage."

"Why haven't you?"

"Killed you?"

He smiled. "The other thing."

"Well, if you want to be a vegetable . . ." She rose to her feet. She moved too fast for him to see her, but he didn't blink an eye or feel any surprise when she was suddenly standing before him.

He stood, slowly unfolding his big body from the chair. She had to look up at him when he was this close to her. She appreciated that he had four or five inches on her. She appreciated his mental strength, and his confidence.

"If I did what I want to right now, you'd be screaming in pain."

"Destroying my mind?"

"Fucking your brains out." Olympias moved closer and touched his injured wrist. When he winced she kissed him. *Does that make it better?* she thought.

His good arm came around her, pulling her close. *Does it?* he thought back.

Olympias's arms came around him, and she fitted her

body close to his. They both forgot his injuries while lost in sensation for a moment.

He made her forget things, important things. Falconer was a dangerous distraction. "You take up too much of my attention," she complained, making herself step away from him.

He smiled. "You do the same to me."

"You shouldn't sound like you enjoy it. We're grown-ups."

"Some of us more than others."

"We have responsibilities to other people."

"More or less—people, that is."

She laughed, when she probably ought to be offended. Damn the man, he made her laugh!

As she laughed, Falconer grew serious. "You're not doing anything to my people. Whatever happens between you and me, you don't touch my people."

He was dictating to her. At another time, or with another person, Olympias would have been coldly furious at the presumption. Or she might have been coldly amused. She couldn't be cold about anything with Mike. There sure as hell was something about those Falconers.

Falconer—

"Shit!"

"What?" Mike grabbed her shoulders. Bitch growled.

Olympias pulled away from him and turned to face the door. The temptation was to take the hellhound and scour the city. She knew what Sara had been keeping from her. She knew who Sara was with.

"Andrew Falconer," she said.

"What about my father?" he demanded.

She almost explained, but it occurred to Olympias that Mike wasn't ready to hear about how a vampire committed suicide. She was going to kill Andrew all right. No one took what belonged to her and lived—but she didn't suppose she could tell Andrew's son about that, either. Not when she needed Mike's help to track his slimy, slave-stealing father down.

"Your father came back to Washington for a reason," she told Mike. "You've been seeing him in your dream-riding."

"Walking," he corrected.

"Never mind what you call it, it's your key to finding your father. It's time you and I went looking for him together. Sit down," she ordered. "We're going to do that thing you do together."

"Thanks for coming," Sara said as Gerry slipped into the booth in the hotel coffee shop. "But I wish you'd come sooner. Like before sunset."

Her beloved was up in the room taking a shower. Much as she wanted to be sharing the experience and scrubbing his hard-muscled naked back for him, Sara had more vital things to do. Things she wished she could have done hours ago, while the fang and claw crowd was harmlessly snoozing.

Curiosity and concern vied on Gerry's expression. "Why haven't you called Olympias? You're the only one who can reason with her. We've been worried."

Sara took a shaky breath. "You've talked to Olympias?"

"I had to find out about a vampire from the Alexandria nest getting killed from Bentencourt. The local vampires are really pissed off, and we need your help to calm the situation down."

He kept saying 'we,' but Sara wasn't sure whom he meant. Gerry had mentioned talking to Bentencourt twice when she'd called him to set up this meeting. Sara sat back in the thickly upholstered booth seat and put her hand down flat on the tabletop. Looking steadily at Olympias's slave, she said as calmly as she could, "Gerry, please understand that I do not give a rat's ass about what Roger Bentencourt wants, needs, or desires. My only interest in talking to you right now concerns *your* mistress, Olympias, the Enforcer of the City." Her voice rose as Sara added, "You do remember her, don't you?"

"Olympias is the problem," he agreed.

"She's certainly my problem."

"She's the whole city's problem. She has to be controlled, Sara. Brought to heel. Someone who understands the changes that need to be made has to be at the helm. He needs your help," Gerry told her earnestly.

Sara stared at her friend and working partner. Gerry had a frightening, fanatical look in his eyes. Oh, dear. "He? Bentencourt?"

"Of course. He's just the man we need."

"Yeah. He's a *man*. We—you—work for a vampire." A vampire Sara'd hoped Gerry would help her get to and reason with on some neutral ground. "I need you to go to Olympias for me. Set up a meeting. Maybe at the cathedral."

"Bentencourt needs *you*. Come with me." He held a hand out to her across the table. "We'll go to him now."

"I don't think so."

Sara looked up and smiled at Andrew, who was the one who'd just spoken. He was so beautiful. She was filled with so much longing at the sight of him that she was barely able to keep her mind on the subject. The only thing she wanted to say was that she loved him. She snuggled up close to him when he slipped into the booth beside her. She was overjoyed when he picked up the coffee mug she hadn't touched and drained it.

"Sorry it's cold," she said. "Want me to call the waiter over to—"

"It's fine." Andrew put his arm around her shoulders. He looked hard at Gerry. "Who are you? Where do you want to take my companion?"

Sara managed to claw out of her happy fog of adoration to say, "He belongs to Olympias."

"You don't have to worry about Olympias," Andrew told her. To Gerry he said, "Leave."

"But—" Sara managed to protest.

"I'll deal with Olympias," Andrew promised.

"How?" She hated that the word came out as a squeak of terror.

Andrew chuckled. "Legally. That's how I do everything."

"Yes, my love. But—"

"Come on." He slid out of the booth and brought her with him.

"Are you ever going to let me finish a sentence?" Sara asked when she was standing beside him.

"Frequently. But not any about your former mistress, at least not right now." His arm was still around her, and he turned her toward the coffee shop door, leaving Gerry seated in the booth. "Right now we're going back to Rock Creek Park to get my stuff, and then we're going to go introduce ourselves to my son."

All things considered, what Bentencourt had to work with was pitiful. It was Olympias's fault, of course. It was her doing that had reduced the population of vampires in the vicinity to the handful that was seated in Rose's living room this evening. Even though they'd all brought their companions with them, the room wasn't exactly overcrowded. Three small nests in Alexandria, Bethesda, and Arlington made up the entire local strigoi population. With Lora's death, that made exactly seven vampires, four companions, and a handful of slaves. What a weak, pitiful bunch of losers—and they were all he had to work with. Which, when he thought of it, was a good thing. For all his gifts, he was still mortal. It would be some years before he was able to raise an army of darkness to serve at his command.

Army of darkness, indeed. He almost smiled at the thought as he sat quietly at Rose's side on the couch. He noticed Gavivi glance his way from her seat on the piano bench. She'd felt his momentary amusement and canted an eyebrow curiously, wondering at its cause. At least Rose hadn't noticed. Her attention was on her own conflicted feelings and on the expectant emotions the other vampires were throwing at her. Bentencourt firmed his mental shielding into a tight mask and gave the faintest shake of his head in response to Gavivi. The mortals were slaves and companions, allowed here only by courtesy— and a great deal of wheedling on his, Gavivi, and Cassandra's parts.

Cassandra literally sat at her master's feet, and Sidney Douglas petted her head absentmindedly, like she was a leashed animal at his side. Cassandra enjoyed the attention, and Bentencourt enjoyed the sight of a vampire behaving as tradition dictated. Rose treated her companion with respect and tenderness that hardly ever made him feel owned. Bentencourt had chosen her for her gentleness, was grateful for her care, but when he was a vampire he'd be a proper master, like Douglas.

Bentencourt had high hopes of bringing Douglas onto his team when he was finally able to establish a proper power base, for the nest leader was also one of the most famous of vampire sorcerers, though the antiquated Laws forced him to be more of a researcher than practitioner these days. True vampire power came from a blending of psychic ability and high ritual magic, though many vampires were unaware of this. Bentencourt wanted to learn everything the sorcerer knew before disposing of him. *That's for the future,* Bentencourt reminded himself sternly. *Concentrate on what needs to be done tonight.*

Douglas had brought the two young vampires in his nest with him, punks in sunglasses and leather who went by the names Coyote and Isobel and held hands even though Rose kept giving them stern looks. Gavivi's mistress, Angela, had brought her nestling Conan along. Alec and Rose were the only ones left from their nest, and both were devastated and furious by the news of Lora's untimely demise.

It was nearly midnight, witching hour and all that. This gathering had been scheduled for nine o'clock sharp, but no one had arrived before ten-thirty. The regal nod he'd

received from Gavivi when he'd opened the door at her
nest's arrival reassured him that at least Gavivi had spent
as much time as possible discussing the situation with
Angela. He'd used the same time to work on Rose. Now
was the time to find out if all his hard work was going
to pay off, but how to get the meeting going without
making it look like he was the one in charge?

"Can I get anyone anything?" he asked, ever the polite
and deferential companion. He started to stand, but Rose
put her hand out to keep him in his seat.

"No," she told him, then looked around the room,
drawing everyone's attention to her. "I don't think this
is quite the moment for my usual hospitality." She folded
her soft white hands in her lap. "I am well aware that I
have the reputation of being something of a—I think the
modern word is wimp."

She held up a hand at the faint murmurs of protest
from the other nest leaders. Bentencourt was sure Rose
was aware that her listeners' emotions were anything but
disagreeing.

There was a tinge of annoyance in her voice as she
went on. "I have always preferred to think of myself as
a woman of peace. Not an easy thing to be, considering
what I am, but I have tried to maintain a veneer of civilization. It has seemed the safest way to deal with the
mortal world, I suppose. Still, I am strigoi, and obedient
to the Laws. I am also the oldest nest leader in the territory, and a daughter of the Nighthawk line."

There was a great deal of consternation in the room
when Rose dropped this little bomb. Bentencourt gave
her an affectionate look when he realized how pleased
Rose was at the attention. So, his girl had an ego as well
as a sense of responsibility. Vanity and pride were even
easier to manipulate than believing one ought to be du-
tiful. Bentencourt noted the speculation as well, especially from Douglas. Vampires were a competitive bunch
when they were allowed to be. Douglas was assessing

how he could use Rose. *Too late,* Bentencourt thought. *She's already spoken for.*

The sorcerer might have caught the thought, because his gaze did briefly flicker Bentencourt's way. But he obviously dismissed the companion's thought as simple jealousy. Bentencourt was aware of the vampire's trying to hide his sudden flare of ambition as he concentrated on Rose. Bentencourt was gleeful with the realization that getting this little group to perform exactly as he wished wasn't going to take the long, hard, tedious, time-wasting debate he'd feared. What he'd done was provide them with the means to scratch itches they already found madly irritating. They didn't have to hate Olympias as much as he did to want to challenge her right to rule.

"We have so much to discuss I'm not sure where to begin," Rose went on. "Perhaps by stating that even by holding this meeting we may be in violation of the Laws of the Blood."

"There is no law against nest leaders conferring with each other," Angela pointed out. "Nor is there a law against—"

"There's a law against disobeying the Enforcer of the City," Douglas cut her off. He gave Rose a hard look. "That is what we're here for, isn't it?" *What you want,* he thought loud enough for even the companions to hear. He looked around at the rest of the vampires. "Olympias has made an arbitrary decision that I, for one, do not intend to obey. My nest is in turmoil enough at the moment." He tugged on his companion's hair. She lifted her head and snarled in response. "My nest needs to Hunt, not pack up and move."

"We could all use a Hunt," Angela said. "It's been three years. She could at least let us Hunt once more before she kicks us out of town."

"I am not leaving," Rose stated flatly. "I do not jump at the Greek woman's command."

"You haven't Hunted recently, have you?" Angela

questioned. Rose shook her head. "Then let us Hunt to-night."

Douglas laughed. "In a show of defiance? Or because it's fun?"

"Yes, and yes," Angela said. "And for two other good reasons. Your girl needs to kill, and there are mortals who need to be Hunted. I'm sure Olympias hasn't mentioned this to anyone—I doubt she's even aware of the danger, since she leaves it to her slaves to deal with what goes on in her city—but I have information that a group of mortals have become aware of our existence. Something must be done to neutralize any threat from these people." She spoke to Douglas. "How's that for prey for your pretty one's first kill? It's our right to take down mortals who hunt us."

"That is the Law," Rose agreed. "Olympias has abused the laws more than enforced them of late. She murdered my nestling Lora last night. She has not seen fit to tell me why. The only conclusion I can draw is that she decided to take the mortal Lora wanted as a companion for herself rather than searching out a new plaything. If Lora had not already asked permission to have this mortal, a fight over him between herself and Olympias would have been lawful, but . . ." Rose's voice trailed away in a despondent sigh. "Olympias simply killed her."

"But a fight to the death over a lover?" Angela asked. "That's ridiculous. There are too few of us to kill over a bunny."

While Rose frowned at the use of the slang term, Sidney Douglas sneered and suggested, "Maybe the Nighthawk wanted Lora for a snack. Get rid of a rival and fill her larder at the same time. How efficient," he drawled sarcastically.

"Don't be disgusting, Sidney," Rose rebuked him. "Remember that the dead girl lived in my house."

"She's meat now," he replied coldly. "We're vampires, Rose," Douglas reminded her. "We kill our mortal cousins—living, sentient creatures of God, with souls and hopes and families. And we eat them."

"They're delicious," Angela added.

If either nest leaders were trying to provoke Rose, Bentencourt caught no surprise in their reactions when she laughed. "I like mine with mustard," she agreed. "I know what I am, Sidney. But I don't kill nice people. I don't worry about a victim's soul when I'm ripping into their living flesh. I enjoy the fear and pain as much as any of you. I simply don't see any reason to discuss it in polite company. Nor do I wish to become meat for an Enforcer myself."

"You could become an Enforcer," Douglas said. He pushed Cassandra away and came to his feet. All the other vampires looked at each other, then at Rose, then at him. "Think of it, Nighthawk's Daughter," he said to Rose. "It is you who could be the Enforcer of the City. The city you love. Replace the one the Europeans imposed on us. She is strigoi. The law of conquest applies to her as much as it does to any of us. If we band together to take her down, hold her subordinate to us, then one of us can take her status, her place."

"That is done with nest leaders," Angela said, not quite a protest. "Taking over a nest is one thing—is it even possible to replace an Enforcer?"

"With another Enforcer," Douglas said. His compelling gaze never left Rose's.

"But . . . but . . ." Angela sputtered. "We'd need to present a case to the Council."

"Would we?" Douglas wondered.

"We have a case," Rose said. "She's killed a vampire without good cause. She's renounced her authority over us by arbitrarily exiling us from our rightful territory."

"She hasn't done anything about the mortals who are hunting us," Angela added. "She hasn't called any Hunts."

"This is very interesting," the young male vampire, Coyote, spoke up. "Sounds like a lot of fun, even, but—"

"—but a vampire has to die for an Enforcer to be born, even us kids know that much," Isobel cut in. She looked over her sunglasses at the other vampires in the room. "Maybe you guys aren't thinking about asking for volunteers, but I for one, haven't done anything that would allow me to be lawfully sacrificed."

"Nor I," Conan spoke up.

"If we're going to replace a corrupt Enforcer, we ought to do it strictly legally," Coyote added. "I don't want to get eaten for the cause, either."

"If it is done, it will be Lawfully," Rose promised. She looked at Alec, who'd so far kept out of the conversation.

Bentencourt had expected Alec to be vociferous on the subject of moving away from his business interests, but other than helping to organize the meeting, Alec had stayed out of it. Wise, cautious move on his part, Bentencourt decided. Alec was a creature of self-interest; the type of power he craved was of the financial sort. Bentencourt judged that Alec would jump whichever way seemed the most helpful to his monetary interests.

"What do you want from me?" Alec asked Rose. "To invite a strig to dinner? The ones I know work for me."

"I am your nest leader," Rose reminded him. "If I ask you to bring me a strig to sacrifice, you will do it."

"I'd rather not," Alec answered, as close to defiant as Bentencourt thought he was likely to get.

A strig would do, of course, but having Rose kill a strig to make the change was not the plan as Bentencourt envisioned it. There was a vampire he already wanted dead, one that would ease Rose's conscience and sense of duty, therefore making it easier for her to go through with the necessary killing. Though he'd stayed inconspicuous until now, Bentencourt gently cleared his throat and touched Rose's hand.

"I hate to interrupt," he whispered when she turned her attention from Alec to him. He sensed her impatience, though he didn't raise his gaze to hers. He kept his voice low, his tone diffident, his quickly spoken words for her, rather than daring to address the gathered vampires. "Andrew," he said. "He wishes to die. He'd be grateful for the honor."

"Andrew." Rose stood to face Douglas. "Do you remember a bloodchild of mine back in the sixties? His name was Andrew."

"I remember him. You fostered him in California, didn't you?"

"He's back in Washington. He came to see Olympias, but she's been ignoring him—the way she ignores everything. Andrew wishes to die," Rose explained before anyone else could jump in with questions or complaints. "If I'm actually going through with this—you do know the proper spell, don't you, Sidney?"

"Would I have brought the subject up if I didn't know the way to do it? Enforcers want us to believe only an Enforcer can change another Nighthawk, but that isn't quite true. Each Enforcer passes the spell to the ones they change and makes them memorize it, but the spell has been written down."

"I see." Rose picked up a tapestry box from the coffee table. She'd brought it down from her bedroom before the nests arrived. She flipped open the lid and showed the contents to everyone. Bentencourt caught a glimpse of a silver dagger resting on red velvet. He knew that all Enforcers carried such a blade, as a symbol of office. He wondered where this one had come from. There was a large cabochon star ruby set in the hilt of this dagger, and its design was quite primitive.

Rose spoke over the collective gasps of the group. "My bloodsire left this with me. He said he might come back for it, but that I could use it if the need ever arose." She sighed.

Douglas grinned like a vampire shark. "You make the sacrifice, Rose, and I will channel the power of the death to make you what you need to be. Then, with your new strength added to all of ours, we'll take Olympias prisoner."

Douglas sounded like he definitely looked forward to the last part. Bentencourt relished the humbling of the bitch far more than anyone else in the room. Let the others do with her as they willed for a while, he'd get a great deal of vicarious pleasure out of it. Let the others have Olympias as their plaything, he'd make sure Olympias knew that her defeat had come at his hands. And she would know that he was Philip of Macedon reborn. This time she would not stop him. The world would be his.

"I'm not going up against Olympias until I've Hunted." Angela broke into Bentencourt's happy reverie.

"We need the added power making kills will bring us," Douglas agreed. He dragged his companion to her feet and pulled her close. "Cassandra needs death."

"Can you manage both spells in one night?" Rose asked him.

Douglas lifted his head proudly. "Of course."

Rose sighed. She looked resigned when she spoke, but her emotions were a combination of elation and anticipation. She hungered for chase and kill. Civilized veneer or not, when it came down to it, Rose was a monster to the core. "Then I suppose we'd better get on with this revolution," she spoke to the other vampires. "While the night lasts we need to find Andrew, and herd these vampire hunters into a trap of our making. Does anyone know where to start looking?"

"I do," Bentencourt spoke up. He hated playing his hand so openly, but his most essential information had not been shared with the other companions. "Olympias's slave told me," he said when all eyes in the room were on him. "She is deeply concerned about the crises her mistress ignores," he added. "And confided her troubles to me when I went looking for news about Lora. Give me a moment to make a couple of phone calls," he said to Rose. "And I will deliver all the prey of your choosing to the perfect place for a Hunt."

"What place might that be?" Douglas asked Rose, rather than address her lowly companion.

"Why, Rock Creek Park, of course," Bentencourt answered, never looking at anyone but Rose. "May I use the phone, my love?"

"The park is acceptable," she told him. "That is where we will Hunt." She rubbed her hands together, then waved Bentencourt toward the living room door. There was a telephone in the front hallway; it didn't occur to her that he could flip open his cell phone and make the calls from here, but, then, he'd counted on that. "Go," she told him. "I want to get this show on the road."

Chapter 14

"COME ON, FLUFFY, get your paw off my foot."

"Her name is Bitch."

Falconer didn't know why he found the annoyance in Olympias's voice so amusing. It couldn't be a safe thing to tease a vampire, but here was a woman who needed teasing. He'd been in her head as much as she'd been in his lately. She was lonely, and stifled—so frustrated with boredom she was ready to pop. A vampire on the edge was definitely not a good thing, for herself, or for the world. He seemed to have made it his job to get her to lighten up, ease the stress level. This could prove to be a suicidal project. He didn't know why he was doing it, other than that he understood what it was like to be weird and lonely, and despite the fangs, claws, and scandalous history, he liked her as much as he was attracted to her. Besides, they had a lot in common, barring the fangs, claws, and scandalous history part; they'd both made messes of their first marriage.

"It's a stupid name for a dog," Falconer told Olympias. "A dog is a dog, or it's a bitch, but you don't name a dog Bitch."

"I did. Now, Fluffy, that's a stupid name for a dog."

"You're right. She's not exactly fluffy. She looks more like Anubis on steroids. How about something Egyptian?"

They'd been halted on the path leading into the heart of the wooded park, surrounded by trees, the way lit by strong moonlight from overhead. Falconer figured Olympias could see better than he could, so he didn't mind her leading the way, even if he was the one who knew exactly where they were going. They'd stopped here to let a group of runners that had come up behind them get passed. Bitch had taken the opportunity to sidle up to him to get petted. She was obviously the sort of dog who thought everybody in the world wanted to be her friend. A good thing, considering her size.

"She's had her name for a long time."

"How long?"

Olympias raised an eyebrow at him. He marveled at how clearly he could see her in the moonlight; she was a beautiful creature of shadow and alabaster. "You want it in dog years?" she asked.

By this time the runners were past them. Olympias stepped out on the path again, but the cell phone in Falconer's pants pocket rang before he could join her. She frowned at him, but he took a step closer to the creek, and pulled out the phone.

"I'm expecting a call," he explained.

The broken right wrist not only hurt, but Falconer had to fumble awkwardly to get the tiny cellular phone open with his left hand. He was not ambidextrous. The phone kept ringing through the time it took him to answer. Olympias glared, and Bitch took this time to squat under a tree. The aroma that floated back on the mild breeze was impressive.

"Hello, Sela," he finally said. "What are they doing? Oh, God. All of them? What do you mean you almost went with them? How did Grace find this out? Who? What does this reincarnation guy know about—the situation? Never mind. Shit. Don't worry about it. I'm already onsite. I'll take care of it. Damn," he muttered after he flipped the phone shut.

"Damn what?" Olympias asked, stepping in front of him.

"Damn, but it's a damn big park," he answered. Which could be a good thing. Maybe Grace, Jeremy, and Donald wouldn't find what they were looking for in the acres and acres of paths, woodlands, and playing fields in the ravine that bordered the twelve-mile length of the creek. It was night and—who was he kidding? They were Walkers. "Damn."

"Should I ask what that call was all about? Or should I remind you that I'm not only telepathic, but I have super hearing?"

Falconer faced the greatest danger to his loons' safety. "I think we should get on with what we came here for," he said to her. "Let's find my father, and then—go somewhere for coffee?"

"You mean get out of the park before your friends show up? What reincarnation guy?" she added.

"Some hypnotist who thinks he was some ancient Greek king in a past life." He eyed the woman who was an ancient Greek queen. "Maybe an old friend of yours."

"I don't have any old friends." She pointed at him. "If you say 'you have me,' I will literally bite your head off." She grabbed him by the shirt front and pulled him within biting distance. "Tell me what's going on. And bear in mind that I have a nasty temper and this has been a bad week."

Any sane man would have been terrified of her strength and of the very real threat. Falconer said, "Not such a bad week. You met me."

"Mike."

"You want bad weeks? I found out my father's a vampire and I've been beaten up by a girl."

"But on the plus side, you met me."

"Yes." He had a bit of trouble answering, as her fingers

were squeezing his throat. "You—realize that—my feet are—"

"Dangling several inches off the ground," she finished for him.

"Thanks." He kicked her, then hooked a foot around the back of her legs. He didn't really expect this act of defiance to work, but the move knocked her off balance, and she fell to the ground. Falconer landed on top of her. He could feel Bitch's breath on the back of his throat the moment he landed, but he ignored the threat and looked Olympias in the eye. "I can see why you don't have a lot of friends."

"I let you do that."

"No, you didn't."

She pushed him off, and he landed in a bush next to the creek. "Ow!"

She was there instantly to help him up. She dusted him off and quickly checked his bandages. "No fresh bleeding," she assured him.

"Your concern touches me."

"As much fun as these courtship rituals are, we don't have time for them right now."

"Courtship ritual? I thought you were torturing me for information."

"Yes to both." Olympias sighed. "You are too much of a distraction. I really don't know why I'm letting you live." Falconer knew that she wasn't joking. He should be afraid for his life, but he wasn't. "Your soul's what's in danger," she said, picking up his thoughts. "If you believe in all that damnation crap."

"Which you don't?"

Olympias shook her head. She hated that she was in the throes of one of the traditional ways vampires fell in love. Stalking was much more fun, but the psychic WHAM! of attraction that almost caused instant mutual bloodsharing was the most quick and convenient method of acquiring a mate. She'd taken companions both ways and enjoyed the process. But this way—the frisson of sexual attractions mixed with actually *wanting* to get to know the future companion was so very—pedestrian, damned near mortal in its normalcy, and about as hard to fight off as the other forms of attraction. Vampires needed to mate and reproduce. She'd avoided it for a long time and hated that the biological and spiritual necessity for companionship had kicked in again. Of course, this was no time to worry about it.

She really hated that she was letting the man distract her at every turn when she had so much else to deal with. She'd come here for a moment of sweet, violent revenge before dragging her slave home to straighten out the current mess the vampire world had gotten itself into. She should concern herself with Mike Falconer *after* his father was dead.

"Are you damned?" he interrupted her reverie. "Is my father?"

He will be in a few minutes, she thought. "Damnation plays a part in vampire religion, but we believe that we're also blessed in that we aren't supposed to face eternal night alone," she found herself explaining to the bunny— her bunny, goddess damn it! Swearing at her goddess reminded Olympias of why she'd thrown Mike into the bushes. She was dedicated to the service of that goddess, and keeping her own kind safe. "I do believe we make our own hells," she said before getting back to the matters at hand. "We dig our way out of them, then start all over again."

"So you do believe in reincarnation?"

"I'm immortal. I'm talking about my own life. I've never died, so how would I know a damn thing about reincarnation? Though apparently someone your crew has consulted about vampires seems to know about both. Your people are too curious and seem to be gullible besides."

He shrugged and winced. "Yeah." He eyed her warily. "I guess."

"And this reincarnation dude sent your people here to look for vampires."

Mike gave up being wary, and said, "So I'm told."

Olympias considered this a moment and concentrated all her senses on searching as far through the park as she could. For all the seeming wilderness of their surroundings, the solitude was a false impression. Rock Creek Park ran through a teeming city, one full of dark energy. The long green ravine wound through areas dense with poverty and crime, and through the scheming centers of power, as well. Heavily traveled roads crossed the creek on high bridges, adding noise both physical and mental to the mix. The area was full of all kinds of life, all sorts of psychic white noise. A lot could be hidden inside that heavy mix of brain soup. Even vampires.

She'd used Mike to help her find Andrew Falconer because the link he'd forged to his father made it faster to pinpoint Andrew's exact location. It had been a good idea, but precious time had been wasted while she and Mike paused for conversations and phone calls. Something hungry moved within all that white noise. She could make out no specific details as yet, could not discern exact numbers, but the faint, dark energy was utterly familiar. She smiled, all teeth, and rubbed her clawed hands together.

"Something wicked this way comes," she said to Mike. "And it seems someone is sending your Walkers into an ambush. Come on," she added, ignoring his questioning protest as she grabbed him by his uninjured wrist. "Let's go find your dad."

"Beautiful night, isn't it?" Sara asked, following Andrew's gaze up to the bright night sky.

He took a deep breath and let it out in a sigh. "Perfect."

It occurred to Sara that within a short time she would no longer be able to compare the difference between night and day. There would be no dawn or dusk for her. There would simply be night. She couldn't mind that.

The choice was hers. She could only hope that many nights in her future would be as perfect as this one.

She was seated on the grass in the clearing where Andrew had made camp. Andrew lay with his head in her lap. They'd come here to gather his things, but had ended up making love on his sleeping bag, without bothering to take off more clothing than necessary. Now, in the delicious, lethargic, sweaty afterglow of swift but terrific sex she combed her fingers through Andrew's thick hair and loved him. Every breath he took charmed her, even when he seemed to sniff the air and lifted his head away from her to look around.

"Look at the moon," Sara said, trying to draw his full attention back to her. "Have you ever seen it so bright?"

Andrew glanced up at the sky again. "Full moon." His tone was more tense than admiring of the bright orb overhead. "Ever notice how the chase scenes in horror movies take place on nights with a full moon?" He rose to his feet, motioned for her to stay where she was, and slowly turned, alertly studying the shadowed clearing. "There's a reason for that."

"What?" Sara barely whispered the word as alarm rose in her. He was teasing her, wasn't he? What did horror movies have to do with—

"Vampires," he said.

Sara jumped to her feet. "Where?"

"Right here, for one," Andrew reminded her. He put his arms around her and pulled her close. He spoke softly as he held her in a comforting embrace. "I'm not certain yet, but I don't think we're the only strigoi using the park tonight."

"Oh, God." Sara began to tremble. "Olympias."

"Very likely."

Why didn't Andrew sound afraid? He obviously did not understand how dire the situation was. Or perhaps he was still at least a little bit suicidal. She had to get him out of here. "We should—"

"Leave," he agreed. "But not until after you talk to your friend."

"Friend? What friend?" He loosed his hold and let her whirl away from him. She looked anxiously around the clearing. "Who? Where?"

"The one you met at the coffee shop. Gerry, I think his name is." Andrew pointed for her. "Behind that tree. Lurking. He followed us here. Don't worry," he added cheerfully. "He's only been here a couple of minutes. He wasn't peeking while we fooled around."

Why was Gerry here? Her first thought was that Olympias had sent him. To set up a meeting, or to drag her home? Then again, he'd acted so strangely this afternoon that—

"It would be better to march up to the tree and ask him than to broadcast your alarm so strongly that it gives me a headache. And maybe others, as well," Andrew murmured as he pushed her gently forward. While she marched toward Gerry's hiding place, she was aware of Andrew silently circling the clearing. Her own senses tingled, and the hair on her arms and back of her neck stood up. Something was happening, but she couldn't decipher the information she was receiving. She couldn't let it send her into a panicky overload, either. She was confident in knowing that Andrew had her back as she reached behind the tree and hauled Gerry out of his hiding place.

"He knows where you are," Gerry told her before she could ask him what was up. "I called him. Don't worry. He'll save you."

Gerry pointed toward Andrew when he spoke, but Sara didn't think Gerry referred to her lover when he talked about salvation. She also noted the cellular phone Gerry held in one hand. "You called Bentencourt?"

Gerry nodded.

"What the devil does he have to do with me?"

"He's going to save you from Olympias. He's going to save everyone from her. He's the one who can do it," he added. Gerry put a hand on Sara's shoulder. His teeth glinted in the full moonlight as he gave her a confident smile. "He's the one we should serve, not Olympias."

Sara was tempted to slap Gerry and tell him to snap out of it. "You claimed you never wanted to be an Uncle Igor," she reminded him.

As a companion herself now, she could pinpoint the reasons she'd always had misgivings about Bentencourt, see what sort of a user he really was. She *loved* Andrew and wanted to help him. Even as a slave she should have recognized that the love that burned through her was a faint, shallow thing in Bentencourt. Somehow he managed to love himself more than Rose, and he loved Rose for what she could do for him.

"The man's a demagogue, and a very gifted psychic."

"He's a genius."

Frustration roared through her. She wanted to take her friend by the shoulders and shake some sense into him. But she felt the night growing darker and a chill coming over her. She needed Andrew desperately, but managed to hold her ground long enough to try one more effort. "Gerry, you've fallen under his spell, but he's no savior of the strigoi."

Gerry didn't argue with her. "He wants *us* to work for him," he said. "He believes in slaves' rights and gradually coming out to the mortal world. The old ways are dead."

"We're all going to be dead in a minute if we don't get out of here," Andrew said, suddenly stepping between her and Gerry. Sara sighed with relief at having him by her side. Her relief was shattered in a moment. "Hunt," Andrew said. "Heading this way." He took her hand.

She felt Andrew fighting to control the natural hunger that rose in him, the need communicated from the vampires prowling nearby. While she was wracked with terror that made her want to blindly run away, she knew that her lover's inclination was to run blindly to join in the kill. "Run," she said. "Run is the operative word."

"You're right," Andrew told her. "We aren't part of this."

Sara was willing to bet otherwise, but didn't want to waste breath or time to explain what she thought right now.

"Run," Andrew advised Gerry.

Gerry tried to block their way. "You can't go!"

Andrew took Sara in his arms and stepped nimbly around the mortal, making for the trees. Sara looked back over Andrew's shoulder when Gerry shouted. "He needs you!"

Then she saw the Hunters pour into the moonlit clearing behind Gerry, who didn't notice them. She would have shouted a warning, but Andrew suddenly pressed her face against his chest, stifling any noise from her. As muffled as her voice and sight suddenly became, it didn't keep her from hearing Gerry's quickly cutoff scream.

"Damn," Bentencourt muttered under his breath.

Gavivi had recognized Olympias's slave when they'd come across Gerry in the clearing. She'd set them on the man with the cry that Gerry was spying on them for his mistress. Furious as they were with the Enforcer, there had been no saving the man, not that Bentencourt bothered to try.

"Damn," he whispered again, even quieter than before.

Rose heard him anyway, put her hand on his shoulder and said, "It's all right. You'll get used to it."

What he saw was Cassandra's naked hips and thighs pumping hard as she raped the man on the ground beneath her. It was all dark blood and pale flesh mixed in the moonlight and shadows. Every few moments she bent down and ripped another bite out of the man's profusely bleeding throat. The smell of hot blood filled the evening air. Her master had made the first deep bite for her, but she now had to use her inadequate mortal teeth to finish the job. She licked the blood and swallowed the flesh in a fit of ecstasy, eating up his suffering and the desire magic had forced on him. Magic kept the man alive for now, as Douglas crouched beside his companion, whispering the spell that brought about the final change. The victim of the sacrifice would come and die at the same time. Cassandra would absorb the dual burst of energy of sex and death, and it would fuel the magic that would turn her into a vampire.

"It's a holy sacrament," Rose went on. "We can't turn away."

Bentencourt didn't want to turn away. He was fascinated, and hungry. He longed to join in an orgy rather than be a spectator at the rite. Agony, terror, and the musk of sex filled him with delicious cravings. And his mouth watered to taste the blood reserved for Cassandra. All around the clearing vampires' eyes glowed, their fangs shown in the moonlight, and they circled the site of the ritual, impatient, lusting for blood and rape. The other companions stayed in the background and stared, as caught up in the excitement as he was—but they didn't have to think. He did.

Bentencourt was impatient to be off. He had promised mortals for a Hunt, he needed to gather the victims together and herd them toward their killers. He hadn't expected Gerry Hansell to be in the park. He hadn't expected the slave to be the first victim. Gerry's death was a minor inconvenience, but Bentencourt hated when something didn't go as planned.

Rose's breath caught in her throat, and she moved closer to the action. Bentencourt had never seen her look more beautiful. He wanted to follow her, to make love to her on the corpse. But he remembered that he had more to offer her than his own worship. He was going to make her into a goddess. He was going to give the nests the Hunt of the decade and earn their gratitude and trust. His climb to power, his revenge against Olympias was at hand.

And why was he standing here gloating when the time to act was now?

While Rose's attention was centered on Cassandra's rite of passage, Bentencourt made his way through the pack of Hunters to start a search for the prey. He was able to think clearer once away from the concentration of hungry emotions. He remembered he was carrying his phone. He found his way to the nearest walking path, found a recognizable landmark, and made a call to Grace Avella. She and two of her friends joined him within a few minutes.

"Are you sure this is safe?" was the young woman's first question.

"Are these members of the Walker Project team?" Bentencourt asked her.

"You told him about the team?" the older of the two men angrily asked Grace. The younger man tapped her on the shoulder and spoke swiftly in sign language when Grace looked his way.

She spoke, and used sign as she replied. "This is no time to argue over security protocols, guys. This is Jeremy and Donald," she told Bentencourt. "He's Roger," she told her colleagues.

"Fine," Jeremy said. "Can we go see vampires now?"

Jeremy was carrying a camcorder.

Bentencourt pointed toward the woods. "This way." He turned to go, Jeremy took a step after him, but the girl and the deaf man didn't follow. Bentencourt looked back and watched their hands quickly gesturing in the light that came down from the streetlights on the busy bridge high overhead. He felt the hunger growing. Soon it would burst out of the woods and out of his control.

"What?" he demanded impatiently of the hesitating pair.

"Don's right," Grace said. "This is stupid. Walking is one thing, but looking for vampires in the middle of the night is insane. Let's go home, Jeremy. We can go vampire hunting at high noon."

"Will they look like vampires then, or pale people sleeping?" Jeremy asked. He held up his camera. "I want evidence. Fangs, shape-shifting—whatever shit vampires do. Walking won't give us physical evidence."

Donald's fingers shaped words. He pointed to the way out of the park.

"Okay, they drink blood at night," Jeremy said to Donald. "They aren't invincible. Remember, one of the pair we saw was killed by the other one. And the other one is a woman."

"There could be a whole pack of them," Grace pointed out. She looked at Bentencourt. "We shouldn't be out here. I shouldn't have talked my friends into this. I don't know how you talked me into this."

Bentencourt almost told the stupid bitch that it was because he was able to control her weak-willed little brain. Instead, he summoned up all the earnestness he could manage and concentrated on Grace. "It's not far." He tried his best reassuring smile, but the girl backed away, shaking her head.

What the hell, Bentencourt decided. He'd bring the Hunt to her and her silent friend. At least he had one appetizer to present to the Hunters. He took Jeremy by the arm. "Come on. I'll show you where they are."

Olympias paused to sniff the air halfway up the ravine. She looked into the distance, as if she could see through the dense patch of woods in front of them. The dark didn't bother her, and her senses were not human. She said, "They've got another one."

He hadn't heard or seen anything, but he didn't doubt that another human had died. Was it someone he cared for? Was his father involved? "You're sniffing blood, aren't you?" Falconer hated to ask, but he needed to know.

A few minutes before she'd come to a sudden halt and reeled against him. He caught and steadied her and heard her whisper, "Blood of my blood." It had sounded very vampiry. He hadn't asked what she meant. She had sighed and said, "Not Sara."

"Sara?" he asked now, when she didn't answer his first question.

She shook her head. "Mortal."

"Sara's not a mortal?"

"Sara is—never mind. The one they killed is gifted. I could feel that."

Fear tightened in his throat and gut, fear mixed with a deep fury. "Vampires are killing my people? One of your kind drew them into an ambush?"

"They're killing mortals without permission, without safeguards," she answered, voice cold as ice. "They'll pay for it."

"Are you so angry because they're killing people, or because they're defying you?"

"Let's stop the killing and then discuss it."

He nodded. "Fair enough." He started to climb up the ravine again, but she put a hand on his shoulder after only a few steps. Her tension was communicated in that touch. At another time he might have offered a hug. Instead, he spun around, alert to danger.

"They've changed direction," she said, and pointed. "That way."

She and the dog disappeared downhill, moving at a steep angle. He hurried after as quickly as he could.

"This isn't right," Andrew said, kneeling to examine the second dead body in the clearing.

Sara knew it wasn't right, but all she wanted to do was run. They'd circled back to the clearing after the Hunters abandoned the corpses to seek out new prey. She hadn't wanted to come here, she sure as hell didn't want to examine the carnage, but she was Andrew's companion. She went where he went. Of course she knew what vampires did—it was just that—

"We have to stop them." Andrew rose to his feet and put his arm comfortingly around her. "Mortals have to die, Sara, for us to exist, and remain sane. It's a fact of our world. I've always been against those who believe it's all right to lose morality when we give up mortality. We're monsters—but there is absolutely no reason in the world for us to attack innocents. I want to be with the pack right now. I *yearn* to Hunt, but not—" He laughed. "Here I am making speeches."

"That's okay," she said. She'd rather he do anything than what he had in mind. "Don't go," she begged. "It's dangerous."

He stroked her hair. "Of course it is, sweetheart. We're vampires."

That was it—and it wasn't. "There's more going on," she told her lover. "I feel it. I never trusted my intuition until I met you, but this time . . . Andrew, this is a trap."

"I realize that. But for who? Olympias?" He nudged the stranger's mutilated body with his foot. "Him? Set by who? We have to find the Hunters before we can stop them and find out what's going on."

Sara banged her head against his shoulder. Andrew was turning into a hero. While part of her found this utterly romantic, the saner side of her wondered how a vampire who'd been depressed enough to want to die a few days before could suddenly want to go off and save the world.

"Love of a good woman," he replied to her thoughts. He tilted her face up to his and kissed her. "Perks a man right up," he told her when his lips drew away from hers. "Let's go, shall we?"

She could feel darkness moving through the park. Even she could sense the hunger all around. Evil was all around, about to burst out of control. He was right, the violence needed to be leashed. Someone had to make the effort to stop it. "You're going to get us both killed."

"Not by this lot," he reassured her. "Olympias—that's another matter. Let's deal with one crisis at a time."

Sara reminded herself that she was used to crises, to putting out fires that could engulf mortals and immortals alike. Because the fangs, claws, and killings were no longer at a distance didn't mean she couldn't deal with them—somehow. She forced down the urge to panic, and offered Andrew a wan smile. "What do we do?"

"Find them first," Andrew answered. He glanced in the direction of the creek. "That won't be hard."

Falconer might have lost sight of Olympias, but he had no trouble tracking where she was headed. He accepted the psychic link without question, at least for now. Maybe they'd have time to talk about it later. He made his way down the hill to one of the walking paths, moving swiftly through patches of moonlight and shadows, distracted by the thought that he wasn't sure following her was a good idea. He needed to find his loons and get them out of danger. He didn't want Olympias to find them without his being present. There was no telling what would happen if she found them before the Hunting vampires did.

He considered trying to use the cell phone to contact Grace, but worried that its ringing might alert the hunting pack to her whereabouts. Besides, even with her number on speed dial, it would take precious seconds of fumbling with the phone that could be used catching up with Olympias.

When the pair of people came hurtling around the curve of the asphalt path, Falconer couldn't do anything but jump out of the way. He didn't move into the shadows under the trees fast enough to avoid a confrontation. One of the runners saw him and turned a frightened glance his way.

"Mike! Is that you? Oh, my God, it is!" Grace's words came out on a sob, and she lunged toward him.

"Shh . . . Ow!" Falconer couldn't stop the cry of pain as Grace's arms came around him in a fierce hug. He could barely breathe from the agony by the time she backed away.

"Sorry! What are you doing out of the hospital? Do you know where we are?" Grace asked as Donald came panting up beside her. Donald signed, while Grace talked.

"What are you doing here? I'm sure Roger's working with the vampires. I think we're somewhere between the zoo and Connecticut Avenue, but I keep getting turned around. It's like this darkness comes washing over me, and I sort of hear voices in my head calling to me, and I run away from the voices. When the dark recedes I'm all turned around again." She leaned close to Falconer and whispered. "I think they're playing with my head. I'm pretty sure Jeremy's dead," she added, and started to cry. "And I don't know why Donald and I haven't been separated. What are you doing here?" Grace asked again.

This time, she paused long enough to let him answer. "Let's go."

Grace looked like she was going to hug him again. She refrained and said, "Can you find a way out? Aren't they messing with your head too?"

"No one messes with his head but me," Olympias said, appearing suddenly behind Grace and Donald. Grace opened her mouth to scream, but Olympias's hand covered her face before the girl could make any more noise. "Talkative little thing, isn't she?" Olympias asked Falconer. "Don't stare at me like you think I'm about to snap her neck, Mike." Donald spun around as she spoke, and Olympias smiled at him.

Falconer could make out the young man's profile, and was surprised when Donald smiled at the tall vampire woman. Olympias nodded to Donald. "Telepathy has its uses," she said to Falconer and slowly eased her hand away from Grace's mouth. "I'm not going to hurt anyone for the next few minutes."

"She can talk to Donald," was the first thing Grace said to Falconer.

"I figured that out," Falconer replied. He kept his wary attention on Olympias. "These are my people," he told her. "I'm here to protect them."

"Where are the other vampires?" Grace wanted to know. "I can't feel them in my head right now. Does that mean we can get away? Please!"

"Where are they?" Falconer asked Olympias. He looked around. "Where's Bitch?"

"Tracking the pack. I think they've spotted more important prey than mortals."

Realization jolted through Falconer. "My father? They're after my father."

Olympias nodded. "Don't know what's up, but I can feel magic starting to build like a thunderstorm growing in my mind."

Falconer rubbed his forehead. "Feels like something trying to pull the power out of me."

"We were lured into a trap," Grace spoke up.

"I think we all were," Olympias answered. "I'm doing the best I can to keep other mortals that were in the park out of it."

"Is that why the place seems dark and forbidding when I look around?" Falconer asked Olympias. "You're sending out psychic vibes to keep people away, aren't you?"

Olympias nodded. "Trying to. Can't put as much attention into it as I'd like, though."

"Is this the vampire that saved you?" Grace asked Falconer. "Is she one of the good guys? Do you trust her?" It was Donald who answered, signing to Grace. "One telepathic dip into your head and you trust her? Don, you're easy."

"You're all going to have to trust me for now," Olympias told them. She wasn't speaking to anyone but Falconer when she said, "I want your help."

Chapter 15

BAD IDEA. DEFINITELY a bad idea, Sara thought as she and Andrew raced across a baseball field with the Hunters on their heels.

He was the one doing the racing, holding her in his arms. She didn't know if her weight slowed him down; she did know that looking over his shoulder gave her far too good a view of the slathering creatures, which wasn't a reassuring sight. There were too many fangs, claws, and animal eyes glowing in the bright moonlight. The companions racing in the rear to keep up with the monsters added to the size of the pack. Every nest in the area must have turned up for this party.

Andrew was right in that finding the vampires hadn't been hard. Getting their attention had been easy. Reasoning with them wasn't likely. Andrew had shielded her behind him when they approached. The gathered nests had turned to stare. Shadows swirled around them, with magic rising like sparks into the shifting darkness. There was the reek of blood on the wind. There was stillness like death.

Then someone with a mouth full of fangs shouted, "Sacrifice!"

Sara saw the faintest glint of silver spark off a silver blade. Then the Hunters rushed toward them. Andrew slung her over his shoulder and ran.

"Why this rebellion?" she asked the night, trying for reason rather than giving in to the urge to scream like a banshee. "What do they want?"

"Us," Andrew answered. He wasn't even breathing hard.

"Me?" she questioned. She was mortal. Maybe they'd recognized her as Olympias's slave and wanted to slice and dice her because of that association. "Then put me down," she begged her lover. "Save yourself!"

"Us," he repeated. "Can't you feel them calling? They've got their claws in my mind."

"They want you to join them? Then—"

"I wish."

Oh, dear. They wanted him? There had been a silver knife. "Only Enforcers carry silver blades."

"I know."

"But Olympias isn't—"

Andrew was tackled from behind before she had a chance to finish. He flung Sara as far as he could away from him as he fell. She hit the ground hard on one shoulder and rolled and rolled, coming to rest on her stomach, covered in dew, her knees and hands scraped by grass burns. It was a minor pain, and she had no time for it. Sara jumped to her feet, but there was nowhere to run. The pack was already spread out in a circle around them.

"Game's over," she heard a man's voice cut through the sudden bays of triumph.

Sara spun toward the voice and found Andrew. He stood in the center of the circle. A trio of vampires stood before him, with one of the companions hovering nearby. Sara recognized the mortal.

"Bentencourt."

She wasn't sure if she'd spoken, or aimed a jab of hatred at the man when she recognized him, but Roger Bentencourt looked her way and waved his fingers at her in supercilious greeting. Rose's companion radiated smug confidence Sara would have found infuriating if she didn't have more to worry about at the moment. Her beloved was in trouble, and she wanted nothing more than to run to him and throw her body between him and those who threatened him. This, of course, would be a stupid, useless maneuver, and Sara kept still and silent, trying to think of something useful she could do to help.

She watched as Andrew looked at each of the vampires in turn, while he lifted his hand slowly and cautiously to push hair back out of his face. "What can I do for you?" he asked, seemingly quite calm.

Sara was surprised when the trio of vampires let him get up, and was very frightened at the way they surrounded him. They were smiling too much, too triumphantly. Everything about them was sharp and glittering. It wasn't just the claws and fangs. Everything about the monsters cut; their smiles were edged like broken glass; their gazes stabbed. Their hunger was palpable, a sick perverted craving they'd turned on one of their own kind. Sara knew it was so, but didn't understand it. Why had the pack chased them down? No, not them, the Hunt had been for Andrew. For now no one noticed her existence but Bentencourt. They wanted Andrew. Vampires did not Hunt vampires. She knew this for a fact—it was the Law. Maybe it wasn't exactly a Law—the Law was that vampires didn't kill vampires. Enforcers stepped in and did very permanent things to vampires that tried to kill each other. They couldn't want to kill Andrew, Sara reasoned, trying to reassure herself.

They did other things to each other, though, didn't they? Perfectly lawful, but perfectly awful things.

Why Andrew?

"No," she whispered. "Please." Where was Olympias? Surely the Enforcer wouldn't let—

"She'd hardly be interested in helping you," Benten-court said, suddenly by Sara's side. She'd been so intent on watching Andrew, she hadn't noticed the companion come up beside her. He took her by the arm, his grip painfully tight. "She's never been interested in helping anyone but herself. Believe me, I know."

"How would you know?" Sara demanded, seething with anger for Olympias's sake.

He laughed quietly. "Still loyal to your mistress?" He gestured toward Andrew. "How can that be? Congratulations," he added. "I see you achieved what you wanted." Of course Bentencourt recognized that she was a companion, one automatically knew one's peers within the strigoi community.

"Not loyal to my mistress, but to my friend," Sara said, realizing the truth as she spoke it. It was a good truth, but this was no time to explore it, or figure out how to convince Olympias of the advantages of this change in their relationship. This was the time to be concentrating on getting out of this mess.

"Hmmm," Bentencourt responded to Sara's declaration and moved away to linger on the edge of the group surrounding Andrew.

Sara thought about the risks for a moment, then followed Bentencourt to stand silently in his shadow. She might be closer to the danger, but it gave her a better view of Andrew.

Andrew held his hands at his side, his body language as unthreatening as possible. "Hello, Rose," he said. Sara followed his gaze as he glanced down. She gasped when she saw Rose Shilling's clawed hand wrapped around the hilt of a long silver dagger.

"I'm going to give you peace," Rose answered.

"I think there's been a mistake."

Andrew took a step backward, but the others followed. The other vampires moved to surround the group in a loose circle, staying out of the way, but able to cut off any attempt at escape.

"You want to die," Rose said to Andrew.

"We appreciate your sacrifice," Sidney Douglas spoke up.

Andrew's gaze flicked to the male nest leader. "Hi, Sid. Still practicing the black arts?"

"I gave up practicing blood magic," Douglas answered, giving Andrew a triumphant smile. Triumph and cruel anticipation wafted off him like psychic perfume. "Since I got it right a long time ago."

"You're going to kill me," Andrew said, with a slight nod. He looked back at Rose. "What has this nutcase talked you into, sweetheart?"

"You want to die," Rose said.

"No I don't."

"I need to become a Nighthawk," she finished, not seeming to have heard Andrew.

"Let's get on with the sacrifice," Angela said impatiently. She glanced at the brightly moonlit sky. "We haven't got all night. We've still got mortals to kill too."

"I wanted to die," Andrew said carefully. He raised his voice so every vampire in the group could hear him. "I do not wish to die."

"You did," Bentencourt spoke up. "You petitioned the Enforcer of the City to take your life. Rose is our Enforcer."

"Don't be ridiculous," Andrew said to Bentencourt. "Rose can't be an Enforcer."

"I will be," Rose said.

Rose Shilling's tone chilled Sara. The nest leader sounded hypnotized. She was totally focused, but not in control of the situation. Dark magic had gotten hold of her, Sara surmised. The combination of the thrills of chase, capture, and kill had worked a spell on her. Rose Shilling was barely in control of the monster inside her. If Rose didn't concentrate hard on the idea of killing Andrew, she would let loose and kill everything in her path.

The other vampires were just as intent on what they

wanted. What did they want? Why were Gerry and the other mortal dead? Why a Hunt? Who needed—? Sara scanned the faces of the vampires and found a new set of fangs sprouted in the mouth of a woman so covered in blood Sara had trouble recognizing her. "Cassandra," she finally whispered. Could the nests have Hunted without permission simply to help Douglas's companion make the transition? No, they weren't that altruistic. This was full-blown rebellion against the Enforcer of the City. A plot to replace the vampire queen with a figurehead. Surely, Rose didn't think she was capable of—

"You can't replace Olympias," Sara spoke up. "Not just by eating Andrew. It's not that simple."

"Thank you for your input," Bentencourt said. "But we already have the details worked out."

"We?" Sara asked him.

"I have the details worked out," he admitted to her. "You and I both know who the brains in this town are." He put his hand on her shoulder and leaned down to whisper in her ear. "Let's rule the world together, my dear. If you survive your lover's death, that is," he added. He actually sounded regretful.

Live without Andrew? That would not be possible. "Get your hands off me," she told the companion.

Bentencourt was amused by Sara's outrage. "As you wish," he answered. "For now." He didn't have time to properly taunt her now, however. Time to get this sacrifice on the road. He went up to Douglas. "The ritual implements are prepared," he politely told the sorcerer. "The sacrifice is here. It will be hard on Rose to wait any longer."

"You can wait an eternity," Andrew said. "I'm not volunteering for any sacrifice. Besides, Sid, you need to be an Enforcer to make one. I don't think you have the fangs for it."

Douglas snarled, his features transformed into a Hunting mask. "These long enough for you?"

"Calm down, Douglas," Angela said. "He's trying to distract us."

"It's not Lawful to kill me if I don't agree," Andrew said, concentrating on getting through to Rose. "I've broken no Law. I've changed my mind about suicide. You're an ethical person. You don't want to do this."

"I—have to." Rose looked around, seeking him.

Bentencourt stepped up to her instantly. "You must do this," he urged.

"But Andrew doesn't want to—"

"He has broken the Law," Bentencourt hurried on. He pointed toward Sara. "See that girl? Feel what she is? Andrew took her."

Rose and the others glanced toward Sara. "A new companion," Rose said. "Proof that Andrew wants to live. We can't—"

"We can," Douglas insisted.

"We've gone too far not to," Angela added.

"The girl—Andrew's companion—belongs to Olympias. She's Olympias's slave," Bentencourt told them. "I've told you about her," he said to Rose. "She's the Gifted one Olympias took as a slave. Andrew took her from Olympias."

Douglas laughed. "Good for him."

"It was still against the Law," Bentencourt went on, concentrating all his persuasive power on Rose. "He is not the innocent he claims to be. He took something without any right to it. This is not how you taught him to behave in your house. What he did is an offense to you as well as it is to the Law."

Rose listened and slowly nodded. "Andrew," she said, turning back to the victim. "You have broken the Law."

"Possibly," Andrew answered. "But not necessarily a killing offense. I plan on taking up the matter with Olympias. You cannot judge me."

"We have judged you," Douglas declared.

Andrew turned slowly all the way around. "Yes. I see where I might be at a disadvan—Good Goddess!" He pointed behind the trio of nest leaders as he shouted.

None of the nest leaders reacted. "Oh, please—" Douglas began.

Only to be interrupted by the shout of "Ghosts!" from one of the younger vampires.

Sara whirled around just as someone else screamed. She saw an amorphous shape, faint, like fog. Then, as she turned, she saw another, and another. Three—things—hovered in the air on the edges of the vampire gathering. Three things that *watched.*

"Ghosts!" the panicked shout rose again.

Sara thought she felt eyes on her, but she was already so terrified she didn't trust any hint of the unusual to be something sinister. It might just be fog and moonlight. She was surrounded by vampires for goodness's sake! It was easy to imagine ghosts thrown into the mix as well.

The vampires took a different attitude. Maybe they could see more into the psychic realm than she could. Fear raced through them like wildfire. One of the male vampires broke and ran, disappearing into the darkness.

Bentencourt started shouting, "Calm down, calm down. There's a logical explanation!" But none of the milling younger vampires listened to a companion.

Gavivi came running up to Angela. "What is it?" she asked. "The souls of those you killed?"

Cassandra dropped to the ground and rolled up in a tight ball; the freshly made vampire was completely overwhelmed.

Rose and Douglas turned to each other.

Andrew took the opportunity to wrap shadows around himself and slip away from the crowd. Sara, totally aware of her lover, quietly followed. It helped their exit when one of the ghosts moved forward, causing one of the younger vampires to scream.

Olympias always found it particularly satisfying to hear a vampire scream. It was a sound to whet the appetite and make the old bloodlust sing in her veins. She had

Falconer and his kids to thank for the diversion, meaning she owed them and she'd have to find a way besides killing them to get them out of her hair. Right now, she moved toward the center of the crowd. She studied the situation while she waited for a little chaos to set in from the ghostly manifestations. She knew how freaked she'd been when she'd first encountered the Walkers in the park. That had only been residue of their astral projections, this was the real thing. The psychic resonance Walking set off was disturbing under normal circumstances. Olympias smiled at the effect it had on vampires keyed up for the Hunt. Amid the screaming, shouting, and milling, she saw that Andrew and Sara recognized a diversion when they were in the middle of one and were quietly trying to make their escape. She admired their taking the incentive, but Olympias hoped Sara and her lover didn't think she'd arranged this for them.

Andrew tried hiding them within a circle of shadow, but Olympias followed them, moved swiftly to intercept them before they made it to the woods. "Don't go anywhere," she whispered in Andrew's ear as she passed them by. She didn't glance back to see if they obeyed as she moved away.

Olympias swerved around a baby vampire girl in a fetal position on the ground. The girl reeked of Gerry Hansell's blood. "Not pretty," Olympias murmured. "Not pretty at all."

Olympias switched her attention to the real danger in this tableau. The sight of the trio of nest leaders in the center of the field wasn't a pretty one, either. The energy that had been draining from all the life and death in the park was drawn toward the male nest leader, Sid the Sorcerer. He was full of power now, bloated on possibility.

Andrew wasn't on the run from her was he? Well, well, well . . .

Looked like Sidney Douglas had some dark, deep magic planned for this evening. The baby vampire was of Sidney's blood. Why wasn't he running to aid the suffering bloodchild he'd just made? Instead, he had his hand on Rose's arm, talking to her low and fast. Angela stared wildly around. She wanted to run, but stank of the fear of failure more. Rose looked more like a zombie than a vampire. A companion had his hand on her other arm, and he was talking to her as well.

What was the matter with these people? And what was that in Rose's hand?

"Let's have a look at that." Olympias appeared in front of Rose and snatched the silver dagger away before anyone noticed she was there.

A second later, Angela screamed.

Olympias supposed she could have asked questions and stabbed later, but Sidney Douglas stepped back, lifted his arms in a ritual gesture and began an incantation. A wave of dizziness hit her even as she struck. The soft point of the silver dagger would not have pierced the vampire's chest on its own. It was the force with which she struck that buried the long blade in the sorcerer's heart. That didn't kill him, but it turned the incantation into a scream. Olympias's dizziness disappeared when the words stopped. Closing her hand around the heat of Douglas's beating heart was a thoroughly satisfying sensation. Ripping it out would have been easier had she fully transformed to her Hunter's Mask and used her fangs to dig out the vampire's heart. This way was a bit slower, but equally effective, especially since it was more painful for Sidney.

"No one tries to pull that magic crap on me," she told the dying vampire.

Watching his face as he died was equally pleasant. She made sure she held his heart up in the moonlight, so he could get a good look at it while his eyes glazed over. Olympias felt the new-made fledgling die moments after her maker. The young one was unable to take the trauma of losing the connection with her bloodsire so soon after making the change. Seeing the ghosts must have already weakened her fragile hold on sanity.

No loss there, Olympias thought. She would have executed the girl anyway, for killing Gerry. The fledgling was hardly to blame for having killed the one her maker gave her, but Olympias would have taken revenge for her slave's death. Justice, she told herself as she turned to the two other nest leaders. Gerry had not deserved to die. Nor had the other mortal the nests hunted down.

Olympias took a moment to assess the situation around her. The ghosts were fading. If Mike was smart he was escorting his people home. More than likely he was making his way toward the vampire riot to have a look for himself. Bitch had left her post guarding the Walkers by this time and came trotting up to Olympias's side. Olympias tossed the vampire's heart on the ground. Bitch sniffed it, and the bodies, but took no other interest in the fresh meat.

Olympias wiped blood off her hands and the dagger on her shirt. She examined the blade and ran a thumb over the huge ruby set in the hilt. "Run and you are dead," she advised the quivering Angela. Then she held the still blood-smeared weapon up in front of Rose. "My son sent me this dagger from India. I gave it to Orpheus. It ought to be in a museum. What the hell are you doing with it?"

It wasn't Rose who answered, but her companion, who laughed. "Your son?" The words were bitter and angry. He looked like he wanted to laugh again, but pressed his lips tightly together instead. He was a balding, plain man, yet there was something familiar about him. He was also frighteningly Gifted. A great deal of power flashed from him momentarily, then he tried to hide it.

Bentencourt hadn't been able to stop the outburst and couldn't regret it even though he knew it was dangerous to confront the Enforcer with his troops in such disarray. He needed to regroup, get out of here.

Bentencourt could not let passion rule him, but the sight of the skinny whore nearly drove him mad. With hatred, and with lust, he had to admit. She'd always af-

fected Philip that way. She hadn't changed. She'd always
been as beautiful as a fine blade, and as dangerous. Philip
always craved that beauty and danger. *I am not Philip,*
he sternly reminded himself. *I am Philip reborn. She defeated Philip, she will not defeat me.* He looked around
and had to pragmatically accept that he may have lost a
battle here, but he could not let this be the whole war.

As long as Rose lived he would be all right, he would
find another chance, even if it took decades. As long as
he had his chance at eternity he would eventually win.
All he could do right now was stand by as the nest leaders confronted the most wicked woman who had ever
lived and hunt for an opportunity to help Rose. Besides,
he loved her, he was her companion. He concentrated on
that love to cover his combined hate and lust for the
witch who'd been wed to Philip.

"Who killed the other mortal?"

Both Rose and Angela reacted with surprise to Olympias's question.

Olympias's grip on the hilt of the silver dagger tightened. "When I ask a question it gets answered."

"Why does it matter who killed—"

Angela didn't finish speaking before the dagger tip was
pressed to her throat. Olympias pressed the claws of her
other hand into the nest leader's shoulder, drawing blood.
Gavivi whimpered as her mistress bled.

"It matters because I asked."

"I did," Alec volunteered, stepping forward. "I brought
him down, but we all shared. It was Lawful death," he
explained as Olympias turned his way. "He was a government agent trying to—"

"I know what he was."

"Don't lie to us," Angela spoke up. "You don't care
about what happens to us. We had to defend ourselves!
The government—"

Olympias whirled back around, swiping the blade
across Angela's cheek.

Gavivi screamed.

Angela gingerly touched the cut while she met Olympias's gaze. After a moment she looked away. "I'll shut up now."

"Wise move." Olympias turned back to Alec. "The killing—not a wise move."

Alec nervously clenched and unclenched his hands. He refused to look away from Olympias's night-black stare. "I acted under the aegis of my nest leader in eliminating a threat to my nest and all the strigoi."

Olympias considered this and slowly nodded. "Nice spin."

"It is the truth."

"Except that the Enforcer of the City called no Hunt and named no prey. You acted on your own," she informed Alec. "You know what happens to those who act on their own."

"I know." The words came out grimly.

"No!" Rose said. "Olympias, please."

Bentencourt winced at his mistress drawing attention to herself. Alec's death would not inconvenience Bentencourt, but Rose's would.

"Let him go, my love," he whispered to Rose. "Please let him go." He took the stunned vampire by the hand and willed her to look at him. "Alec has accepted responsibility," he told her. "He made the choice to Hunt. You did not order it."

Rose's lips moved as though she was going to protest, but then she sighed and her shoulders slumped as if hundreds of years of weariness weighed them down.

Olympias accepted this sign of defeat from Rose and turned back to Alec. "Now . . ." she said—and changed.

Bentencourt knew that Nighthawks were as different from vampires as vampires were from mortals. He'd known, but he had not *understood*. The creature that Olympias became was a thing of pure nightmare horror. He'd always wondered at the legends and rumors; now he knew what it was that frightened vampires. "Impressive," he murmured, but refused to give in to the urge to panic. This was no time for it. "It's only Olympias," he reminded himself. "She will not win."

"She already has," Rose said, but he ignored her.

Alec made no effort to flee or defend himself when the Enforcer leapt on him. He barely even screamed. Maybe he didn't see what use it would be. Bentencourt loathed the vampire's easy submission to fate, but he welcomed the distraction.

"Now!" He ran, dragging Rose behind him. She came, but her steps dragged. If she'd wanted to she could have used her strength and speed to aid their flight. Instead, she only followed his lead, her will broken. "I won't let you die," he told her. "Help me!" he pleaded, but no response other than Rose putting one foot in front of the other, running at the best pace he could set. Even with such minimal cooperation, Bentencourt hoped to have them out of the park before the Enforcer finished feeding.

Olympias heard Rose's companion urging his mistress to flee, felt the rush of air as the pair sprinted away, and raised her muzzle from her victim's chest to watch Rose's reluctant retreat. It was amazing and amusing to see how much influence the plain little man had over the nest leader, but she didn't let herself be amused for long. Rising from the kill, she loped after them. She grabbed the companion around the waist and threw him against a fence that ran along one edge of the playing field. She heard him land with a painful jolt, but forgot about the mortal as she turned her attention back to Rose.

Olympias brought the nest leader down with a hard tackle and flipped Rose onto her back. Rose automatically responded with fangs and claws, instinctively fighting for her life now that it came down to conflict between her and the Nighthawk. Good for her, Olympias thought, and raised the dagger to strike.

"Don't you dare!" Sara suddenly screamed in her ear.

An instant later, Andrew kicked the dagger from Olympias's hand. "Ouch!" he shouted, when the movement resulted in the back of his leg being ripped open by her claws. The silver dagger went flying into the darkness. Andrew fell onto his knees. Olympias stood to confront Sara, but she kept a foot on Rose's chest, just in case the vampire tried to escape again.

Olympias reverted to her normal shape so she could shout. "What the hell do you think you're doing?"

"Saving you from making a mistake—as usual!" Sara shouted back.

"Hon, do you think this is a good time to—"

"Hush," Sara cut Andrew off.

Olympias was so taken aback by the sudden assertiveness of her slave that she held off breaking Sara's neck long enough to ask, "What are you talking about?" She jerked a thumb at Andrew. "What are you doing with him?"

"Same thing you're doing with me?" Mike Falconer suggested, as he came up to the group. He'd stayed in the background while Olympias served out violent justice to the vampires who'd committed the murders, but now that his father had entered into the fray, he decided it was time for him to do the same. He put down a hand and helped Andrew to his feet. He quickly looked over a man who seemed half his age. "Hi—Dad."

"Let's talk later," Andrew suggested.

"You won't get a chance," Olympias threatened. She glared at Falconer. "What are you doing here?"

"You're supposed to say 'thank you for helping me' at this point," he answered.

"How do you manage to appear as a ghost?" Andrew asked. "It nearly scared me out of my skin the first few times I saw you. Great vampire riot," he added. "Good work."

"Thanks. Olympias's idea," Falconer added, giving the devil her due. "She's quite the strategist."

"Thank you," Olympias finally said.

She was seething, and even though he'd watched her commit some atrocities in the last few minutes, Falconer couldn't help but be amused. "You don't play well with others, do you?"

"No." Olympias decided to ignore her mortal for now, and concentrated on Sara. "You're in a very precarious situation. You know that, don't you?"

"I know everything," Sara said. "That's why you aren't going to kill me. Or Andrew," she added, looking at her lover.

Olympias grabbed the girl's jaw and forced Sara to concentrate on her again. Rose squirmed beneath her foot, so Olympias moved and let Rose get up. "If you know *everything*," she questioned the woman who had been her right hand for years, "why didn't you tell me the nests were staging a revolt? Were you using it as a cover to escape with your lover?"

"You know, that would have been a good idea—if I'd realized sooner that the nests were being manipulated into taking you down."

"If I hadn't killed Sid a few minutes ago, they might have succeeded. Why an uprising? Who'd dare pull something like this?"

"I can answer those questions. But let me go first," Sara requested. "I can barely talk with you gripping my jaw."

"I ought to rip your face off."

"Then I couldn't answer."

Olympias dropped her hand. She wondered if she should be asking her questions of Rose, who stood lethargically beside her, but intuition told her that Sara did know more about Rose's actions than Rose herself. "I'm waiting," she told Sara.

"It's all your fault," Sara said. "But the person to blame is Bentencourt."

"Me? Who the hell's Bentencourt?"

"I've told you about him. Rose's bunny boy."

"Bunny boy?" Mike asked.

Olympias ignored him.

"My companion," Rose said. She sighed. "Roger Bentencourt. Why are you blaming Roger?" Rose asked Sara. "He's only interested in trying to save me."

Andrew stepped up behind Sara and put his hands on her shoulders. "Listen to her," he said as Sara relaxed against him.

Olympias's impulse was to tell Andrew to get his filthy hands off her and swat him away from her property, but it wasn't a strong enough impulse to act on. Maybe it was more habit than impulse. She was aware of the psychic connection between the pair. She hated it. She also could feel no trace of the connection she'd shared with Sara. Well, that had been a tenuous one anyway. Olympias felt more attachment to Mike, whom she hadn't even shared blood with, than she ever had to the woman who'd been her slave. But Sara was hers, and—

"I'm listening," she said. "Make it quick."

Chapter 16

Sara took a deep breath and talked fast. "This is your fault because you haven't had any personal contact with the nests in years. An Enforcer needs to enforce. They're vampires, you know; predators itching for opportunities to Hunt. Telling them to leave town was a solution, but it wasn't a good one. Maybe I should have pointed this out, but it would have made life easier for both of us. You always have too much on your plate to really be the city's Nighthawk. You need to concentrate on keeping the government from knowing about the strigoi and supervising the other Enforcers. That may even be too much for one vampire administrator to handle. You do a good job of delegating, but there's things—like the local nests—that a mere slave shouldn't be asked to handle. Into a tense and not well-supervised situation with the nests came Roger Bentencourt. He saw the power vacuum and took advantage of it."

"How?" Olympias asked.

"He's the reincarnation guy, right?" Falconer asked. Sara nodded. "He's the one who lured my loons out here to get slaughtered," Falconer informed Olympias. "He found out about us through Grace and set us up."

"He gave the nests a Hunt," Sara said. "Something you haven't done in years," she reminded Olympias.

"But—" Olympias hated being put on the defensive. Her claws itched to spring forth and rip into any dissension.

"Bentencourt's persuasive," Sara went on. "That's his strongest gift. He has this charisma that he focuses on people. He gets them to do what he wants by making them think he cares about what's best for them."

"Yes," Rose said softly.

"Gerry was seduced by him," Sara said. "When Gerry found me in the park, it was because Bentencourt sent him looking for me. Bentencourt tried to get me to tell him things."

Olympias gave her a sarcastic look. "Tried?"

"There were things I had to tell him—such as your order for the nests to move. You used me as liaison, remember? My contact with the nests was through the companions. Bentencourt sought me out with the excuse that he worked for Rose. What I think he was doing all the time was playing everybody." Sara looked at Mike Falconer. "Bentencourt had contact with you?"

Falconer nodded. "I suppose he knew about me. He knew about the project through one of my people. He had her convinced he could teach the group how to— never mind. I do know he met one of my people doing past life regression sessions."

"You told me he thought he'd been an ancient Greek king," Olympias said. "He's the reincarnation guy."

Sara did not understand the sudden sharp smile that lit the Enforcer's features, but she hurried on with her theorizing. "My guess is that he set Lora onto Falconer when she felt the urge for a companion. That his aim was to get you to kill Lora all along, as a way to foment more unrest among the nests. He coaxed me into telling him about Andrew and decided to use Andrew to make his own Hunter. He used the order to relocate, and everything else he could come up with, to foment revolution." Sara recalled with anger her own fear for Andrew and herself, the deaths of Gerry and the other mortal, the deaths of the three vampires. She was amazed at the scope of the destruction wrought by Bentencourt's ambition. And it had almost worked. She looked back at the smiling Enforcer. "The object all along was to destroy you."

Olympias was not at all shaken by this revelation. "Yeah. He's tried it before."

Sara was taken aback by this offhand statement. "You said you didn't know Bentencourt!"

Olympias shrugged. "I don't. But I think I know who he thinks he used to be."

"Philip," Falconer guessed. "Philip of Macedon. He's the reincarnation of your husband."

"Delusions of grandeur most likely," Olympias said.

"But if *he* believes it—" Falconer began.

"He never loved me," Rose interrupted mournfully. "Never." She looked to Olympias for an answer. "How can a companion not love?"

"Sounds like Philip," Olympias said. "A seducer, a manipulator, always good at finding weaknesses and playing off rivals. Easy to love, hard to forget," she added. "Always in need of killing." She stuck the dagger through a belt loop in her pants, laced her fingers together, and stretched her arms.

"I'll do it," the forlorn Rose spoke up.

Olympias looked at her. The nest leader was disheveled, bruised, blood-spattered, all magic and energy drained from her for the moment with the devastating turn of events. Olympias had been going to kill her a few minutes ago. It would have been easy then, a routine matter of dispensing the swift justice of their kind. Only it turned out Rose was one of Orpheus's kids. Had to be, or how else had she come to be a member of the Nighthawk line, and possess the dagger? Rose wasn't a thief, and Orpheus had always been uncomfortable with silver daggers becoming the symbol of the Enforcer organization. The original hippie had never been comfortable with the idea of organized government.

"He's not an establishment kind of guy, is he?" Olympias asked, pressing the dagger hilt back into Rose's limp hand.

"Bentencourt?" Sara asked.

"Our bloodsire," Olympias clarified.

Rose lifted the dagger, though it seemed to weigh a ton. "You want me to kill Roger with this?"

"Hell, no," Olympias answered. "He doesn't deserve the honor." Olympias sniffed the air for companion scent as well as searched the area with her psychic senses. Angela's girl was sticking close to her mistress's side, and Angela was standing quietly where Olympias had left her, with Bitch standing guard over the rebellious nest leader. Sara was right here, her newly altered state shining out of her as bright as a new penny. "Hmph," Olympias muttered and turned her concentration farther afield.

"He's heading out of the park," Rose announced. She turned and pointed back toward the wooded ravine that went steeply down to the pathways that ran along the creek. "I can feel him moving away from me."

"Toward Adams Morgan?" Sara suggested.

"Lots of mortals that way," Andrew added. "Not a good place for vampires to cause a scene."

"He won't get that far," Olympias promised. She whistled for her dog. "Stay here," she ordered, and she and Bitch took off toward the woods.

"Wait here," Andrew ordered Sara and ran after the Enforcer.

Sara and Falconer exchanged looks as the supernatural beings disappeared in a blur of motion. His father's girlfriend gave him a wild grin. Falconer shrugged, and they followed Olympias and Andrew after the quarry.

Why aren't I calling in the Special Forces? Falconer wondered as he ran. Somewhere along the line he'd totally shed the military skin he'd worn most of his life and slipped easily into the weird underground loony bin where he must have always belonged. He was a loon. Loons didn't belong working for the government. Loons had to stick together. Besides, never mind that they were vampires, you couldn't call in an air strike on your family. All he could do was help the vampires save the world from some guy with delusions of godhood, he guessed.

All was not yet lost. No matter how bad it seemed, there were contingencies, different ways to achieve his goals. Rose was too weak, and Sara proved useless. Grace was a selfish child, Angela a coward, and Douglas unbelievably easy to kill. If not for the weak tools at his disposal, Olympias would be in his power now, Bentencourt told himself as he moved cautiously down the steep slope.

He had to move carefully. He might be away from the killing field, but he certainly wasn't out of danger. He feared falling or a sprained ankle almost more than he did the inevitable pursuit. He knew he could get away if—

If, if, if, there were many dangers yet facing him tonight, but he knew he had a chance. If Olympias killed Rose, then it was all over. If the psychic backlash from her death didn't kill him it would certainly fry his brain. Olympias could hunt him down at her leisure, then, for he would be as helpless as she was during the daylight. Rose wasn't dead yet, so he had hope that Olympias would be talked out of such a usefully ruthless act by Sara. He'd only stayed crouched next to the fence long enough to hear the beginning of the argument. With each passing second that brought him closer to the walking trails he grew more certain that Olympias had made the mistake of being merciful.

He would survive if he made it to somewhere populous and public. There was a chance she'd try to kill him in a crowd, but it would be more dangerous for her. Olympias had to protect the knowledge of the strigois' existence at all cost. She was limited in what she could do among people.

He would survive if he had enough time. Come the dawn, the danger to him would be over, and the danger to Olympias would just be beginning. He knew where all the vampires lived. The nests were weakened. He could move through the daylight and dispose of all that remained at his leisure. He'd kill Olympias first. He should have done so already, but the plan to play kingmaker had seemed so much safer until he put it in action.

They were all too weak. That was why vampires did not rule the world: they were cowards, fools, and weaklings. Bentencourt knew he would do better next time. He'd hunt up one of Alec's strig friends, convince the lawless vampire to turn him and protect him until he could function on his own. Chances were good that he could—

"Hi, there," Olympias said behind him.

In front of him, two glittering points of fire coalesced into a pair of inhuman eyes.

"Where do you think you're going?" Andrew Falconer spoke on Bentencourt's left.

Fear and adrenaline spiked at the sights and sounds coming out of the dark. Bentencourt dashed to the right, but his foot caught in the undergrowth, and he went down. There was nowhere for him to run, but Bentencourt scuttled away on his back, using hands and feet to move down the steep hill. They let him move a short distance, savoring their love of the chase, no doubt. He wasn't going to give up.

Then the glittering eyes loomed over him again, and he made out the huge head and sharp muzzle of the largest dog he'd ever seen.

Bentencourt threw up an arm to protect against the animal's fangs, but it didn't attack. Instead, Andrew grabbed the arm and dragged Bentencourt to his feet. Bentencourt looked at the vampires, expecting to see fangs and claws set to rip him apart. The pair hadn't bothered to change. He was only a mortal after all.

"You're nothing," Andrew answered the thought.

"I nearly got you killed," Bentencourt spat back. He wasn't going down begging for his life. He turned to face Olympias. "I nearly had you in my power."

"Nearly don't count, hon," she answered, and smiled that familiar, triumphant smile. "In this town winning is all that matters. I dreamed about you a few nights ago," she added. "Well, not you."

"I am Philip of Macedon!" Bentencourt proclaimed.

"No. You're dog meat." She looked at the huge hellhound. She said, "Bitch. Kill."

Falconer arrived with Sara as the hellhound's muscles bunched, and Bitch leapt. When he heard the sound of the dog's fangs snapping shut in the man's throat, Falconer very nearly threw up. Somehow, this killing affected him more than watching Olympias rip out vampire hearts.

"Fluffy?" he whispered and the memory of Olympias saying *"She's nice until I tell her not to be"* floated through his mind. Now he knew what Olympias meant. Bentencourt died quickly, and Bitch licked blood off her muzzle and trotted back to Olympias. At least the hellhound didn't seem to have any interest in eating her kill. Which was more than could be said for vampires.

"She prefers dry dog food," Olympias answered Falconer's thought. "Did that man taste nasty?" she asked the dog, bending down and rubbing Bitch's head and ears. "You want a big treat and my best pair of shoes to chew when we get home? I think you deserve that. Stay," she then told Bitch, and turned to Andrew. "Your turn."

There was a blur of movement, and the next thing Falconer saw was his father pinned to a tree, with Olympias's hand around the other vampire's throat. Falconer took a step forward, and Sara rushed past him.

Olympias poked a finger against Andrew's chest. "You took what's mine," she told him.

"I did not!" he shouted. "Not exactly," he added, with

a sudden calm Olympias found infuriating.

Sara tugged on her arm. "Let us explain. Please."

Olympias glanced at Sara. The girl was crying, but her spirit shown with defiance.

Andrew managed to speak again before Olympias could smash his throat. "Maybe Sara belonged to you once, but barely. It had been years since you touched her. You can't maintain a relationship without sharing blood—even with a slave. But if you shared blood, she wouldn't be a slave, she would have been your companion. You didn't want it, you never told her, but she deserved it. She gave you her loyalty—"

"I still do," Sara rushed to put in. She still clung to Olympias's arm. "You don't need me the way Andrew does, but you do need me."

"You need me too," Andrew added.

Olympias didn't know what they were talking about. She didn't know why she was listening. It had been a hell of a night. She was exhausted, even with the fresh blood and sense of triumph coursing through her. It wasn't that long until dawn, and all she wanted to do was take Mike home, have a fantastic bout of sex, then sleep like the dead while Sara—

"Who do you think's going to clean up tonight's mess?" Sara jumped into Olympias's revelation. "You?" Sara laughed. There was only the slightest edge of hysteria in it.

"Let me go," Andrew said, far too calmly for someone in his situation. The young vampire certainly had presence.

Olympias backed off. It wasn't as if she couldn't kill him anytime she wanted. It was disgusting the way Andrew and Sara rushed into each other's arms. Olympias crossed her arms beneath her breasts. "Talk," she told the happy couple. "Fast."

"You could kill me," Andrew admitted. "Though custom dictates that what I did was not a killing offense."

He held up a hand before Olympias could respond. "A fine would be more appropriate."

"A fine?" And who was this kid to tell *her* what was lawful and appropriate?

Andrew nodded. He had his arm protectively around Sara's shoulders. "I should have asked to buy Sara from you first, but you know how irrational we can behave when the companion bond forms. Sara is my first companion. I reacted to the need before thinking through the consequences."

Olympias considered telling Andrew that his nose was starting to grow, but said, "Go on."

"If you kill me, you'll lose Sara. You cannot afford to lose Sara. And I think you need me for several other reasons." He glanced toward Mike. "Him, for one."

"I wouldn't take it kindly," Falconer spoke up. "I don't want to find out my father is alive—undead?—only to lose him before I find out whether or not *I* should drive a stake through his heart. Give us a chance to get to know each other. By the way, I feel like I'm marrying into the Addams family," he added.

"Marrying?" Maybe it would be easier to kill all three of them and run away and hide somewhere. Olympias spared Mike Falconer a glare. "We'll talk about us in a minute." She turned her attention back to Andrew Falconer and Sara. "I know I need Sara," she had to admit. "But what good will she do me as your companion?"

"I can still work for you," Sara spoke up. "I love my job, Olympias." She squeezed Andrew's waist. "You're overworked. You need help. Andrew's a Nighthawk."

"What?" Olympias shouted, and thought the word came out loud enough to be heard the length of the park.

"I didn't know it until tonight," Andrew went on in his infuriatingly calm way. "I had planned to offer my services to you in any way you wanted to use them. To purchase Sara's companionship the way Jacob worked to acquire Rachel."

"How—biblical," Olympias replied.

Andrew shrugged. "I used to hang out in Miriam's nest. Speaking of nests," he went on. "You've acquired one tonight, you know. With Douglas gone and Angela not exactly trustworthy, the pair from Douglas's nest need someone to take them in. Rose isn't capable of running a nest right now."

"I can arrange to send Rose out to Helene Bourbon's in Oregon to recover," Sara piped up, showing her usefulness.

"I don't want a nest. I've got too much to—"

"That's the point, isn't it?" Andrew hurried to state his case. "Sara's told me about how much you are personally responsible for, how much you have to delegate, how thin your resources are. If you keep doing things as you have been, others like Bentencourt are going to try to take advantage of the situation. Don't send the local vampires away. Show me how to be a Hunter, train me as junior Enforcer. I know I'm not ready to make the change yet, but I can keep an eye on the locals. Sara, the other slaves, and the nestlings can serve as needed. And you and—" Andrew gave a not altogether approving glance between Olympias and Mike. "You and my son seem destined for a commitment. From your treatment of Sara, I guess you've tried not to take companions for a while. You know how that always turns out. You end up with the bond when you least expect it. Companion relationships work out best for the long term in a stable household."

Maybe she would kill the self-righteous little fangboy. Kids on their first companion were always so know-it-all smug about relationships. She wanted to be around when Sara changed and went off to lead a life without him. How content with the status quo would he be then? Would he mouth platitudes about Laws and curses and all that goddess worshipping crap she was sworn to uphold?

"So you want to become an Enforcer?" she asked him,

aware that this might be just the punishment Mr. Andrew Falconer the prim and proper deserved.

"If I've been granted immortality I want to do something worthwhile with it," was his earnest answer.

The worshipful look on Sara's face shining in the dappled moonlight almost made Olympias gag. Had she been that in love with Orpheus? Or Philip? She glanced at the reincarnation guy's corpse. Had she really killed Philip for a second time? Was she destined to be haunted by him for eternity?

Nah.

"Besides, who cares?" Right now she was in love with Colonel Mike Falconer. Lovers came and went. The trick was to appreciate them while they were there. She'd only been trying to avoid that survival trick, maybe out of nostalgia. Live for the moment or go senile, that was the vampire creed. Maybe it should be a law.

"Fine," she said to Sara and Andrew. "Do whatever you want. Get us a bigger house," she ordered Sara. "Maybe we'll all move into Rosie's place. And get the park cleaned up before the mortal cops show up. And— get out of my sight."

"You're going to let us live?" Sara asked, while Andrew gave her a steady, grateful look.

"Go," Olympias said. "Before I change my mind."

Andrew picked up Bentencourt's corpse and shepherded his companion back up the ravine. Olympias heard Sara talking to someone on her cell phone as they went.

Falconer said, "What about us?"

"Want to go home and have some nookie?"

"Yeah, if my ribs don't give out," he said.

"I'll be careful."

He put his big, warm hands on her shoulders, though he winced from the broken wrist when he did it. "But what about us?"

"Can the discussion wait until tomorrow night?"

"What about my people?"

"I owe them," she answered. "They'll be safe."

"Define safe."

"I don't know!" She didn't want to think anymore tonight. "You'll resign your commission. People will forget that the Walker Project ever existed. Maybe we'll introduce your loons to my two new nestlings—we'll do something where nobody gets killed. But tomorrow."

He gave her a long, hard look that reminded her annoyingly of his father. "Fair enough," he agreed. "What about us?"

He put his arm around her and led her toward the exit to the park. She could have moved a lot faster without him being there, but she loved being surrounded by his very large presence. Tall as she was, his size made her feel safe and protected, emotionally at least. Bitch padded along beside them.

"What about us? After tonight? I don't know," Olympias admitted. "I'm not going to bite you until you ask me too. I like us the way we are for now."

She sensed that he was not at all insecure about this, or in the least bit frightened. He was willing to play it as it came. "We could use some time alone to get to know each other. How about we get out of town for a while once things settle down?"

Olympias thought about this for a moment, then said. "Actually, I have been planning on being away for a few days with Bitch while the werewolves are in town."

"Don't you mean Timberwolves?"

"I'm not talking basketball, Mike. You ever been to Las Vegas?" she asked before she was called upon to explain about the controversy involving werewolves and hellhounds.

"Not for a long time," he answered.

"I've never been there. Why don't we take a long driving trip out there?" she suggested. "I'd like to see all the lights and fancy hotels along the strip."

She'd especially like to know if there were any monsters roaming the streets of Las Vegas and find out what had happened to the city's Enforcer. She'd probably get a report on the situation long before she and Mike arrived in town, but if she didn't, she didn't think Mike Falconer would object to a working vacation. He was an action kind of guy who'd been working at a desk too long. So was she.

And Bitch was just going to have to get used to sleeping on the floor.